The old memories grew stronger, took on flesh and bone and walked through my mind.

Creatures with dark skin and broad wings, shifting from one shape to another—it had all been a dream, I was certain of it, or a nightmare. Still, at this moment, it felt so real that I drew one arm about Tucker's shoulders and together we started to back away from the ridge and the bright setting sun.

Just then the wind picked up; it circled through the trees in a low moan, black branches scratching lavender sky. Beneath it all I sensed something different, almost unearthly.

The dog spun in a circle, barking and snarling, as if he had cornered something that now flew through the trees, a fluttering dark shape.

I stumbled and caught myself, pulled Tucker even closer.

I could see it then—the thing that I had dreamed about—with great black wings spread wide and a long body with fierce talons. Thick muscles spread across its chest and it swooped between the trees at a furious speed.

As if hunting . . .

By Merrie Destefano

AFTERLIFE
FEAST

MERRIE DESTEFANO

FEAST
HARVEST OF DREAMS

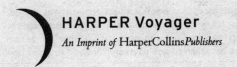

HARPER Voyager
An Imprint of HarperCollinsPublishers

This is a work of fiction. Names, characters, places, and incidents are products of the author's imagination or are used fictitiously and are not to be construed as real. Any resemblance to actual events, locales, organizations, or persons, living or dead, is entirely coincidental.

HARPER Voyager

An Imprint of HarperCollins*Publishers*
10 East 53rd Street
New York, New York 10022–5299

Copyright © 2011 by Merrie Destefano
Cover art by Gordon Crabb
ISBN 978-0-06-199082-3
www.harpervoyagerbooks.com

First Harper Voyager mass market printing: July 2011

Harper Voyager and ❯ is a trademark of HCP LLC.

Printed in the U.S.A.

10 9 8 7 6 5 4 3 2 1

For my son, Jesse

Acknowledgments

Many thanks to my wonderful agent, Kimberley Cameron, and my talented editor, Diana Gill. Thanks to cover illustrator Gordon Crabb, graphic designer Amy Halperin, and to the rest of the amazing staff at HarperCollins: Ellen Leach, Laurie Connors, Pam Jaffee, and Will Hinton. Big hugs to my pals at the Supernatural Underground: Tracey O'Hara, Terri Garey, and Karina Cooper; and to my writer buddies, B.J., Rachel, Becky, Mike, Kate, Nancy, Leann, Andrea, Jeremy, Paul, and Brandon. Also, a hearty thank you to Sgt. Roy Mason of the San Bernardino County Sheriff Department for helping me with my research, and to the town of Big Bear, California, for providing inspiration for the fictional town of Ticonderoga Falls. As ever, thank you to my husband, Tom, for being incredibly supportive as I continue to pursue my dream of making up stories. And a special thank you to all of my readers—you make the impossible possible.

FEAST

Part 1

*Dream no small dreams for they have
no power to move the hearts of men.*
—Johann Wolfgang von Goethe

Chapter 1

Russet Shadows

Ash:

She was just a girl—bony, pale-skinned and wild—when we stumbled upon each other in the woods, the wind shimmering through the trees around us. She was nothing like her parents, both of them sleeping back in their rented cabin, the stench of rum and coke seeping out the windows and doors.

She should have been scared when she saw me, appearing suddenly in the russet shadows, but I could tell that she wasn't. Her long dark hair hung in a tangle, almost hiding her face. In that moment, I realized that she lived in a world of her own.

Just like me.

"Do you work at the inn?" she asked, her gaze running over my form curiously.

I nodded. Somehow she had recognized me. True enough, we'd seen each other often. I did work at the inn, and I brought her parents fresh linens and coffee every morning. But this was my free time and I no longer wore human skin.

"You're different. Not like the other one."

I frowned, unsure what she meant. I cocked my head and then followed her pointing finger with my gaze. She gestured toward a trail that led deep into the woods, all the way to the edge of my territory.

"Have you gone that way?" I asked, concerned when I saw her yawn.

She nodded and stretched, all of her barely as tall as my chest.

I heard him then, one of my wild cousins, calling to her. She lifted her head and listened.

"He wants me to come back." She shifted away from me, started to head down a path that led to shadows and darkness. In that instant, a stray beam of sunlight sliced through the trees, fell upon her milky skin and set it aglow, almost like fire. That was when I saw them.

She was surrounded by imaginary playmates. Transparent as ghosts, an arm here, a leg there, a laugh that echoed and followed after her.

I quickly glanced at her forearms, bare for midsummer, and they bore no mark. No one had claimed her yet. She was still free.

I could have claimed her for myself right then and to this day I sometimes wonder why I didn't. But she was so small—only seven years old, much too young to harvest, though my wild cousin wouldn't think so.

His calls were growing more plaintive, more insistent; the trees began to moan beneath his magic, and I grew angry that he would consider intruding on my land with his wanton hunt.

She walked away from me then, and without thinking, I followed her, just like one of her imaginary playmates. They jostled alongside me, all of us watching her, hoping for a moment of her attention.

The trees parted to reveal a wide grove up ahead of us, filled with thimbleberry and wild peony, their fragrance drifting toward us, intoxicating as incense. I saw him then, right there at the edge of my territory, the land that I had claimed nearly a century earlier with my own terrible curse. He was one of the barbarians who regularly raided the other mountain villages and he stood akimbo, his dark skin glistening in the dappled light, his wings spread broad and proud.

She gasped and stopped walking.

He must have disguised himself when she'd seen him earlier. Pretended to be a woodland creature, a fox or a squirrel. But now he had grown confident in his spell over her, bold enough to expose himself for what he truly was—a dangerous predator daring to steal from me.

She glanced back toward me and whispered, "He looks like an angel, don't you think?"

What did she think I looked like? I wondered.

"He's beautiful," she said.

"No, he's not."

Even from this distance, I could see his brutish features, the flattened nose and splayed legs, the long fingers with broken claws and the yellow teeth. His stench carried on the wind, unwashed flesh and carrion blood. Centuries of poor breeding had spawned beasts like this and I could see that he was near as old as I was, probably near as strong too. His eyes began to glow, pits of bright fire in the shadowed glen, and he lifted his chin, in both defiance and melody. A song drifted from his lips, sweet as clover honey; the chanted poetry began to wrap itself around the girl like ropes of silk. With just this tiny sliver of magic, the creature had her under his spell.

Her eyes fluttered and her limbs waxed soft and supple, her knees began to bend beneath her. I grinned wide when she fell to the ground, asleep and safe.

For she was still on my land.

The fool hadn't known that you must tempt children nearer before you begin to sing, for the magic of home is too strong for them, a fact I knew all too well. That was how my own curse began, nigh on a century ago—by breaking all the laws.

"Give her to me," my cousin growled, a fierce expression folding his face. His shape wavered when the sunlight grew stronger, passing from behind a bank of thick summer clouds. His naked skin sizzled and he drew away from me into the shadows. "She is *my* spoil. 'Twas my enchantment!"

"No. And you know it well. All that which lies within my boundaries is mine and mine alone."

"'Twasn't always that way, though," he teased, trying to draw me out to battle. "Time was your mate shared this land with you, until you killed her."

My blood turned to venom. I left the child on the ground and stepped nearer the forest's edge. With one hand I reached through sun and shade until I gripped him by the throat and squeezed. I had been wrong, he wasn't nearly as old or as strong as I was.

"You are wrong," I said through gritted teeth, "though I thank you for reminding me."

Both of my hands were about his throat then, tightening, driving the life from his ragged carcass as he flailed and clawed. I held him, breathless as if he had plunged beneath a pool of icy water, watched his strength fail, all the while enjoying his torment, until I heard the child moan behind me.

She was waking up.

"Begone, foul beast," I said in lowered tones. "Leave and never return or I promise you, I will finish what we have begun on this day. And you will cross over into the Land of Nightmares, never to return." I released him and he fell to the ground like a sack of dead rabbits, loose and unmoving. Only his eyes glaring up at me and the shallow movement of his chest proved that life still flowed through his bones.

I turned my back on him, shifting my skin at the same time, assuming the familiar features of Mr. Ash, caretaker of the nearby inn and groundskeeper of the forest. I sang my own soft enchantment as the child opened her eyes, changing her memories just a bit so she'd forget about the wild creatures she had seen here today.

She wiped a hand across her forehead and yawned.

"Miss MacFaddin," I said, a tone of surprise in my voice. "Have you taken a nap in the woods?" I reached a hand down to draw her to her feet.

She nodded as she looked around us both, a bit confused.

"I did," she answered, her brow furrowed as if she didn't believe her own words.

Some enchantments take instantly. Others take days. Eventually, she would forget that she had seen me in my true shape.

"Let me walk you back to your cabin and safety, young lady," I said, putting one hand ever so gently upon her shoulder.

She glanced up at me through that wild tangle of dark hair, her eyes filled with mystery and curiosity and something that I don't see very often. Gratitude. Some part of her still remembered what she had seen, I realized, and that thought made me strangely glad.

We parted at the forest's edge, her cabin in sight. She turned at the halfway mark, when she was fully surrounded by green meadow; she waved at me and smiled. I saw her imaginary friends gather about her, only this time I could see who and what they were.

A cowboy, a princess, a faery, all pale as ghosts.

And another shadowy creature, new to the pack, stood away from the others, wings folded neatly at his back.

This last creature was me.

Chapter 2

Ticonderoga Falls

Ash:

A bell on the door jangled and a hush fell across the room. I stood near the counter, a pile of odd supplies stacked before me as I waited for old Mr. Hudson to snap to attention and tell me how much I owed him. Then the room filled with a hint of early frost, mingled with the fragrance of sunlight and fallen leaves, and somehow, without even turning, I knew that she had just walked into Ticonderoga Falls' only grocery store.

Twenty-five years later, she had returned.

I wanted to look around and see how she had grown, see if those imaginary friends of hers still tottered just at the edge of sight. But I kept my eyes downcast instead, focused on the counter and the bag of sugar and the pound of coffee.

She laughed and a smile teased the corner of my mouth. Another voice joined hers, a young boy.

"Samwise is watching us, Mom. Look," he said.

Then I swiveled on my heel, took all three of them in one glance.

A tall woman hesitated at the end of one of the crowded aisles, dark hair falling in tangles around her shoulders, a small boy at her side with hair the color of autumn birch leaves, while a dog stood just outside the window, grinning in at them, a leash tethering him to a lamppost.

She looked up and her gaze caught mine. No memory of me flickered in her eyes, but then why should it? I'd changed my skin since she'd been a little girl. I'd had to. Couldn't stay the same person in this small town, not when I'd easily outlive all the inhabitants and their grandchildren.

"This all you'll be needing, Mr. Ash?" Hudson said behind me.

"Mr. Ash?" she asked, taking a step nearer, still not seeing any resemblance between me and the creature she had met in the woods so long ago. "Are you related to the caretaker who used to work over at the bed and breakfast?"

"My father." The lie slipped from my tongue easily.

Her expression softened and she held out her hand. I took it gently, held it in my palm, perhaps a moment longer than I should have, but she didn't seem to mind. "He was a friend of mine, once," she told me. "My family and I visited here. A long time ago."

"Mr. Ash is the caretaker now. A fine one, too," Hudson said.

Caretaker. Not the word I would have chosen.

"Really. Well, we might be seeing one another then. I just rented the same cabin my parents and I stayed in."

I wondered if she was like them, if she would fill the rooms with the stench of alcohol and fighting. I didn't think so. I had a feeling she was different. Her hands danced through the air when she talked, as if she were pulling words from the ethos. Steam and smoke curled from her fingertips—a phenomenon only my kind could see—and I tilted my head with curiosity, trying to look deeper.

It would have been much easier if she belonged to me.

"I'll check in on you later," I said. "Make sure you have everything you need."

"Will you be staying for the Hunt—" Mr. Hudson asked, but I cut him off before he could finish.

She's an outsider, you fool.

I shot him a quick glance and his eyes flashed wide at his mistake. He wore his sleeves rolled back and part of a long, jagged scar peeked out on his left forearm—my mark. He and about half of the town were mine.

He stammered for a moment, then righted himself. "I meant to say H—Halloween. Will you be staying?"

"No." She didn't seem to notice his awkward speech. "Not that long. We'll be leaving in the morning."

"That's too bad," I said, meaning it. I glanced back outside and noticed that there was no husband waiting for her in the SUV parked at the curb. No ring on her finger either, although a band of white flesh told me that there had been one.

I pushed my groceries aside. "You can go first. I'm in no hurry."

"Thanks," she said as she set her things down on the counter. Her shoulder brushed against mine and I could smell the fragrance of her dreams, she stood that close. The hunger in my belly stirred and I longed to cast a spell of sleep right there and then, to stop time and take her in my arms, to lead her into that vast land of imagination where humans dwelled almost half of their lives.

The land I could never visit on my own.

I watched her every movement, quiet as a trespasser on gated property: the hazel eyes that shifted from green to brown; the hair that hung across her cheek until she brushed it behind one ear; the way she reached for her son's hand and found it instinctively, without even looking; how she frowned unexpectedly when she opened her wallet and saw a photo inside that she must have forgotten about.

Her fingers grazed the picture of her son standing beside a man who looked almost exactly like him, a lake in the near distance. Both of them grinned and held fishing poles slack in hand, a tiny silver trout glistening at the end of the boy's line.

This was the man who wasn't in the car.

She took a deep shuddering breath, heavier than a sigh, then pulled out a credit card and closed the wallet. Mr. Hudson ran the card through a machine, and with a cheery voice, he handed it back.

"I hope you enjoy your stay, Mrs. MacFaddin," he said.

She winced. "Miss," she corrected him. "Miss MacFaddin." Then she wrapped one arm around the paper sack, balanced it on her hip, turned and left the store, one hand still possessively clinging to her little boy. I continued to watch her as Hudson bagged my purchases. Dark hair surrounding her like a cloud, she put her groceries in the car, then strapped her son in the backseat. At that point she came back and untied the dog, pausing to ruffle his fur and kiss him on the snout.

Her fragrance grew even stronger then. Perhaps she had slipped back into her own world. A small host of transparent creatures emerged from the shadows and gathered around her, although these were different from the imaginary friends she'd had as a child. These had more substance, as if she'd spent countless hours—maybe even years—with them.

One thing lifted my spirits as she drove away and I left the shop, heading back toward the bed and breakfast. She wasn't a little girl anymore, that much was certain. She now carried the sorrow of a broken life.

And now she was old enough to harvest.

Chapter 3

Deep Dark Secret

Maddie:

We drove through a cavern of trees that blocked out the sky. Pine and oak leaned across the road and caught one another's boughs in leafy hands, forming a canopy. In twenty-five years, the town hadn't changed. The people still acted as if they were one breath away from revealing some deep dark secret. Even though the words—whatever they were—never escaped their lips, their eyes seemed desperate to speak.

Almost as if someone or something was forbidding them to talk.

I shivered slightly as I drove over the winding blacktop road. It curved and dipped and tried to evade me, spinning off into a myriad of forks and unmarked turns—almost as if someone were trying to hide the path through this village.

Tucker fidgeted with his PlayStation in the backseat, and Samwise curled beside him. All the good that was left in my life had dwindled down to what was contained in this car.

Maybe not, I told myself. *Maybe I'll find what I'm looking for here.*

I pulled two granola bars from the bag of groceries on the front seat, tossed one back to Tucker, then rustled the other bar open with one hand and took a bite. That was when I missed our street. I drove for a few more blocks before I realized my mistake, cursed below my breath, then slammed on the brakes and pulled into a driveway to turn around. For some reason, the GPS hadn't worked since we'd arrived this morning. I fumbled with a map that lay on the seat next to me.

That was when my phone rang. I switched on the Bluetooth.

"How's it going?" A familiar voice said in my ear.

My shoulders sagged. It was my agent. "I'm heading for the cabin right now," I said. I traced a nearly invisible hairline road with my finger, tried to figure out how I had gotten off the main road. Two pickup trucks flew past me—must be rush hour up here—before I was able to pull out again.

"So, anything yet?"

"Simon, I haven't even unpacked yet, so, no. Nothing."

I crammed my half-eaten granola bar in my pocket. The map crinkled across the steering wheel as I backed the SUV out onto the two-lane highway, the narrow blacktop spine of this little mountain village.

"No worries, Maddie. You'll get your mojo back soon. I know it—"

He meant it, I know he did. But we both also knew that if I couldn't break through my writer's block soon, my career would be over.

"I didn't really call to talk about that, though," he said. "It's just that, well, I didn't want you to hear about it on the news—"

"Simon, if you've got something to tell me, just say it. I mean, my life already sucks, right? How much worse can it get?" I said, waiting for my agent to say something. For a moment, I thought I had lost his signal.

"Simon?"

Then I saw the cabin up ahead and I felt a sense of relief. It didn't last long.

"He got married, Maddie. Yesterday, in Las Vegas."

I slowed to a stop in the driveway of the cabin where my parents had taken me on one last holiday, where they fought and drank and made love like teenagers, trying desperately to hang on to the love they thought they had.

"Maddie?"

I got out of the car, opened the door for Tucker.

A chill autumn wind cantered through the trees that surrounded us. Much too cold for October, it howled against my light jacket. I knew that I should have felt some emotion, but in reality everything felt flat and hollow.

"Did you hear me?" Simon asked.

"Yeah," I answered, my voice cracking. "So who was the lucky girl?" My ex had plenty to choose from. Hollywood was just one big dating smorgasbord for a director of his caliber.

"Lacey."

I sat on the front steps of the cabin, the air in my lungs coming in short staccato puffs. Meanwhile, the dog loped across the grass, frolicking with Tucker. They chased each other, my son pulled the German shepherd's tail and the dog turned, leaped through the air, giving Tucker a big sloppy kiss right on the nose. Both of them laughing, mouths open, tongues hanging out.

A kiss.

Wasn't that how it had all started? Wasn't that what I had seen in the tabloids, month after month? My ex with his tongue down my best friend's throat. A photo taken when I'd been on a movie set in Romania. Back when I and the rest of the world were pretty sure that I was still married. Had been for eleven years.

Since then I hadn't been able to write, couldn't even come up with a decent character. It felt like somebody had crept in during the night and stolen all of my ideas.

All that was left was a blank page.

And an empty bed.

"You know, I've heard rumors about that town you're staying in," Simon said, breaking the silence. His tone was suspiciously upbeat. "It's supposed to be filled with inspiration. All the Hollywood writers used to go up there, back in the seventies, whenever they . . ." He paused. He'd unwittingly crossed back into dangerous territory.

"Whenever they ran out of words?" Nobody but another writer could fully understand the terror of the blank page. There had to be therapy groups for what I'd been going through.

"The reporters are hunting for you," he said then. "That's why I called. I thought I should give you a heads-up, before one of them tracks you down for an interview or something. Look, I'm sorry. About it being Lacey, I mean."

I stood up and walked away from Tucker, cupped my hand around the phone, instinctively lowered my voice. "They deserve each other," I said with a long sigh. I cradled the phone on my shoulder and rubbed my hands together. Maybe it was going to snow. I wondered whether I still had the tire chains for the SUV or if they had ended up in Dan's Mercedes by mistake. My ex-husband had just married my former best friend and I was grinding my teeth together, and right now, more than anything, I wanted to go search the cargo compartment for those damned chains. I didn't hear the soft approach of my son until he stood in front of me, hair the color of toffee, eyes just like his father's.

Tucker stared up at me and my heart nearly broke in two.

"I'll call you back later," I told Simon, then I flicked the phone off.

"Mom? Can we?" Tucker asked.

Somewhere along the way, I'd missed the question.

"Can we go for a hike before we unpack?"

Samwise seemed to sense the answer was yes even before I did. The dog spun around in a black-and-tan circle, yipping at the unending stream of crows in the sky. I shoved my cell phone and Bluetooth inside my pocket, then pushed a smile into my eyes. A real smile this time, one that talked about Christmas and birthdays and body surfing at Santa Monica, one that remembered reading the entire *Lord of the Rings* trilogy out loud when Tucker was three years old. One that knew he was the best thing that had ever happened to me.

"Absolutely," I said.

He slid his nine-year-old hand in mine.

"Come on," I told him. "We're going on a hunt for a new story, something magical, something wonderful, something so incredible—"

"—that they're going to make a movie out of it," he said.

"Exactly." I turned my face from his for a moment so he wouldn't see the tears in my eyes.

Then, as if he knew exactly which way to go, Tucker pulled me toward a section of the forest that seemed to open like a door as we approached. The trunks stepped aside and boughs swung out of the way, arching overhead like a secret tunnel into another world. All the trees whispered and sighed in the breeze as I stepped onto the path.

It almost felt like the forest had been waiting all these years for me to return.

Chapter 4

A Century of Magic

Ash:

The house held a century of magic twisted into its cupboards and narrow crevices. It remembered me, the old me, I know it did. I know that somewhere in its wooden heart, it woke up and wept on the day of the curse. When my wife lay crying and dying and hoping that I would find her, this old house had watched every moment. An unnatural wind followed me from room to room, like a sigh, moving curtains, sometimes tossing small objects from tables. My clan says it's nothing but my own magic, gone awry from the curse. But they're wrong, of course.

I think hauntings start like this.

A spirit stays too long in one place, with bad intentions, like I did, and then they get stuck. Might be torment for the humans, but nobody ever seems to wonder how the house feels about it.

Sometimes I think I've succumbed to the enchantment of my own curse.

I put the groceries away, stretching, my human skin feeling too tight. Probably because I saw her—*Maddie*. She was disturbing my thoughts, intruding into memories I didn't want dredged up. The look in her eyes, and that mouth—how had that little girl grown up into something that lovely? It just wasn't right.

"Not much right in this world," a voice spoke at my side.

Sage, my sister, emerged from the shadows, unexpected, as always. She loved to catch me by surprise. I didn't even have her room ready yet.

"Don't need a room, you know that. I'll just stretch out on one of those green boughs, watch the stars, wait for the moon to rise, full and sweet."

Music sparked in her voice, casting even more memories about the room. "You're early."

"Half a day, give or take. We all left early this time. You have anything sweet in your cupboards, brother? I've got a craving for human food." She flexed her shoulders. "The flight was wearisome and long." A pair of wings fluttered at her back, broadened to stretch almost the full width of the narrow room, then fell into place, neat and tight between her shoulder blades.

I cut her a thick slice of white cake, heavy with frosting, put it on a plate and handed it to her. She ran a slender finger along the icing, then slid it into her mouth with a smile. She ate with her fingers, an act some humans would call uncivilized. But in my land, only the host is allowed a knife and fork, too many fierce fights have started and ended over the use of cutlery during meals.

"Where's your human?" she asked, her mouth full, a smear of dark frosting on her cheek.

Sage was walking behind me now, as we went up to my private chambers at the top of the house. Three flights of stairs, through the door to my room, and then we were outside again, on the widow's walk. I always feel better outside, with the wind in my hair and the trees close enough to smell. I think it's instinctive—it's much easier to fly, to escape, when you're outdoors.

The moon greeted us, near full and commanding, making

it difficult for me to think clearly. It rested at the top of the tree line, a swollen silver disc challenging her sister, the sun, for possession of the earth and all within it.

"I'm not sure where he is," I answered, as I stared down at the green across the street where the cabin was situated, just opposite the bed and breakfast. Maddie was down there, talking on a phone, her son and dog playing in the leaves. Without thinking, I closed my eyes and pulled her fragrance into my lungs, estimated how far away she was, how long it would take me to get to her. I've always thought of humans as prey. It's hard to stop.

"You've let Driscoll run wild, over hill and dale," my sister said in her best accusatory tone. "He should be sitting right there, at that desk, ready to greet me with a bow and a shiver, but he's not. And you've grown thin because of it."

"I've grown weary of his dreams is all."

"And the old dreams, the ones of Lily. Are they gone?"

I sighed. This was a familiar argument. I didn't answer.

"That's what I feared," she said. "They'll make you sick, if you keep on. Dreams that old should be forgotten."

"You want me to forget my wife?"

"She's dead, Ash, been dead longer than most humans have been alive. Nothing in the curse says you can't mate again, though you always seem to cast your gaze in the wrong direction."

We were both staring down at Maddie now, I, with rumbling in my gut, my sister, with distaste.

"Mayhaps a good hunt will set your bones at ease," she said, a hopeful gleam in her eyes.

Even now it was difficult to focus on the words my sister spoke, for part of me was lifting my head toward the moon and catching that human's fragrance on the wind. Her dreams were growing stronger, I could feel it.

But something that beautiful had to be avoided.

I'd learned that lesson once already.

"How many are coming for the Hunt?" I asked, forcing my attention back onto my sister.

Sage leaned against the railing and stared down at webbed fingers. She seemed to be counting, lips moving. "Four, I think. No, five, including me."

I raised an eyebrow, waited for details.

"Sienna." A female, one of her handmaidens. Sage always traveled with an escort, ever since she had married Willow, one of the High Princes, himself. "Thane and River." No doubt the cause for the carrion stench that hung thick in the forest today. I already regretted sending an invitation to those two.

Then I realized that Sage had stopped talking. She made a long, dramatic pause, and lowered her voice as if someone was listening to us. As if any of the humans cared about my indiscretions.

"And Elspeth."

It should have made all the difference. My daughter was coming here; the half-breed child I had abandoned, the one I had kidnapped from her human mother and then exiled into a foreign land—my homeland. It should have caught my attention, caused me to wonder why she was here, why now. But it didn't.

Because that was when Maddie and her boy and their dog headed toward the creek and the Ponderosa Trail—toward the outermost boundary of Ticonderoga Falls. Hadn't Driscoll warned them? Didn't some part of her still remember? It was dangerous to go too deep into the woods, especially on days like today. When the moon was almost full, and the Hunt itself hung ready and eager on the horizon.

At that same moment, a crow circled overhead, crying and cawing until we both gave it our attention. Then, with a great flourish, it swooped down to land beside Sage on the railing. And before either of us could blink, the bird's black feathers and beak faded away. A shape grew in its place, a shimmering shadow that transformed like liquid silver until finally, a lovely young woman sat on the railing, legs crossed at the ankles. With a slender waist and long hair the same color as the raven, her voice sounded like wind rushing through the trees.

It was Elspeth. My daughter. Wearing the same vexing grin I saw on all the local teenagers. Her human features were growing more pronounced with each passing year.

"A fine entrance," I said.

Then movement on the green below caught her eye. In an instant her posture changed, her fingers curved into talons and her breathing slowed. The wild, untamed stance of the Hunt caught me by surprise.

My daughter was growing up. Much faster than I had expected.

Chapter 5

Invitation in Hand

Thane:

We flew through the silver doors of home, fair and square, with an invitation in hand. We soared through night skies, never tired, never weary, always knowing that somewhere up ahead, that exotic land called Ticonderoga Falls waited. Eager as newborn fawns testing wobbly legs, we followed the wind currents down and ever down, my blood-brother, River, and me. I knew that I should have stopped to pay my respects to Ash of the Blackmoor clan, for this land truly belonged to him. Though he was kin, there'd be a high price to pay if I broke the clan rules so early.

But I had plenty to do on this journey and following rules wasn't part of it.

I had to explore the wilderness, all of it, on my own first. Had to figure out what I really thought. I wanted to know if all those tales told around the fires of home were true or not. So it wasn't until River and I set foot atop that high mount, resting our wings for the first time in near a full day, that we took in all that belonged to our cousin, Ash.

There we stood, wing to wing like the brothers-in-skin

that we were, scanning the valley from riverbed to cloud-scraped peaks, both of our mouths hanging open in amazement. Then, while the sun colored the afternoon sky, we sniffed the air, prowled the wood and changed our skins to mimic the myriad creatures that lumbered through the forest.

Bear. Coyote. Mountain lion.

And all the while, we smelled the humans, just far enough away that we couldn't see them. I knew they were all tucked away and safe, hidden behind wooden doors and closed windows, all scattered throughout the village.

We had been invited to the Hunt, yet I hungered for more.

So, I cast one arm toward the east and one toward the west. "Choose," I said.

River stared at me like I had lost my mind. He didn't know my plans. No one did, yet.

"Let's fly the perimeter boundary of his land, then come back here before the sun ends her journey."

He grinned. "Aye, and we'll see all that Cousin Ash has. We'll be that much more ready for the Hunt."

I nodded.

"West," he said and we both knew that he wanted to fly away from the harsh rays of the sun. No matter to me. I'd be happy flying into fire itself, to get what I wanted. We both soared off then, our wings always brushing up against that bright silver edge of Ash's territory, clearly marked by magic for intruders to see—just like a wolf sprays urine on trees and rocks to warn other packs away. We passed over trees beyond counting, plus two rivers, then soared through a narrow mountain pass until we saw the beginnings of the village, a cluster of wooden houses here and there. All neat and tidy, with root gardens and fruit trees, metal vehicles that growled when they rolled over rivers of black tar. All the human dwellings thrummed with dreams, both the waking and the sleeping sort.

For the first time in five seasons, the hunger in me felt like a good thing.

Trees rushed past, a mere wingspan below us, and the sound of the river called, sweet as song. An ache burned in my gut and I realized, with each beat of my wings, that both my brother and I were searching for prey.

We hadn't meant to do it, but couldn't stop ourselves, nonetheless.

And now the scent was growing stronger. Man-flesh, somewhere nearby.

"There!" River said, pulling me to a steady halt and pointing down.

My brother always has been a good tracker.

It was almost right below us—a human male. Pushing his way through the brown-shadowed pines, hiking over a twisted wood-chip trail, all by himself and tired of it by now.

My heart quickened and I slid my tongue along my bottom lip.

The human had so many dreams—worlds within worlds—all spinning about him like copper circles, wheels and spirals, glowing like sparks, like fire.

I nodded at River and we sailed to the forest floor, silent as the wind, our skin and wings blending perfectly with the dappled shadows. Together we landed with a soft thump, one on either side of the path, watching him through a wall of black oak and coulter pine.

The human stopped, hands on his hips, sweat staining his shirt. "What was that?" he called out, head cocked. "Is someone there?"

An unnatural quiet fell upon the wood—it always does when we hunt. All the birds and animals hold still, even the wind refuses to blow.

I could have sung an incantation, dropped the human to his knees with a single chanted word.

But I've never had patience for hunting like that.

Instead, I lunged through the bracken, ripping branches and bushes out of my way with a mighty fury. I landed full on his chest, and sent him tumbling to the ground. The man was strong and worthy of the chase. He bounded to his feet and scrambled off, wood chips flying in his wake.

Both River and I laughed, the sound rattling through the silent wood.

I gestured to my brother, then we set off, each of us flying through the trees on either side of the trail.

Meanwhile, the human raced up the path, chest heaving. He almost fell once, then managed to steady himself and dashed off even faster than before. He glanced over his shoulder, looking for us.

That was when I left the cover of trees. I flew right in front of him—when his head was turned—and he crashed into me, tumbled to his knees. I grabbed him by the throat, lifted him high like a prize until he squirmed in my grasp, eyes pleading. River howled, flying out from the wood behind us.

"Let him go," my bother pleaded. "Let him run again. I want to catch him this time."

And so I released the human. He darted around me, leaving the trail and heading straight for the thicket, for the falls.

"Hurry!" I called to my brother. A dead human was no good to us. I followed behind them both, laughing as River taunted the man, as my brother swooped down to nip at him with sharp teeth, teasing him with screeches and hollers. Then just as I'd feared, River let him run too far.

The man reached the cliffs and the falls. He paused for only a second, then leaped toward a watery death and the narrow canyon below.

I spread my wings, stopped time with a Veil, then flew through the glen, past the hissing white waterfall. I swooped down and down again until I was right beneath him. With a grin, I released the Veil, then caught the human in my arms.

"Sleep," I sang as we sailed through forest gloom, back toward the trail where there would be room to feast.

The human tried to struggle against me. He blinked his eyes, tried to strike me with a wooden fist. But in a moment, all his muscles fell slack, his jaw loosened and his head slumped forward to his chest.

His breathing deepened and slowed, though I knew that he was yet awake.

I set him on the trail, where a broad meadow opened at the edge of the forest, and we kept to the shadow of the wood, avoiding sunlight as much as we could.

"Time to pretend we're not Darklings," I told River. He snickered. Legends come and go about my kind and we usually give in to whichever one is most popular.

I opened my mouth wide, let my fangs grow, and then just before the human fell into a deep sleep I sank my teeth into his neck, leaving behind a trail of blood and two puncture wounds.

He screamed, though we sought to muffle the sounds a bit too late, and I slammed my hand over his mouth.

Then the dreaming began. I watched as it pulled him down through rippling layers of images and threads of memory, all of his wishes and hopes and fears fighting for attention, struggling to be on center stage. Every forbidden fantasy and every secret longing lay exposed, like ripe fruit that ached to be picked and devoured.

The human writhed and moaned—half asleep, half unconscious—beneath the weight of the dream. Like it was too much. Like his body would burst.

At that moment, I summoned the dream, held one webbed hand out to catch it when it bubbled from the human's lips. I ate my fill without stopping, until I was glutted, and I would have eaten yet more, but that was when a new sound broke through the vale: thrashing and scrambling, and the mixed scent of human and beast wafted through the wood.

Someone else was coming toward us on the trail.

I pulled away from the human to listen. Distracted, I heard laughter in the near distance. Two more humans were approaching. And a dog.

"Stop. We must leave," I said, turning back, but that was when I realized that it was too late. My brother had feasted until the human had no more dreams left. The creature lay quivering on the ground before us, like a babe sleeping through a nightmare. He was dying with soft, whimpering cries.

"You've taken it all," I growled.

River wiped his mouth with the back of his hand. "I couldn't stop," he said, a look of terror in his eyes. And now the creature stretched out on the ground before us—no more than an empty shell, a brittle skin with bones inside.

Dead.

Meanwhile, the wild and noisome racket drew even closer.

Chapter 6

Birds of Prey

Maddie:

Tucker and I hiked higher and higher on the trail that led through the forest, the sky now burnished with the fiery shades of sunset. The muscles in my legs ached and my lungs burned from the thin mountain air. Sunlight glinted off a cropping of rocks to my left and I lifted a hand to shield my eyes. Just then—when I was raising my arm—I thought I saw two shadows drop from the sky, broad wings spread wide.

Like massive black birds of prey.

They were probably eagles or vultures, but something about their shape made my heart skip a beat, though it was hard to tell whether it had been from fear or excitement. I stopped and scanned the foliage around us, trying to see the birds again. I turned off the Ticonderoga Trail, leading us in a different direction, following the creatures that I had seen.

Something lived in these wooded hills, I was certain of it. And I needed to find out what.

I hadn't truly put it all together yet, hadn't realized how desperately I was hoping that something waited for me in this pine and cedar wilderness.

Something important. Something legendary.

Something that would finally help me break through my writer's block.

I paused on the trail. Was I being foolish? If so, it wouldn't be the first time. Sure, I wrote about magic, but that didn't mean it was real or that I could capture it in a jar and paint it on the page.

That was when I noticed that the trails were now shrouded in darkness. None of the paths on this side of the mountain were well marked and several veered off into shadows that never brightened, even in the middle of the day.

It might not be that easy to find our way back.

That was when Samwise pushed past me, and with a bark, the dog bounded up the path.

"Hey!" I called out to him, suddenly knowing where we were—on the Ponderosa Trail. This was exactly where I had been before, as a child. I rubbed my temples, trying to remember. I had seen something in the woods on that day, someone peering at me from behind a thicket of trees, eyes that had looked familiar. I had fallen asleep and had a strange dream, one I was never able to forget or fully remember. "Come back."

The dog stopped and looked at me.

We had made our way deep into the timber. I caught glimpses of sky between the trunks and I could hear the falls now, so close it was almost deafening. The path curved up ahead, then seemed to pitch off the face of the earth. There was no way to know what waited around the bend. Still, somehow I knew what might be there—a shadow-dappled plateau, trimmed with wild grasses and flowers.

For the first time a shiver ran up my back. There was something in the plateau, something dangerous. I knew it. We had to turn back. *Now.*

"Come back!" I shouted again to the dog, but he wasn't

listening. "Sam!" Apparently the dog couldn't hear me over the rushing waterfall.

"I'll go get him," Tucker said, but I grabbed him by the collar before he could launch away from me.

"No, stay here!"

Then the old memories grew stronger, took on flesh and bone and walked through my mind. Creatures with dark skin and broad wings, shifting from one shape to another—it had all been a dream, I was certain of it, or a nightmare. Still, at this moment, it felt so real that I drew one arm about Tucker's shoulders and together we started to back away from the ridge and the bright setting sun. He strained at my grip, eager to get the dog.

Just then the wind picked up; it circled through the trees in a low moan, black branches scratching lavender sky. Beneath it all I sensed something different, almost unearthly.

The dog spun in a circle, barking and snarling, as if he had cornered something that now flew through the trees, a fluttering dark shape.

I stumbled and caught myself, pulled Tucker even closer.

I could see it then—the thing that I had dreamed about—with great black wings spread wide and a long body with fierce talons. Thick muscles spread across its chest and it swooped between the trees at a furious speed, as if hunting. Then it paused to glance down at the dog.

There was a gut-wrenching moment when I thought it might attack. And I knew instantly that Samwise would lose the battle.

Chapter 7

Dark and Deep

Ash:

Something sizzled through the sky at that moment, a warning cry. Just as the three of us paced the widow's walk, keeping to the shadows, my sister chattering away and I marking the steady movement of the moon through the heavens. We all knew that the Hunt would be here soon and we were waiting, eagerly.

But just then—when there was a pause in our conversation, when my sister's gown stirred in the breeze, carrying the fragrance of home, bringing a myriad of memories that I would rather forget—the scream of a human echoed from the forest.

The sound vibrated and shredded, bit and clawed; it circled through the air and shook me to my senses. No matter how hard I tried, I could not ignore it, for it was my duty to protect this land and the inhabitants.

Yet, as horrid as the cry was, the sound that followed was even worse.

Silence, dark and deep, rushed through the forest like an underground river.

My human guise melted away, my wings unfurled wide and ready for flight.

Somewhere nearby, somewhere deep in the woods, life was being drained from a human, dream by dream, until soon there would be nothing left. No hope. No future.

Not even a heartbeat.

I slung my head back toward the heavens, caught the moon full in my gaze, and I loosed a wild territorial howl. Without a word or an explanation, I left both my sister and my daughter behind and soared off into the darkening sky, looking for the poacher that had hunted on my land.

I swept through the woodland thicket, dodging back and forth between trees, following the river. Beneath me, the water sparkled, reflecting my image, twisting it into song. Despite the stillness, I knew almost immediately that Darklings had been here, I could smell them. Right here in the midst of timber and sunlight; they had been hunting and harvesting. I could smell the berry-sweet odor of dreams stolen too fast, almost spoiled, almost bitter.

Then wind picked up and the scent drifted away.

In its stead, only the odors of dry crackling leaves and rushing water remained.

The air shimmered below me and the curtain of trees seemed to ripple. In an instant, I spread my wings and soared to the forest floor. There I saw it, walked through it like a doorway. Just at the edge of my territory, a wood-chip trail led through stands of fir and spruce toward an open meadow. Here, the fabric of reality twisted with the stench of stolen dreams; they hung heavy and thick as fog. I closed my eyes and inhaled.

Then I opened my eyes wide, searching for more clues and finding them. In between the fallen leaves and pine needles and shaggy moss, I saw the ghostly images that dreams leave behind. Their faint outlines wavered before me, evaporating on the breeze. A human male had been here—someone who walked with dreams of fire—and now the fragrance of smoke tangled with the sweet scent of overripe dreams.

Too late, I recognized another smell.

Life.

Maddie, her boy and their dog. They were here on this trail too, stumbling along, laughing, just on the other side of the ridge. They hadn't seen me yet.

But their dog knew I was here. I'd had been in such a hurry to catch the poachers that I had forgotten to mask my own scent. And now the animal sprinted up the trail toward me.

In a panic, I spread my wings and tried to fly away. At the same moment, I lifted one hand to cast a Veil—to stop time, to hold everyone and everything still—and my mouth opened to speak poetic words of enchantment.

But I wasn't quick enough.

Chapter 8

Laced with Magic

Ash:

I lowered my hand, the Veil complete. Everyone and everything around me stood still, as if carved from rock. Nothing moved, no animal, no bird, no human. Not even the wind. With a velvet-soft thump of wings, I sank to the ground and entered my own magical incantation, drops of light spinning about me as I walked, my own words of poetry still weaving through bark and leaf and sky.

Maddie stared straight ahead as I approached, at the empty spot in the forest where I had been only a moment earlier. I passed her dog, still on outstretched legs, head in the air, jaws open wide. Leaves stirred as I walked, pine needles crushed beneath my weight, spilling the fragrance of the forest around me. The boy stood held in place by his mother's firm hand.

I walked haltingly toward Maddie. Beneath her fear I could smell the sweetness of her dreams and her stories; laced with magic and dark twists and turns, they all had one thing in common—a happy ending.

Something I wasn't sure I believed in anymore.

With one hand, I cupped her face. Did she tremble at my

touch, did she recognize the gentle brush of my flesh against hers or was that my imagination? The not-full moon hovered at my back, her silver light singing in time with my own poetry, reminding me how much I longed to harvest, how long it had been since I had eaten anything but the old dreams. My sister had been right, though I would never confess it to her or any of my clan.

The old dreams of Lily, those I kept in a secret cache, had become like poison. With each one I grew weaker. If I kept this up, I would soon become a phantom, trapped between worlds. I would become the ghost I had pretended to be for so many years and I would haunt Ticonderoga Falls forever.

Unless my appetite could once again be stirred.

I winced at the thought, my old wound causing me to curl over, bending at the waist. I almost lost control of my Veil and it began to melt around the edges, silver flashes of light growing nearer as the magic collapsed in upon itself.

"Be still," I murmured, my strength failing as the pain waxed full. The Veil responded, staying just strong enough to continue holding all three of them motionless.

I leaned closer, fighting the temptation, though it was near impossible when the phantom mists of someone else's dreams still drifted through the forest. My lips rested beside Maddie's ear and I whispered.

"Stay," I said, speaking the words I had longed to say from the moment I first saw her in the store. "Stay in Ticonderoga Falls for one more day. Then you'll be free to go. I give you my promise. I only ask that you stay for the Hunt. Please."

With a great reluctance, I pulled away. She was caught in that still and silent world between breaths, and there are rules about how much you can tell your prey to do.

Rules bind our worlds together, hold the moon and sun in place.

I know that now. Wished that I had known it long ago.

With a leap and a mighty surge of wings, I broke my spell and I soared away from her, into the heavens, high above the trees. Where I could resist her fragrance once more.

Chapter 9

a Secret Wound

Thane:

Dreams still hung in the air, mingled with the odor of spilled blood. The forest hung quiet and fixed in place, as if frozen by an invisible glacier. I crouched in shadow and rock, my flesh pressed thin and my bones crumpled into distorted, unrecognizable shapes. Even my face had been flattened in this narrow space between stone and boulder. Part of me watched a space between two thick lodgepole pines where River and I had hidden the human carcass, buried beneath a blanket of leaves before we had sailed off through woodland green.

And the other part of me watched all that happened back on that wood-chip trail.

Ash soared between thick trees and cast a Veil. Then my dear cousin dropped to the forest floor and approached the woman. At that moment, when it looked as if he recognized her, he suddenly winced and crumpled near in two, and the Veil he had cast—a mediocre piece of workmanship—began to melt.

That was when I knew that the stories from home were true.

Ash crouched in pain from a secret wound.

This sudden weakness in my cousin was exactly what I had been hoping to discover. It was worth my entire journey to Ticonderoga Falls.

Cousin Ash recovered, then mumbled a brief snippet of poetry and held his Veil in place. If it had been me, I would have sailed away, right then and there. But that's not what he did.

I watched him with great care, trying to puzzle out his motive.

He pulled himself straight, cast a mournful gaze toward the human woman, then he leaned nearer to her, but to what purpose? To kiss her or whisper in her ear?

There was some secret between them. I needed to discover what it was.

Ash broke the spell then, sooner than I expected, and he flew away.

The human woman and her boy and their dog woke up, groggy at first and easily confused. I sang a brief song to them from my hiding place, twisting the wood in their mind, turning the trails into a maze that would lead them astray.

"Stay here," I whispered over my shoulder to River. "Mayhaps Cousin Ash is still nearby. I'll go out and test the air, see if his scent is yet strong in the timber. Wait 'til I return and say whether it be safe."

"Aye," my brother growled from his enclosure. "But don't be long."

Then I left him and I melted into twilight shadows.

Chapter 10

a Dark Tide

Maddie:

Time bled and changed, turned into something liquid, and I got caught up in a daydream. I must have stopped, right there on the trail, lost in some reverie, for when I finally came to, everything looked different. The sky and the trees wavered around me. Shadows grew longer—like a dark tide, they spread out across the forest floor until the whole expanse before me lay black and gray. I stretched, then yawned. It felt like I had been asleep, standing in the same position for a long time, my muscles stiff, as if a single instant had stretched out into a year.

I turned around slowly, searching the wood, now filled with the song of birds and the soughing of wind through pine needles. The mysterious creature had disappeared. Just a heartbeat ago, something had been flying through the trees, something dark and sinister. *No.* I paused and ran my fingers against my cheek. *Not sinister. More like a long lost friend.* But whatever I had seen, it now felt like nearly half an hour had passed, plenty of time for that winged beast to escape.

In fact, I could still hear the echo of my own words hanging in the air. I had just called out to the dog and he now snapped his head toward me, ears up. He charged back down the slope, a black-and-tan blur, running to me.

"What did you see, Mom?" Tucker asked, yawning first, then looking around. "What was in the woods? A coyote?"

"No," I answered. I grabbed the dog by the collar, clipped on his leash and pulled him close. "It was just my imagination, there was nothing there."

But there *had* been something, I was certain of it. And as we turned to head back toward the cabin, it felt as if something still lurked in the woods, watching us. My skin prickled. My thoughts scattered as we stumbled down the trail, amidst shifting shadows, beneath a sky that deepened to the color of pomegranate. And there was something that I couldn't quite remember, almost as if I had left the stove turned on or misplaced my keys.

The trails now looked foreign in the fading light. As soon as we came to the first fork, I realized that I didn't know which way to turn. I paused and glanced around, trying to get my bearings, looking for some familiar landmark but seeing none. Meanwhile, the dog blundered ahead, too impatient to wait for me. He jerked the leash out of my hand, and we had to traipse after him. I hoped that he might have an uncanny sense of direction that would be able lead us safely back.

Unfortunately, his uncanny sense of direction led us right to a rabbit that scurried off into dusky shadows. The path we were on took us to the river's edge.

"We didn't come this way, Mom," Tucker said with a heavy sigh.

"I know," I said.

Sunset bled into twilight, the sun sold her kingdom to a handful of wayward stars and a bloated moon. And none of them gave us enough light to see where we were.

"We'll find our way back, no problem," I told him with a bravado I didn't feel. "All we have to do is head back down the mountain. Eventually we'll find a trail that will lead us to the cabin."

"I'm hungry," Tucker said. "Maybe we can find some berries or something we can eat." He paused beside a suspicious bush and began to finger through the leaves.

I dug deep into my pocket, pulled out that half-eaten granola bar and handed it to him. Just then I heard something rustling in the thicket behind us, saplings wisped and cricked beneath the weight of something large stealthily moving nearer. A fragrance carried on the breeze, like toadstools and cobwebs.

Samwise growled and strained at the leash.

Some woodland creature was following us. I reached for Tucker's hand, pushed him in front of me on the trail.

"Come on," I told him. "Let's go."

He tried to scramble over the rocky terrain, now sodden with water. His feet slid beneath him and he almost fell into the creek. I grabbed him by the jacket, pulled him back onto the path. He was tired, both of us were. The only one with energy left was the dog and he kept snuffling at the bushes, growling low, his hackles up.

That was when I noticed a flash of light, bobbing and weaving through the thicket up ahead of us.

"Is somebody there?" a voice called. A safe, familiar voice.

"Here!" I shouted back.

Light was spilling through the trees, drawing nearer.

Meanwhile, Samwise growled even louder, teeth snapping at twilight dusk and I could barely hang on to him. His leash slipped through my fingers but I managed to grab it with my other hand.

"No, boy! Don't!" I didn't want him to charge after whatever was following us. Could be a bear or mountain lion. He wouldn't survive a fight with something like that. "Stay."

Then I saw that it was Mr. Ash coming toward us, the caretaker at the inn. He must have hiked off the main trail, just like us, down through vines and thorns, for his shirt was torn and he had a gash across one cheek. He turned the flashlight on us as he approached. At that moment, when his light cascaded into the bushes all around us, I was finally able to see what had been following us through the woods. It was only a shapeless outline; still I could make out something huge—much taller than me—with broad shoulders, less than an arm's length away from us. Then the light shifted and instantly the creature's shape melted into the surrounding darkness.

It vanished.

Whatever had been following us just disappeared.

I shuddered. Samwise sniffed the ground curiously.

Mr. Ash was beside us then and the sense of danger was gone, almost as if it had never existed.

"You're off the main trail," he said, though it sounded almost like a question. "Lost?"

"Yeah," I answered, rubbing my hands, noticing a chill bite in the wind. "I'm not sure how we ended up down here by the river."

"Come on." He reached down to Tucker and easily pulled him into his arms.

"How did you know we were here?" I asked. We were headed toward the summit that led back to the Ponderosa Trail. I was winded from the climb and my words came out separated by long pauses for air.

"You didn't unpack your car." He carried Tucker, who was already asleep in his arms. Samwise scampered alongside the two of us, weaving between us from time to time. "And there were no lights on in your cabin, so I figured you must have gone for a hike."

I smiled reluctantly.

"Be careful of the woods, Maddie," he said, his face masked in shadow, his tone serious, his flashlight aimed steadily before us. "These paths aren't as friendly as they look. It's easy to get lost on the Ponderosa Trail. Be best to stay off it."

I nodded. The moonlight fell down through the leaves and

branches, outlining him in silver light. He was a handsome man, more handsome than his father, broader at the shoulders and maybe a full hand taller.

"I'm glad you came along when you did, Mr. Ash—" I said, though I didn't like to confess we had needed saving.

"Please call me Ash."

"Ash." The name settled in my mouth, at once familiar and sweet. "I think some wild animal was following us, though I never saw it clearly. It disappeared when you showed up."

"There's not much tame and safe in Ticonderoga Falls." He grinned at me in the moonlight, and he chuckled, low and soft. "That's one reason why I love it here."

That was when we cleared the last stand of trees.

The sky and the surrounding landscape had darkened to violet. We now stood at the edge of a twisted black wood and, save the beam from his tiny lamp, we were engulfed in darkness. I shivered as a brisk wind greeted us and we stepped away from the forest.

"Come, you're almost home," he said, and he put one hand gently on my shoulder.

From the moment he touched me I felt safe, something I hadn't felt for a very long time. Then together, we walked toward the cabin, silhouetted in the near distance behind the rising moon.

Chapter 11

Autumn Skies

Thane:

One moment Ash was walking the human woman and her boy through the wood, the next he was a winged shadow that flew through autumn skies, nightmarish and dark, carrying the fragrance of wind and rain. River joined me and together we hid in the forest gloom, both of our faces turned toward the little cottage on the green, watching as it lit with yellow light, as Maddie and her son transformed into black silhouettes.

We'd been so close to catching her earlier; if Cousin Ash hadn't come along when he did, surely we'd have harvested her by now. She would have been delicious. I was sure of it. Even the trees and the wind had seemed to sense it.

And now she was walking toward the bed and breakfast, crossing the green meadow and then the road. Her boy remained back inside the cottage, playing in the front room with the dog.

All the while, I could see Sage watching us from the widow's walk. She knew we were here, hiding in the wood. A shiver of regret ran through me as I realized that it was now too late to go back and dispose of the dead human.

Chapter 12

A Glass Jar

Maddie:

The door swung closed behind me and from the moment my foot crossed the threshold, I felt like I was in another world. Outside the moon cast broad silver beams, the forest clung possessively to the colors of summer and the air was electric. But here, inside the Ticonderoga Falls Bed and Breakfast, I felt suddenly trapped.

Like I had just walked inside a glass jar and someone had spun the lid closed.

It's my imagination, I thought, forcing myself through the foyer into a large entryway, toward the registration desk. I've always hated Victorian houses, with all their nooks and crannies, pantries and closets, their doors within doors and hallways that seem to lead nowhere. Hitchcock got it right when he staged *Psycho* in that mausoleum. Ever since that movie, my heart would ricochet in my chest whenever I saw turn-of-the-century architecture. Like this place.

Part Victorian Gothic, part Queen Anne romantic, part Herman Munster scary.

I crossed the lifeless room filled with swirling dust motes, shadows melting in corners, time standing still. My body the only thing moving as reality seemed to shift around me.

The rules are different here.

I stopped, remembering that thing I had seen back in the woods: Talons and skin the color of night—

My pulse sped and something flickered in the back of my mind, something that hadn't happened for so long that I almost didn't recognize it—an idea for a new character.

"Did you want something?" Professor Driscoll, the owner of the bed and breakfast, gloomed in the shadows, blending in like a chameleon. He crouched behind the desk, a wizened old man staring over wire-rimmed glasses. With his bowed stance and unflinching grimace, he looked like he had eaten something bad for lunch.

"Yeah, I—" I reached the registration counter, remembering that wild animal that had followed us in the woods. I swallowed with difficulty, my throat suddenly dry.

"Speak up." Driscoll tilted his head, probably aiming his best ear in my direction.

"I want to rent the cabin for two more days."

"No." He shook his head. "You went off the Ticonderoga Trail. I warned you not to go up by the falls. That bridge isn't safe after all the rain last week and I'm not gonna be liable for some idiot who tumbles over the edge out there."

"But I—how do you know I went off the trail?"

"It's written all over you. Eucalyptus leaves in your hair, red clay on your shoes. That stuff's only on the Ponderosa Trail."

I ran a hand through my hair and, sure enough, I pulled out a leaf. "Okay, I won't go up that path again. I promise." But even as I said it I knew I was lying. I suddenly needed to see what was up there, hoped that I would see that flying creature again.

Leathery wings, body that hovered in midair, staring at me.

I just wouldn't go at night next time. And I'd take my pepper spray.

Driscoll squinted his eyes, watery and pale blue and

bloodshot like he hadn't gotten enough sleep. He watched me, almost as if practicing the ancient art of telepathy.

"I'd really like to stay." I pulled out my credit card and set it on the counter between us.

He glanced nervously toward the stairway landing. I thought I saw someone up there, a tall figure watching us. But if anyone was there, he vanished almost instantly, retreated down the hallway. Nothing but shadows up there now.

"Fine," the old man said as he grabbed my card, then swiped it through a machine nearly as old as he was. "I'll send fresh linens over in the morning. Just remember what I said about staying off the Ponderosa Trail, or I'll come over there and help you pack up your things myself."

I chuckled as I signed the receipt, imagined him tossing my clothes into a battered suitcase, fumbling with the cords on my laptop, wagging a finger in my face. "Yes. Sir." I found myself studying his face, the stubble of a day-old beard, craggy blue shadows on gaunt cheeks. He'd make a great character—the tortured pawn.

He lowered his brow. Perhaps his telepathy had finally kicked in.

I folded the receipt, tucked it in my back pocket and nodded good-bye. Then I headed toward the door. Eager for fresh air.

Chapter 13

The Great Puppet Master

Professor Eli Driscoll:

The door swung shut with a thump. For a long, painful moment it felt like all the oxygen had been sucked out of the room, like Maddie MacFaddin was the only true living creature in the world. Then I caught my breath. My body sagged back in the chair, limp. I closed my eyes. If I had been a praying man, there would have been a litany of words pouring from my lips right then, I would have been begging for release. I'd have scuffed my knees on that polished wooden floor, would have braided my fingers together and clasped them to my chest.

But prayers meant nothing to me.

The only thing that mattered was the curse.

I knew this reprieve was temporary. I felt like a prisoner who finally got to walk around in the yard, who could let his head fall back and stare up at the sun. This long, delirious moment of quasi-peace was marred only by the fact that it wouldn't last. It would shatter, break into a thousand unrecognizable shards, I might not even be able to remember that the Beast had left me untended.

Sometimes it was so lonely when that happened. Like a horrid vacuum.

But right now it was sweet as sugar, sweet as a thick caramel sauce drizzled over vanilla cake, sweet as a baked apple swimming in buttery molasses—

That was when I realized I wasn't truly alone. The Great Puppet Master was still inside my head, listening.

"Leave me alone!" My words echoed through the cavernous room. No one answered, but I heard laughter upstairs, faint and condescending. "Just leave me alone," I muttered again, words running together, falling over one another, "let me run the bed and breakfast on my own, quit giving me orders. I'm sick of it, I'm going to leave if you don't stop crawling around inside my head—"

"And where would you go, human? How far do you think you would get before one of us tracked you down and brought you back?" It was the female, still wearing gray skin and silver eyes, walking down the stairs like a prowling cat. I didn't turn, didn't look. Didn't want to see her with those leathery wings, folded neatly at her back.

"I don't belong to you—" I said, careful to keep my voice low.

"Oh, yes you do, sweet little man." She was almost behind me now. I could smell her, like a field of wildflowers. I longed to look, to drink her in, to let myself be mesmerized by her alien beauty. "You are mine and I can harvest anytime I want. Would you like to take a little nap, right now?"

"Leave him alone, sister. He's terribly sorry, he never meant to talk to you like that." The Beast itself was speaking, making sure that she remembered who I belonged to. Always and forever.

I kept my eyes focused on the floor as they drew even nearer, as if I could make all the bad nightmares go away by pretending they weren't real. There were three of them now, not two. *How many would there be by the end of the night?*

"You're sorry, aren't you?" the Beast asked, moving closer. I nodded my head. They were surrounding me. Even if I wanted to run, I couldn't get away. Then I sensed something. The air grew softer, calmer. I glanced at them from the corner of my eye, saw that they were all wearing human flesh now, human clothes. Pretending to be what they weren't.

The front door opened then, the cold fresh night air swept into the room. That woman, Madeline, walked in again. She stopped for a second. I glanced up at her.

"Sorry," she said, seemed to feel an awkward silence. "I think I left my credit card."

The monster called Ash, the one who owned me and all of Ticonderoga Falls, stood behind the counter. He found the card, held it in his hand, lifted it, stared at the woman.

A cold electricity flowed through the room.

The woman walked toward him with a grin, lifted her head and sniffed. I could smell it, layers of shadow, the heady fragrance of the forest at dusk. The scent hung in the air like droplets of water, sparkling, spinning. She had to walk through the mist to get her card and her eyelids blinked like she was fighting a dream.

One hand outstretched, fingers wrapped around her card.

Ash didn't let go until she looked into his eyes.

"I'm glad you decided to stay," he said with a grin.

"Me too," she answered.

The wrong answer, of course. I could feel it, vibrating beneath the floor. Gears set in motion, cogs and sprockets instead of emotion, metal and sparks instead of flesh. I couldn't look at the monster's face, it just wasn't allowed in situations like this. So I stared at the woman instead. I wished that I could tell her to run, wished my mouth would open and a warning would come out.

She pocketed the card, turned and left.

She didn't notice the silent plea in my weary, sleepless eyes. Didn't hear the word *run* get tangled and erased by the Beast's machinery. Silver wires laced through my brain, stole my strength. Forced my knees to bend, to stay in the chair although I longed to follow her out the door, to see the stars, to walk so far away that no one would know my name.

I should have cried *help*. Next time I would.

Then, as soon as Madeline walked out the door, electricity sizzled through the air and the transformation took place. Fake human flesh dissolved like ashes in the wind. And I was surrounded by monsters once again.

Chapter 14

Human Blood

Elspeth:

The house sighed and moaned, shutters rattled and boards creaked as soon as the human woman stepped outside the door. A restless hush teased lace panels, making them dance, ghostlike, against wooden floors. I followed the human woman out of the house to the wraparound porch. There I stood quiet and still as a shadow, watching as she jogged back toward her cottage, toward the child and dog that waited for her. Then I glanced back through the leaded-glass window on the front door and saw my father inside, wearing his true Darkling skin. I saw the fear on Driscoll's face.

Stupid, weak humans.

I kicked the railing that ran the length of the porch, then quickly glanced down to make sure I was wearing the right skin. *Can't be calling attention to myself unless I'm dressed properly. Can't embarrass Father.* I leaned against a column and felt the vibrations that flowed through the house. Every time I visited earth, I was drawn back here, to the Driscoll mansion, no matter how I tried to fight it. I hated this house, hated every piece of furniture and every painting, hated the stench of human pride that had soaked into every crevice.

Hated the fact that I was the only one in my clan who could walk through doors or windows uninvited.

Hated my human blood.

"Shouldn't hate what you cannot change, my pretty."

One of my cousins stood behind me. Thane. I gave him a quick glance and a nod. Ran my gaze up and down his shape, then wrinkled my nose. Broad shoulders and long limbs, narrow brow and probing dark eyes. But his feet curled up at the toes and his skin had a green cast. He never could get the human form quite right. Didn't have the eye for shape or color.

Barbarian.

He snickered and took an unwelcome step closer, placed one long finger under my chin. "You don't want to hear the word that comes to mind for you, love."

My spine turned rigid, fingernails curved into claws.

"Better learn how to hide that anger, little one. Or you'll lose the Hunt." His breath was hot on my face. No one ever got this close to me. "And then your father would be displeased. Might not give you a seat at his table."

"Your father spent so much time training you, did he? Oh. I forgot. Your clan doesn't train for the Hunt, do they? You're supposed to work in the fields or the factories. Beasts of burden. I heard that you and River haven't even been taught the gift of discernment—"

"Fair and square, we've had our training, sure enough. Wait and see, my precious. Wait and see who goes tumbling through midnight sky because they can't keep up with the rest of us."

"I'd race you now, if the humans weren't still awake. Perhaps we should cast a sleep enchantment together and then see who—"

"Elspeth." My aunt Sage stood beside me. Tall and majestic and beautiful, everything I would never be.

I lifted my chin, could still feel the warmth of Thane's

finger pressing into my skin even though it had been gone for several heartbeats.

"I'm sorry, Cousin Sage," Thane said with a sweeping bow. "I was merely hoping to get her blood ready for the Hunt."

Perfect words, mocking tone. My cheeks reddened. *Damn human blood.* Never obeyed when I needed it to. I tried to make my skin ivory pale, like that human woman who had just walked past.

"It would be good for all of us to stay focused on the Hunt," Sage answered. She glanced at the sky, at the track of the moon, the position of the few stars brave enough to shine when the Queen of the Heavens reigned. "One human hour. And then we will have dinner."

"Dinner?" Thane frowned.

"A ritual," she said. "Ash's human needs to eat and we may as well watch." A devilish grin spread across her angelic features. "After all, he watches us eat often enough."

Chapter 15

The Killing Room

Ash:

The moon crested the tree line until she hung, full and sweet, in black heavens. She called us to obeisance and the rest of my clan heeded. They gathered in the back garden for a brief ritual. Meanwhile, I prowled the halls, searching for my own version of redemption. I slid a key in the lock, turned the knob, then pushed my way through the door to the study. I thought about opening the louvered wooden shutters, letting in a sultry bank of moonlight, but changed my mind. I preferred the darkness. Besides, I didn't want to see all the dead things hanging on the wall—all the bright winged creatures inside wooden frames and the animal heads with glass eyes.

The killing room.

Even after a hundred years, the stench of death never left this place: a peculiar odor of potassium cyanide, plaster of Paris and hydrogen cyanide hung in the air.

This was the room where Lily had died.

She came for a party, but got murdered instead.

I pulled open a desk drawer, fumbled with a false back

panel, fastened my fingers around a small sphere, then clasped it in my fist. With my back to the wall, I placed the sphere in my mouth, bit and swallowed, ignoring the bitter taste and the foul odor. She would be here soon and that was all that mattered.

The dream melted in my mouth.

"Forgive me." I whispered to the shadows that began to move and shift, as the room itself began to glow beneath the dream. "I wasn't always like this."

"I know, my love," my wife answered.

She slid into the room, tall and beautiful and whole, her gown glimmering, casting its own light in the darkness. In a few steps, she was at my side, nestled in my arms.

"There was a time when I was invited to the best parties, when my smile charmed all the ladies, both young and old. When I told stories that kept the children up late at night, as we knelt before the Evenquest fires, beneath the stars of home."

"I remember. Children would run to greet you," she said, the curve of her smile dazzling, her neck a perfect arc of alabaster flesh. I leaned in to kiss her and she closed her eyes. "They would laugh and jump into your arms." Her voice was a husky whisper now, a waterfall of words.

I didn't want to speak. Didn't want to break the spell.

"You're not really here, are you?" I said.

"No." But the smile remained and I could still taste her skin on my lips.

I remembered a dance we had attended in Germany once, long ago. She had worn a peacock green dress and pale human skin, her hair a tower of glistening gold. Everyone had watched her as we both waltzed together over gleaming floors. Then she had tripped, caught her slipper in her gown, and nearly fell. In the confusion, she forgot what skin she had been wearing, and as she came to her feet again, she was now a round-bellied merchant with a swollen red nose and a ragged frock. People around us shrieked in terror.

Monster, they had cried. *Doppelganger!* Lily and I had

fled, laughing, bursting through the doors to the great hall and then sailing up into moonlit skies. For weeks afterward, we had laughed whenever one of us remembered the incident.

It had been her only flaw. Sometimes she forgot what skin to change into.

And now, in the dream, she put her head on my chest. My dear sweet dead wife. Even in the dreams she had no heartbeat. And she was so very pale.

"But the children didn't always run to greet you." She was gazing up into my eyes now. Why did the truth grow more brittle with age? She didn't used to speak like this. Not when she was alive. "Remember? The Boy was frightened of you, the first time we met him."

I stared into the darkness that surrounded us, wished the morning would come, that the bright sun would devour me whole and that this torment would be over.

"It took a long time for me to woo him," she continued, "to get him to trust you. There was always a dangerous glimmer in your grin, my love, something hiding between your words. That is what attracted me to you in the first place."

But it wasn't true. I had never been that way around her, my precious bride. "Your true memories are fading, blossom," I said with a catch in my voice. "The dreams are growing old, turning bitter with age. You were never like this."

"Then tell the Boy to make you some more dreams. Throw the old ones away."

It always came to this. You'd think I would learn to stay away from this room and my hidden cache of golden dreams. And now, it was time. I had to tell her.

"I only have a few dreams left," I said. "And the Boy is dead."

Her eyes widened. A moment passed when she didn't move, then tears formed on her lashes, her lip quivered. "Nay. Young William lives. I know it."

I shook my head.

"When?"

I shrugged. I had lost count of human years. "Fifty years, maybe. I don't remember."

She pulled away from my embrace. "Why didn't you tell me that he was gone?"

"I do tell you, my love. Every time I see you. And then you forget."

She turned away. "Don't come to me again, Ash. Let me go. I don't want our time together to always end in pain."

"Yes, my love."

She was facing me again, arms about my waist. "Kiss me, sweetheart. Hold me one last time." It was always our last time, now and forever. It was all the Boy had been able to give us, a lasting torment that neither one of us could end. I had bound the Boy's father in the curse, then the Boy got caught in the web by mistake.

Her image began to fade. The dream was breaking, growing thin like river ice in the spring.

"Tell Young William that I love him," she said. Already she had forgotten that the Boy was dead.

Then she was gone.

And as soon as she left, the pain in my side flared up, the wound tore just a bit, shining bright silver in the unlit study.

This was the room where she had run, a hundred years ago, during a game of hide-and-seek with Young William. It was the same room where William's father met with the members of the local lepidopterist club. Lily had panicked when a group of men unexpectedly sauntered in from the back parlor, smelling of brandy and cigars. Startled, her disguise of a nine-year-old girl had fallen off and without realizing it, she turned into a faery.

It was the disguise that Young William had always preferred. It was the skin she wore when visiting him in the grove—gossamer wings, her body small enough to sit upon his outstretched palm.

In the flash of an eye, William's father had caught her in a tangled net; with rough fingers, he sealed her inside a killing jar. Then, when all life had fled her, the old man pinned her to a board, like she was just another giant blue swallowtail caught on an African safari. He speared a pin through her side. And her wound matched the one I wear to this day— the gaping hole just beneath my ribs that travels straight through to my back.

I paused before the window, opened the shutters and let the moonlight pour down upon me, burning my flesh. I didn't blink, didn't turn away when the silver light scorched my flesh.

The moon spoke a different language in this room, all her kindness gone, for this was the place where I had failed my beloved. This was where my curse had fallen, like stars from heaven, beyond my control. It bound me to this place, where I had tormented the Driscoll family for three generations.

And now I ripped my shirt open and let the moon scourge my skin, the pain of a thousand cat-o'-nine-tails blistering my flesh and forcing me to my knees.

Knowing all the while that I was a fallen creature and worthy of my torment.

Chapter 16

Sketchbook

Maddie:

Moonbeams fell through the kitchen window like a sheath of silver arrows. All the dinner dishes had been washed and put away, and it was now that quiet time in the evening when my imagination stirred and came to life. This was when stories used to leap onto my page from the crevices and shadows. Sometimes the characters themselves bloomed full and large from the corners of the room, sometimes outlined in white light, sometimes transparent as ghosts.

But that hadn't happened in a long time. I hadn't even been able to come up with a decent story idea since the divorce.

Until tonight.

The door to Tucker's room hung open and a pool of light washed across the floor. I hesitated in his doorway, sketchbook in one hand. Part of me felt like a faceless silhouette, an outline of who I used to be, a pencil sketch waiting for someone to ink me in, make me real again.

Just then my son glanced up and his smile said something else. It erased all of my jagged edges.

"I had a feeling you weren't asleep yet," I said. "Whatcha reading?" I entered his room, walked past the dog curled on the floor.

Tucker yawned, looked down at the paperback folded on his lap, almost as if he had forgotten what book it was. But it was always the same book. For the past two years. Over and over.

The Hobbit. He lived in a hole in the ground. I wished I could find one.

"What's Frodo doing now?" I asked, sitting beside him on the bed.

"Bilbo," he corrected me. Another grin came out of hiding.

"Your favorite character, huh."

He nodded. "And Samwise Gamgee."

As soon as he heard his name, the dog stood up and pushed his way in between us, then laid his head on the bed. He stared up at Tucker. Waiting.

My son leaned down and kissed Samwise on the nose, then whispered, "Good boy."

The dog's tail thumped, beating the air. Tucker's grin widened, revealing a space where one of his front teeth was missing. I brushed the honey blond hair back from his forehead and kissed the spot in the center of his brow, the spot that belonged to me.

My kiss on his brow. My seal of protection. Against all the monsters who looked like his father or one of my best friends.

"Can I see?" He pointed to my sketchbook.

"You promise not to get scared?" I asked in a teasing tone. I flipped the spiral book open to the page I had been working on for the past hour. Tucker's eyes widened as he stared at the splash panel sketch.

"Is there more?"

"Here." I handed him the sketchpad. He was always my best critic. If this new character had potential, he would see it.

"Wow." The word was so quiet I almost didn't hear it.

With a fingertip he followed the storyboard, from panel to panel, reading the notes in the margins. This version was too rough for dialogue, the character wasn't fully developed yet. I still had to figure out his goal, obstacle, conflict, arc, etc.

But apparently, right now, the character alone was enough.

Tucker got to the last page of pencil drawings and flipped it over, as if disappointed when there weren't more. He frowned. Looked up at me.

"Is this your next story?" he asked.

I nodded, still not sure, waiting to hear what he thought.

"This guy's wicked! He's better than Batman or Wolverine or Hellboy."

I grinned.

"How soon are you gonna be done with it? This is better than your last one—"

I was laughing now. Better than my last graphic novel that won an Eisner Award and was currently in production over at Universal Pictures.

"You seriously need to let me read this. Will this one have words?" he asked, referring to a series I did two years ago with no dialogue—just sound effects and a small amount of narration. That one was being considered as a mini-series on HBO. I was hoping they could get somebody like Zachary Quinto for the lead.

"Yeah, it'll have words." I watched as Tucker flipped back through the pages. He studied each of them and then finally ended on the beginning splash panel.

A dramatic woodland scene covered the page, thick stands of ponderosa pine, a knot of hedge nettle and thimbleberry and mossy shadows, and there between the trees—half running, half flying—was a dark, dangerous creature, sweat glistening on leathery wings, eyes watching from the tangled wilderness.

Every time I looked at it, my heart raced and I remembered that thing back in the woods, the familiar look in its eyes. I felt the way the air had shimmered and how the sky darkened, almost as if time had stood still just long enough for it to escape. One hand had stretched out toward me, palm open.

Something had sparkled in the air.

I had to go back. Tomorrow. I had to see if it was still there, somewhere.

Tucker yawned again, settled back against his pillow. I took his paperback book, set it on the nightstand, then turned the light to a lower setting. He had nightmares if I turned off all the lights.

Fortunately, tonight both he and the dog were asleep before I even left the room.

Sketchbook in hand.

Chapter 17

Lulled into Slumber

Maddie:

Weariness rolled over me. Without meaning to, my head slipped back and rested on the sofa cushion. I stared at my sketchbook for a moment—at that splash-panel creature—until the picture faded, until the pencil lines began to move and change. Everything changed. I tried to keep my eyes open, but everything started to fade.

I fell asleep, the transition between the two worlds simple. The real world intertwined with that of my imagination, and a surreal landscape suddenly unfolded around me.

I was in my car, staring out the window, trying to focus on the undulating switchbacks, vistas that alternated between primeval forest and rocky cliff. We were heading up into the mountains for a long deserved vacation. Tucker was asleep in the backseat, PlayStation clutched possessively in one hand.

Don't fall asleep. Not now.

But in the end, I knew it didn't matter whether I stayed awake or not. I fell prey to the faltering light that sifted through the branches, allowed myself to be lulled into slumber, let the dream wash over me, a serenade of beauty. Just like I had allowed myself to fall in love.

Wake up.

I glanced across the car, saw a surreal landscape sweeping past, purple trees, green sky. The colors were wrong, but they often are in dreams. My younger sister was driving, much too fast, but then it wasn't my sister after all. The face was blank, all features erased except for a pair of silver eyes. *You were in love,* my sister asked. I nodded, *we were all in love once, a long time ago.* I held a box of photos in my lap, black-and-white pictures of my life. The images melted, turned garish and gritty, like cheap tabloids sold on street corners.

The dog is barking. Something must be wrong.

The box of pictures spilled onto my lap, fell across the floor, took root and blossomed, became a garden of images: a picture of that corner office where I had been able to see the sticky glitter of Hollywood; a photo of that delirious holiday we had spent in Cancun; a snapshot of Tucker's last birthday, back before my world had exploded in tabloid headlines.

GET UP!

A picture of a man who smiled too easily at all the wrong people, most of them women.

My eyes flickered open.

Wake up, wake up, wake up!

I had a crick in my neck and my mouth hung open, slack. But I wasn't awake. I couldn't be.

Because a shadowy monster blurred across the living room and the dog was barking, growling, snapping. Samwise was pushing Tucker's bedroom door open, he was pummeling across wood floors, legs spinning, mouth open, teeth bared, running toward that dark hole in the universe, that leathery thing that was sucking all the light out of the room.

I sat up and swallowed, blinked away one nightmare for another.

"Sam?" It was the only word I could get out, my mouth filled with the glue of sleep.

Growling. Snarling. Leaping through the air toward the Beast.

Wings spread wide, darker than night, a shadowy creature filled the room like a great, monstrous crow, blacker than black and heavier than a nightmare. It pressed me down and I couldn't move, couldn't even feel my heart beating anymore. The dog was frozen in the air, leaping in a broad vengeful arc, jaws open and ready to rip that nightwing beast to shreds. He had a piece of it in his mouth, dark blood spraying.

A woman was screaming.

And then suddenly there were two of them. Wings spread, blanketing the room in a black-ink hell and whispering cold.

Chapter 18

The Edge of Twilight

Ash:

We sat poised on the edge of twilight, eating—
this houseful of monsters who barely tolerated one another.
Plates passed from hand to hand, moving around the circle
like the shadow on a sundial. Driscoll glanced at me from
time to time, a glimmer of fear in his gaze. I merely nodded,
a king in my court granting reluctant permission to my subject's each and every move. The two of us were connected
in a silent, secret way, the ancient curse shackling us with
invisible chains.

Driscoll always preferred to see me dressed in human skin.
So, of course, I rarely appeared to him that way.

Tonight we all sat in full Darkling attire, revealing ourselves as the beasts we truly were. We dined on baked apples
and sugared rose petals and pastries with thick raspberry
icing. We drank blackberry wine and munched on cham-
pagne grapes and fresh strawberries. Through it all, I was
the only one at the table allowed to use both knife and fork.
Even Driscoll had to gnaw on his chicken and potatoes with
bare hands.

It isn't truly a curse unless you find some way to drive them mad, inch by inch, moment by moment. And madness always was the goal. I could have lived anywhere, like my wild brothers and sisters, those without homes or humans of their own, those who prowled the edges of Ticonderoga Falls like scavengers. But from the beginning, I chose to be civilized.

I took one family, and just one, to haunt. Forever.

The Driscolls of Ticonderoga Falls.

So right now, I pretended to pay attention to the pointless chatter about the Hunt. It looked like I was listening, I was sure of it.

Because in truth, I was.

I was listening to the Legend as it whispered overhead and throughout the village. Somewhere, someone was telling the tale about my fall from grace, leaning over a back fence or pausing on a street corner, one neighbor was reminding another about what had happened right here, nearly a hundred years past. And as the words were spoken it was like they had ripped off yet another pound of flesh. Sparks glimmered and I held a hand against my old wound, covering it anew with a fresh Veil.

Just then I heard something else. I tilted my head.

Yes, there, a silver crackle, the sound made when a Darkling unfurls his wings, when he folds reality.

But the pitch was off.

I glanced around the table again. My daughter, Elspeth, had slipped away a few moments earlier, said her shoulders ached from the journey, had even shown me the bruised flesh where wing met bone on her back. But bruises can be faked.

I stood, inadvertently kicking my chair to the floor, an act that silenced all their conversation. Driscoll cowered as I swept past, the others merely stared at me with a curious expression. In a heartbeat, I was on the porch, head lifted, smelling dark sky, searching for my daughter's scent.

My human flesh dissolved, blew away on the chill autumn

wind. Wings spread, I hovered in the air, listening, searching.

"What is it?" Sage appeared on the porch behind me.

"Hush!" I ordered.

That was when I heard it. A scream. Coming from Madeline's cottage.

Elspeth. Screaming.

I cast a Veil, strong and bright, one that would slow everything and everyone down. It froze a corner of Ticonderoga Falls like insects in bits of amber. Like my people, my powers come from human dreams. Anything they can dream, I can do.

Then I soared over field and forest, following the scream that wouldn't end. In an instant I stood before an open window and saw Elspeth inside. A dog soared through the air toward her, teeth bared. The creature already had my daughter's arm clamped in its jaws.

Foolish child!

I flew into the room and grabbed the dog, then pulled it away from Elspeth. "Sleep," I whisper-sang in its ear, a song meant to calm a faithful beast that tried to protect someone it loved. I gently closed its jaws, wincing when I saw my daughter's blood in its mouth, tried to wipe it away with my hand. Then I placed the animal on the floor, carefully, in a position that would look natural.

When I lifted my head I realized that she was watching me. Maddie was awake.

All she would see was a blur. Still, she shouldn't be seeing even this much. I glanced down at a sketchbook on her lap.

She had been drawing a picture of a Darkling in the forest. *Me.*

But I couldn't stop to act on it. Life and limb, they were what mattered. *Harm no human, no beast, during harvest.* Rules had to be followed, or the harvest would turn bitter and foul in the mouth. Would bring famine. Pestilence. Plague.

I spun around, faced my child, grown now and lovely as the moon herself. Disobedient and foolish and bleeding—

she was too much like her father. Because of her human blood, she too had been captured by my Veil. I ripped off my shirt, wrapped it around her wound and folded reality so that we could both fit through the open window.

Then I flew away, with Elspeth in my arms.

Chapter 19

Shimmering and Silver

Maddie:

One moment I crouched on the sofa, unable to move. My dog hung frozen in the air, biting a black-winged beast that filled the room. Then there were two beasts and an unbearable cold frosted my skin. For a brief flash of time, I recognized an unmistakable odor. But it didn't make sense.

It was the forest, a fresh mash of green leaves and moss, sunlight and wind. The fragrance filled the room, made time stand still.

Then, suddenly I could move again. I blinked and let the wet fragrance of the wood fill my lungs. The darkness and the wings that had blocked out the light were gone now. Samwise was no longer growling.

In an instant, nothing was the same as before.

Now the dog was sleeping on the floor beside me, curled up, tail tucked to his nose.

The window hung open, shimmering and silver, as if a great heat had just passed through the room. But all was still. I stood on shaky legs. Then I walked through the house to make sure no intruder was inside, made sure Tucker was safe and asleep. I tested and closed and locked every window and door.

And then finally, I stopped and knelt beside Samwise, so deeply asleep that I couldn't rouse him, even when I called his name. That was when I saw it—the only proof that what had just happened hadn't been my imagination.

A few flecks of blood colored the dog's muzzle.

Chapter 20

Silver-Gray Skin

Ash:

My wings pummeled the air. I flew through mist and shadow, between white fir and lodgepole pine; I followed a mountain pass, deeper and deeper through evergreen vein toward the village, all the while wishing that I could go faster. The clouds of midnight shadowed the vale, threatened snow, spoke promises of brittle cold. The only warmth was my daughter, a crescent of flesh that nestled too still in my arms, eyes closed.

She was caught in her Darkling skin—eyes the color of the moon, skin like a stormy sky, hair like the blue-black raven.

Eyes that wouldn't open, flesh growing colder.

Was she asleep? Why hadn't Sage told me about this?

I soared low through moonlit skies toward the center of Ticonderoga Falls, toward the one human I trusted.

Wake, human! I cried through vellum wind, calling my friend to rise from slumber, to be ready. *Get out your precious silver instruments and bandages. Have all the medicines ready.*

The village came into view then, tiny houses tucked amidst the trees, streets that followed the curve of the mountain like ribs. Bits of fog shrouded buildings, erased alleys, wrapped me in wet frost as I descended, wings flapping, reality folding like a black cloak around me. As soon as I landed I took the shape of a human, a long cape draped over my shoulder that shielded my daughter, still trapped in her Darkling skin. A small whitewashed building emerged from the fog, placard creaking in the wind, sign hanging in the front window.

CLOSED, OPEN AT 9 A.M.

I beat a fist against the door. Once. Twice. Just about slammed it down again, when the door swung open. I almost hit my friend in the face.

"Hey." Dr. Ross Madera stepped back, hair messed, glasses perched crooked on his nose. "Could you please try a cell phone next time? That dream telepathy thing of yours is awful—"

I pushed my way inside the door, past the doctor, toward one of the inner rooms. I wrinkled my nose at the horrid stench of antiseptic and detergent. Human medicine was primitive at best. I gently placed my daughter on a long stainless-steel table.

"You know I'm not really qualified for this," Ross said as he followed a step behind. "I'm a veterinarian, not an M.D. I'm not supposed to treat people."

I lifted the cloak to reveal my daughter's Darkling features: silver-gray skin, dark hair, gray-black wings, slender pointed ears, webbed fingers. "She's only half human," I said. "And I can't take her to a doctor. Not when she's wearing this skin. It's Elspeth."

Ross nodded with understanding. There were few secrets between us. He stared at my daughter, looked at the shirt that bound her wound, the blood soaking through. "What happened?"

"A dog bit her."

Within a few minutes, Ross had gathered everything he

needed into a neat pile. He started cleaning and dressing her wound, sweat beading his forehead. Then he paused and glanced up at me. "She's going to need stitches," he said.

I nodded.

"I can give her a topical anesthetic, but I don't think I should take a chance on anything stronger. I don't know enough about your anatomy. I can't have her jump while I'm sewing her up—"

"I can keep her under until you're done."

Then I sang a soft enchantment and the room sparkled with dots of light.

Ross bent over her again, then began the slow, delicate process of stitching her flesh together. "Do you know if the dog has its shots?" he asked.

"Shots?" I gave him a blank stare.

"Rabies shots. Where did this happen?"

"In one of the cottages Driscoll rents."

"Then the dog's owners must have filled out some paperwork when they registered. Ask Driscoll. I need to know if that dog has its current rabies vaccination."

"I'll go get the dog."

Ross sighed as he stood up. The stitches were finished and Elspeth's arm was now wrapped in layers of white gauze. "You don't think that might look a bit suspicious?"

"I can make it look like the dog ran away."

"Check the paperwork first, would you? If you show up here in the morning with a dog—"

Just then Elspeth moaned and her eyes fluttered open. She tried to sit up, grabbed for her injured arm, then saw that it was wrapped in a bandage.

"Lie still for a few minutes," Ross said. "I'll go see if I can find some more topical anesthetic for the pain." He walked out the door and I could hear him rummaging through drawers in the next room.

"What did he do to me?" she asked me when we were alone. "My arm burns."

"Who taught you to hunt?"

She grimaced, then lay back down and closed her eyes. "I didn't do anything wrong."

"You didn't mask your scent. You walked into that house smelling like a human. If I hadn't gotten there when I did, that dog might have killed you—"

"I don't need a babysitter."

"No. You need a father."

"Really? Well, I wonder where I might find one of those. Maybe Aunt Sage will take me shopping in the morning, I hear humans buy and sell almost everything—"

"It's my fault."

"What?" She sat halfway up again and stared at me. I never apologized, never said I was wrong. It caught me by surprise too.

"I should have taught you to hunt, myself," I said, wishing I could take back the years I had ignored her. But I never thought she would get hurt, thought that the Elders back home would have done a better job than I could. Apparently I had been wrong about that. "I didn't realize that you would be so—so—"

"Human?"

"No. Stubborn, like me."

She grinned and threw both arms around me, then let out a little yelp when she accidentally pulled her stitches. She laid her head against my chest and I ran my hand over her hair. For the first time, I realized that this whole father-daughter thing was going to be a lot more difficult than I expected.

Part 2

Our truest life is when we are in dreams awake.
—Henry David Thoreau

Chapter 21

Back in the Wood

Thane:

The evening slipped away. One moonbeam after another slid through black branches, teasing and calling, until finally, the Mistress of the Night disappeared. I slumped against the wall, one curved claw absently drawing patterns in the dust on a side table. The time for hunting was over. The shelter of sweet black night gone. Still the moon continued to call to me, even after her sister, the ever-brilliant sun, crested the nearby hills.

A breeze circled through the woods, a moan and a sigh of wind, then it swept back toward the Driscoll mansion, carrying with it the stench of death. It seeped through windows and doors, curled down corridors until it found me. Standing alone in the front parlor.

I closed my eyes.

It was the dead human in the woods. Already his body was beginning to decompose, to cast the foul odor of rotting meat into passing air currents.

I heard a soft footstep approach, cautious, hesitant. A familiar face loomed in the narrow doorway. River.

"Do you smell it?" my brother asked, keeping his voice low. He glanced behind him to make sure no one else was about.

"Of course I do," I replied, bitterness in my voice.

And then another voice drew near, singing morning poems, clear and sweet.

Sage.

"Good morrow, lads," she said, opening drapes, then walking through sunbeams as if they were paths of butter, never a grimace of pain when the searing light touched her flesh. She was more cunning than she seemed on the surface, just like her brother. "Just one more day of sun. The Hunt begins tonight."

She smiled at both of us before shifting her skin, until she became little more than a shadow, the same shape she had been most of the evening. Then she slipped off into another room, near invisible, her scent masked and her heartbeat stilled.

She was watching us, had been ever since she spotted us in the wood last night.

"Fair and square," I cursed. It wouldn't be long before one of the Blackmoors discovered the moldering heap we had left back in the wood. But I couldn't let that happen. Not yet.

Chapter 22

White Shadows

Maddie:

Mists rolled over the landscape, laid on top of each other like sheets of tissue paper, muffling sound and replacing the night with eerie white shadows. The sun tried to break through. One part of the sky seemed slightly brighter, seemed to say, yes the sun still exists. But the mists won the battle. They moved and shifted, curled around the cabin and blocked out any connection with the outside world. The only thing I could see from the kitchen window was the wrought-iron weather vane that perched atop the Ticonderoga Falls Bed and Breakfast.

I tried to warm the cottage with a fire in the living room and the thick fragrance of scrambled eggs and bacon. Apparently it worked. My son stumbled to the small kitchen table as if summoned from the dead. He yawned and scratched his head while I poured him a glass of orange juice, then loaded his plate with food. Everything was fine, for a few minutes. He was eating, drinking, waking up.

Then he looked around, as if something was missing.

"Where's Samwise?" Tucker asked between bites of jam-laden toast.

"Outside. Finish your breakfast, sweetheart."

"He should come in," he said, sliding from his chair, then heading toward the door.

"No! I mean, not yet."

Tucker stopped in the middle of the living room, stared out the window at the dog, his leash tied to one of the porch rails. "Why can't he come in? And why is he wearing his muzzle?" He whirled around, looked at me with a concerned expression. "Did he see a mailman? Mom, I told you, Sam never bit the mailman. He just barks a lot and acts like he might, but he never does—"

"I know. He didn't see a mailman. Finish your breakfast."

He opened the door to the porch, stood in the doorway. "I wanna see Sam."

"No!" I raced across the room and slammed the door closed. "I need to—he got in a fight with a wild animal last night, and he's been acting funny this morning. We have to take him to the vet after we eat."

"What wild animal? Is he okay? Is he hurt?"

"Tucker—"

"I don't want any breakfast!" He was crying now, putting on his shoes and his jacket. "I wanna go to the vet and make sure Sam is okay."

I glanced out the window, saw the dog stare at me with pleading brown eyes, tail thumping so hard I could feel the vibration on the floor. I sighed, then took my car keys and handed them to Tucker. "All right. But you have to listen to me, understand?"

He nodded, wiped his nose on the sleeve of his jacket.

"Go out the side door and unlock the car. Get in the passenger seat. I'll get the dog and put him in the cargo area—"

"But he never rides back there—"

"Tucker. You'll have to stay home if you don't do what I say."

"Fine! But there's nothing wrong with him. I know it. Just look at him."

He went out the side door, slammed it behind him, then jogged to the car. I opened the front door, edged my way onto the porch, gingerly untied the leash from the railing and held the dog at arm's length as I led him to the car.

Just look at him.

But that was the problem. I couldn't. Not since this morning when I woke up and found him prowling through the house, hackles up, sniffing imaginary tracks and growling. Then he had stopped in front of the window, the same window I had left open last night, and raised himself up on hind legs, paws on the windowsill. At that moment the eerie morning mists had crept into the room, surrounded the dog, and like a shadow he had grown—until he was almost as big as that thing I had dreamed about last night.

It all had to be a dream, right? The winged creature, the dog turning into something that looked like a werewolf, the blood on Samwise's muzzle, the way he kept prowling through the house. Looking for something or someone like he wanted to rip the flesh off its bones.

I had cried out his name, fear in my voice, and instantly he had changed back, turned around and run to me, faithful dog ready to protect.

But was he the same? Was it all my imagination?

I swung open the rear door to my Lexus SUV, made sure the cargo net was stretched and secure so Samwise wouldn't be able to get in the passenger section. This was the part I had been dreading. For the past year the dog had been unable to jump up into the car because of hip dysplasia. I always lifted him in, all eighty-five pounds of him.

He stood alongside the rear bumper, tail wagging, looking just like the dog I had raised from a puppy.

But what was going to happen when I took him in my arms, when his face was right next to mine? Even though the dog was wearing a muzzle, I was terrified.

"Come on, boy," I said, holding my arms outstretched.

Instead of walking into my arms, he just laid his head on my hand and stared up me. It was the move that could get him anything he wanted, whether it was a bite of hamburger or a walk on a rainy day, it always worked.

It was as if he was trying to tell me that he would never hurt me, not me or Tucker. He was still the same old Samwise that I had rescued from the pound, that I sang to sleep when he was a puppy.

"I'm sorry, boy," I said.

Then I lifted him into the car and closed the door behind him.

The Lexus eased through winding two-lane mountain roads, headlights carving twin beams of light in the heavy fog. A surreal village appeared house by lonely house, then disappeared as soon as the SUV lumbered past. Just yesterday, I had driven into town to get groceries, and now today everything looked completely different. Ominous. Quiet. All the Halloween decorations that I thought looked cute yesterday looked almost spooky today. Carved pumpkins lined the porches, scarecrows and skeletons hung in the trees. Someone had dressed up their front yard to look like a miniature cemetery with Styrofoam headstones. A trio of ghosts made out of gossamer fabric swung in the damp breeze.

"Maybe we should get some candy while we're in town," I said. Tucker just stared out the window, his hair sleep tousled. I hadn't realized until now that he was still wearing his pajamas.

I wasn't going to win any Mom-of-the-Year awards today, that was for sure.

"There it is." A small whitewashed building appeared, with a sign out front that read Tooth and Claw. Strange name for a vet. I parked on the street. "Stay in the car."

"No." Tucker was already hopping down from the seat to the ground.

I sighed, wishing that my son behaved as well as the dog. Then I got out, went around to the back of the car and opened the tailgate. There was Samwise, ears down like he'd been a bad dog, tail wagging, begging me to please, please forgive him for whatever he had done. I felt like a monster as I lifted him to the ground, then took the leash in my hand—but I had to do this, had to make sure that he hadn't been infected with some unknown wild mountain strain of rabies. Or worse.

Tucker opened the door to the vet's office. Two other people already waited inside. One had an old white dog with patchy fur, while the other had something inside a box—scratching and sniffing, a cat maybe, or a rabbit. Samwise lifted his head toward the box and took a whiff. Curious to see what was inside, he strained at the leash, dragging me across the slippery floor.

"No!" I said, doing my best to maneuver the dog toward the counter. I suddenly regretted thinking that the dog minded me better than Tucker. Neither one listened to me very well.

The woman at the counter raised her eyebrows. "Does he bite?" she asked, looking at the muzzle.

"Not unless you're a mailman." Then I lowered my voice. "I need to see the vet. Something got into my house last night, a raccoon or a bat or maybe a bear—"

"A bear?" The woman repeated the words in a loud voice. *So much for a low profile.* "Well, I don't actually know what it was. Could have been a flying monkey for all I know. I only saw it for a second, but my dog bit it and there was blood and I think—"

"Sounds like chupacabras," the man holding the box-animal said. "But there wasn't a full moon last night. They only come out during a full moon, that's what I say. Every other day of the month is—"

"—That's enough, Joe. No need to scare the tourists away." Then the receptionist pointed to an open door. "Take him in there. The doctor will be right in. But you better wait out here, young man," she said to Tucker. "Just in case your dog needs a shot."

I settled into an uncomfortable molded plastic chair, hoping I wouldn't have to wait long. Surprisingly, only a couple of moments passed before the doctor came in. He gave me a half smile and closed the door. He was unshaven, his clothes were wrinkled beneath his lab coat and he looked exhausted. Didn't anybody in this town get any sleep?

"I'm Dr. Ross Madera," he said as he shook my hand. "I understand you think your dog bit someone last night?"

"Something. He bit some*thing.*"

"Right. I'm sorry. That's what I meant." He flashed a charming grin. "I guess I think animals are people. Do you want to tell me what happened?"

"I woke up last night and there was this big, I mean *really big*, animal in the living room, with wings and claws"—I expected him to laugh at this point, but he just nodded his head—"and then my dog came running out of the bedroom, growling and barking, and he jumped up and bit it. Whatever the hell it was."

"I see. Are his rabies shots current?"

"Then it just disappeared—" I paused. "What?"

"His rabies vaccinations, are they up to date?" He smiled again.

"Yeah. But then this morning, the dog started running around the house, growling and sniffing—"

"Was there blood on the floor?"

"No, just a little on his muzzle. But I wiped it off."

"He could probably still smell the blood and thought that the animal, whatever it was, was still in the house."

"That's all? He was smelling the blood?" I sank back into the chair, felt the tension flowing out of my body, hadn't even realized that there had been a knot in the back of my neck. "I thought he was rabid or something. Believe it or not,

I even—I even thought that I saw him turn into a shadowy monster himself. As big as a werewolf."

"No." Dr. Madera gave me an astonished look, then he glanced down at the dog. "That's impossible. That couldn't happen."

I laughed. "Which part's impossible? That a monster broke into my house or that my dog turned into a werewolf?"

He didn't say anything, almost as if I had caught him off guard. Then suddenly some idea flashed in his eyes. "Did you go for a hike down by the creek recently?"

"Yeah."

"It's possible that you wandered into a patch of deadly nightshade. It used to grow down by the falls. I'm not saying it's common, but it could have gotten onto your skin or in your nasal passages. Nightshade's been known to cause hallucinations."

"Really? So my dog's okay?"

"We'll give him a round of antibiotics, just to be safe." He wrote something on a chart, then stared down at my paperwork for a long moment, silently mouthing a few words. My name. I'd seen this before—that strange flicker of recognition, the connection with my pen name, although it usually happened at sci-fi conventions. And it was almost always a teenage boy, teetering on the awkward precipice of manhood.

"Madeline MacFaddin." He lifted his head. "You wouldn't be Mad Mac, would you?"

I was going to smile, maybe flirt just a bit, but that was when Samwise decided he'd had enough. He jerked the leash out of my hand and lunged for the door. With a fierce head butt, he shoved it open and then scrambled into the reception room.

"Sam, no!" I jumped from my seat and tried to grab the leash, but it was already out of reach. The dog was skating across the highly polished floor like he was on a mission. That was when I realized that the animal-in-the-box, a long, furry, weaselly-looking creature, had just pried its way out of the box and was now scrambling up the desk. The receptionist stared at it wide-eyed, then it leaped toward her head. The woman screamed and ran. As if that was exactly what it wanted, the creature scurried down the hallway after her.

And now Samwise bounded after both of them.

"Stop! No! Stay!" I tried every command I could think of. "Sit! Get over here, right now!" Tucker jumped up from his chair and together we both chased after the dog. "Leave it, stop, down, sit, sit, sit!"

Finally, one of the commands took hold.

The dog lay down at the end of the hall.

One paw on top of the ferret, holding it in place.

We drove through foggy tree-lined corridors, over a swift flowing black road, past postcard-perfect nineteenth-century bungalows. Only a few cars were out this morning, white beams of light that appeared suddenly, heralding the approach of another living being. Then the other car would pass and the dreamlike landscape would once again turn gothic, almost as if the entire village had slipped back in time. Once we were finally back inside the cabin everything was normal, raucous and chaotic and normal. Sam bounded from room to room, playing with Tucker, chasing a ball, stopping to drink from his bowl and then dashing off again. All was forgiven. The horrid muzzle had been taken off. Tucker laughed and tumbled and almost broke a lamp.

Just like it used to be.

Before.

I made lunch for Tucker, then paused beside my laptop, glancing at the papers on the desk. I stared at the splash-panel sketch of that creature in the woods. Could this be the same beast that had broken into the cabin last night? Whatever it was, it had never actually hurt me or the dog. Scared me witless, but that was all.

Could it be the same creature I had seen when I was a little girl?

I grabbed my iPhone and shot some photos of my sketches, then attached them in an e-mail to my agent. The description of the project was brief, just a hook and a few potential titles. *Nightshade. Nightwing.* They'd probably already been used, but it was a start. Then I took a closer look at the drawing. The trees weren't right. Neither were the bushes or the undergrowth.

I glanced out the window.

It was almost one o'clock. The fog had thinned a bit and it didn't look like rain or snow. I could hike down to the creek, take some photos of the surrounding woods, get a better idea of the setting, and still be back in time to make a late lunch for myself.

If I was really lucky, I might see that thing again.

Might even get a photo of it this time.

Chapter 23

River of Black Silk

Ash:

Down in the human world—where the seasons spin like an unending wheel—there, a car drove through the fog, headlights like glowing eyes. Tires crunched gravel, a door opened, then closed with a hollow metallic thud. It was like the sound of battle armor, chain mail and clanging swords, reviving violent ghosts of the distant past.

They were home. Maddie and her boy and their dog.

There had been no rabies. No dangerous strain of wild venom flowed through my daughter's veins. I knew that already, had made Driscoll search for the papers before the moon finished her journey. Elspeth was safe.

For now.

My daughter lay curled on her side, wounded arm propped on a pillow. Her Darkling skin faded while she slept and all of her features turned human: pink flesh, dark lashes, lips the color of poppies, hair like a river of black silk. Right now she looked almost exactly like her mother—a human that I should have avoided. Instead, I had given in to my hunger and drunk so deeply of her dreams that no one else had been able to satisfy me.

And now, because of my transgression, I wondered what would happen to Elspeth. What Darkling or human would ever love or care for her, bewitching creature caught between two worlds—

Bewitching me even now. Making me forget how much I despised humans.

"How is she?" Sage landed with a gentle thump on the widow's walk, then stood in the doorway to my room.

"Sleeping," I answered, as if it were a horrid thing. "Why didn't you tell me that she sleeps?"

Sage moved closer, her long dress whispering. "You wanted me to tell you what you already knew? That your daughter is half human?" Silver eyes glimmered, stared through me.

"Why didn't you teach her to hunt?"

"We did." She crossed the short distance to the bed, feet not touching the ground. A detail she forgot about from time to time.

"She didn't mask her scent," I said. "She could have been killed—"

"But she wasn't. You were there to save her, to teach her. It's time, brother."

"No."

"Elspeth is different from us. Her bones are heavier than ours." Sage knelt beside the bed, ran a gentle hand over my daughter's hair. "She can only fly for short distances and then she has to rest. Sienna and I took turns carrying her on the flight here. She's not strong enough to return. This must be her home now."

"I told you. The humans—they won't accept her."

"They've accepted you, my love."

"It's not the same." I turned my back on her, brooding, remembering, wishing I could change everything.

"The humans haven't accepted me," I confessed then as I watched another car make its slow approach through streets drenched in cloud.

"They fear me. To them, I am a beast."

Chapter 24

The Land of Nightmares

Driscoll:

Dr. Ross Madera stood on the wraparound porch, one hand on the carved brass doorknob, as if dreading what waited on the other side. I could see him through the leaded-glass panels on the door, watched him shiver, as if pushing his ghosts behind him, as if shouldering his way through a large crowd.

Sometimes the price of friendship is too heavy to bear.

But I have no empathy for his choice of friends.

The knob turned, almost on its own, as if the door itself willed him to enter. They waited inside—like a pride of lions: Ash's clan, here for the Hunt. They had spread across the parlor and I was doing my best to crouch behind the desk and stay hidden.

Ross stood in the doorway, now, fear on his weathered features. I knew that he barely made it from one day to the next and that thought alone made me smile.

None of the Darklings bothered to hide behind human flesh when the door opened—they all kept their glowing eyes, papery skin, the wings that rustled and sang. Meanwhile, a single-note chant, poetic and hypnotic, circled the room, haunting and eerie in both simplicity and depth. I felt like I could listen to it for a thousand years and never hear it repeat, never grow weary of it. Sparks hung in the air, liquid, and fragrant.

They were probably testing enchantments, holding time still.

Ross took a timid step across the threshold. One of the females, wild and beautiful, smiled at him with silver-gray lips. It was Sienna, Ash's cousin and one of Sage's hand-maidens. She walked closer, touched webbed fingers to the intruder's brow.

She was probing, looking for his secrets.

I knew that Ross had enough secrets to satisfy even the most wanton Darkling. Tales of war in faraway jungles, short men with almond eyes, children who had banded together to carry death. Burning villages and rice paddies and protest-ers back home who hadn't cared about the war. Helicopter blades that had sliced blue-black sky, a foreign language on the radio. Men who had tumbled down to the ground, far below—the imprint of Ross's hand on their backs. Always and forever, falling. Always and forever, dying. The secret desire Ross had: to be shoved out of the door next, sucking night sky, praying to the god of gravity to be merciful and swift.

Sienna smiled now, as if she had joined him in the Land of Nightmares. She drank in all of his pain and seemed to beg for more.

"Sienna. That's enough." Ash's voice sounded, some-where up above. On the landing, perhaps.

I flinched and huddled closer to the floor, peered from the side of the desk.

But she ignored Ash. She traced a finger from Ross's temple to his lips. There, she let it rest, eyes focused on his mouth, as if willing him to speak of it, out loud, the horrors of war, the sleepless nights.

"What does it mean to not be able to sleep?" she asked,

head cocked as if gazing down a microscope at some new form of bacteria.

"Stop!" Ash was beside them both now. "This one belongs to me. He bears my mark." He took Ross's arm, lifted it, pulled back the sleeve to reveal a six-inch scar on the human's forearm. "The Hunt does not begin until I say."

Then he pushed Sienna back, fire in his touch. Yellow flames licked her shoulder; they traveled the full length of her arm before disappearing.

She cried out and shrank away from Ross. A hiss slithered from her lips, but she didn't fight back.

No one challenged Ash. No human. No Darkling.

Ever.

"Come."

Ash led Ross away from the flock of Darklings, up a stairway, to a room where they could talk. They turned their backs on the whir of leathery wings, retreating into the safety of friendship.

And at the same time I retreated as well, through the kitchen and up the back stairs to my room. Maybe, if they couldn't see me, I could be forgotten. I needed to hide. For there would be no safe place in all of Ticonderoga Falls once the Hunt began.

Chapter 25

Dancing Burning Beast

Thane:

The stench of fire and scorched flesh filled the room. Thin trails of smoke followed after Ash as he ascended the stairs, venom in his gaze when he looked back at us from the landing. Meanwhile, flames sizzled on my sister Sienna's skin, bright and burning—a gentle, flickering, liquid heat. I watched her, my heart fascination growing.

I hated the sun; her light blinded me.

But this dancing, burning beast was different, this thing called fire, this smell of charred flesh.

The Hunt does not begin until I say.

But it had already begun, yesterday in the green shadowed wood, when my brother had killed that human male. The creature had died with a pleading whimper, all because River hadn't been able to control his appetite. And now his body lay cold and alone beneath a shallow pyre of leaves.

We had to dispose of the body, before one of the Blackmoors stumbled upon it.

I reached for Sienna, urged her to come closer, then I soothed her raw flesh with an incantation. She shuddered and cursed as she leaned into my embrace, brother and sister-in-skin. At the same time, the human-named-Ross disappeared in the gloom upstairs, safe behind yet another closed door with my dear Cousin Ash.

I rested my lips near Sienna's ear, then whispered, "Perhaps you can harvest the human tomorrow."

She pulled away and shook her head.

"You shouldn't let Ash's mark stop you," I said.

"'Tis the law," River said. "We dare not cross him again." My brother joined us, tall and weedy, thin of flesh but strong of sinew. His gaze flicked from Sienna to me and then toward the empty staircase. Perhaps making sure Ash was gone.

"Wrong to break a blood oath, you mean," I said.

River nodded.

"But haven't you broken his law already? And isn't that why we're here? To live. To hunt. To find our own little patch of dirt like Cousin Ash. No matter what we have to do to get it," I said, all the while watching the expression on Sienna's face as she took a cautious step toward the stairs.

"I've never seen such vivid, dark dreams," she spoke with longing in her voice.

"My pretty cousins." I put one hand on each of them, lowering my voice to a conspiratorial tone. "This right here, *this* could be our home. These humans could belong to us."

Sienna turned toward me, eyes like the golden fields of home, lips parted, teeth like porcelain daggers ready to hunt. "This land *could* be ours," she agreed. "And that human, the one who dwells in the Land of Nightmares—"

"He could be yours, my love," I said. "And so he shall be. There's just one thing that we need to take care of first. We can't let our dear Cousin Ash grow suspicious too soon."

Chapter 26

Glittering Machinery

Ash:

Ross Madera sat in a wicker chair before the fire, sipping a cup of tea. Outside, the fog spiraled, caressing the windows as if it longed to enter. Inside, the flickering fire colored the room. It accented the lines in Ross's face, making him look older, more tired. Or maybe he had been slowly aging and I hadn't been paying attention. Humans wear out much faster than Darklings. They are so fragile.

"Is Elspeth still sleeping?" he asked. His hands shook slightly, but it was obvious he was trying to hide it.

I nodded.

He set his cup down with an awkward clatter, then he stood and walked to the window. He stuffed his hands in his pockets. "I hate coming here, especially when your family is visiting."

"Everybody has a side of the family they're ashamed of. You just met mine," I said, sifting through the human's thoughts. All I could see was the war, bits of it strewn about the room, alongside the hand-carved Belter furniture and Tiffany lamps. A headless body here, an M–16 assault rifle there, a tank rumbling through the wall. I had to concentrate to sort reality from the waking hallucinations. "Did the nightmares come back last night?"

This was what had brought us together, how we had become friends. I knew how to navigate my way through the horrors of the dream world, and Ross knew how to maneuver through the tangled mess of human civilization.

"Not until I walked in here."

"I apologize for my cousin," I said. "Sienna has a preference for bad dreams."

Ross flinched when one of the pine logs in the fireplace snapped and cracked, sent a shower of sparks against the screen. "I came to tell you that Elspeth should be fine—the dog doesn't have rabies."

"I know."

"But there's something that you don't know." He turned to face me. "Apparently that dog caught something from your daughter. He turned into a werewolf or a dog shape-shifter or something. You ever hear of anything like that before?"

I ran my tongue over my teeth as I remembered another fog-shrouded wood, another country, another century. It had been a very long time ago, before I met Lily. A wolf had chased one of my brothers through the Black Forest, leaping, biting. Then later the local villagers had whispered tales of a wild beast that came out at night, a wolf that changed into a great hulking, shadowy monster. I, myself, had never seen it, but I knew that it was part of the Legend that had followed us throughout the centuries.

"You're not answering and that usually means I'm right," Ross said.

I crossed to the window, then stared down at the smoky mists. I tried to see the little cottage on the connecting green.

"There's something else you need to know." He stood beside me now, shoulder to shoulder, like we were brothers-in-skin before a hunt. We were united from the many dream journeys we had taken together, a kinship that none of my clan would understand. "That woman, the dog's owner—"

Just then Maddie appeared, walking through the fog. The breeze cleared a path for her, fingers of white cloud trailing in her wake, as if she were created to dwell in a surreal landscape. Or as if she had created this one herself.

"—She's pretty famous, sort of a cross between Stephen King and Neil Gaiman—"

I followed her with my eyes, felt hunger burning in my gut, even stronger than before. It was an unusual sensation, something I hadn't felt in years.

"—She just finished working on a TV series with Joss Whedon—"

Maddie walked toward the forest, surrounded by wheels and spirals and sparks. A whole universe of transparent glittering machinery followed behind her, as if she were building a new world when she moved. My heart skittered in my chest, my blood burned. I could barely concentrate on what Ross was saying.

"So, you better be on your toes during this hunt. I know things sometimes get a bit wild."

"Life and limb," I murmured, repeating the Darkling creed like a litany. "We know the rules: don't harm a human—"

"Look, I remember what happened six years ago—"

I still couldn't bring myself to turn away from her, noticed again how beautiful she was, in form and thought, a ragged hole where her heart should be. Strange how humans wore their wounds on the inside, how they tried so valiantly to hide them. I unconsciously covered the ever-present wound in my side with a hand, knowing that it would never go away. It would be an eternal testimony to what I had lost.

"—when they found Jim Hernandez out in the woods," Ross continued, "half naked and mad."

"Moon madness," I said. "Someone accidentally harvested too long. He recovered a few days later."

"All I can say is, nothing better happen to Madeline Mac-

Faddin during this hunt or your sweet little mountain king-dom will come tumbling down around you. You'll have the woods filled with humans, from Hollywood paparazzi to L.A.'s finest men in blue. All hunting for *you*."

A breeze cleared the fog a bit more, swept away another patch of haze, revealing a small crowd of teenage boys that loitered in a cluster of trees by the side of the road. All dressed in black and blue jeans, they stared at the cottage, at Maddie.

"Damn. I didn't expect word to get out this fast," Ross said. "It was probably my receptionist. Two of those boys are hers."

"Why are they here?"

"They're her fans."

Just then Maddie noticed the boys standing by the road. She jogged out to greet them, laughed and signed a few au-tographs, then posed for a few group photos taken with a cell phone one of the kids pulled out of a back pocket.

Then she waved good-bye and headed off, alone, toward the woods.

Toward the Ponderosa Trail.

Where just yesterday she had seen me in my true skin.

Chapter 27

The Safe and
Narrow Path

Maddie:

A chill of mountain air, crisp and electric, flowed into my lungs. All around me, a battalion of nameless pines towered, trying to hide the sun between lacy branches. They swayed and murmured, threatened to swallow me as I stepped onto the path—so obvious yesterday, shrouded today as if dressed for the grave. I felt the promise of adventure, like a wilderness kiss, luring me closer.

All this was necessary. To know my character. To meet him face-to-face.

I hiked down toward the stream, surrounded by the primal fragrance of evergreen. Fog rolled between the trees, muffling all sound, covering my tracks, hiding any evidence that I had even been here.

I found myself wondering if reality sometimes folded, if it could change into something malleable and indefinable, like liquid metal waiting for the mold.

I knew there were things that lived in the dark, things

that could never be fully understood. Things that wanted to lure you away from everything safe. Just like in the story of Hansel and Gretel, you could be surrounded by a dangerous wildwood, while a bear trap with rusty hinges waited for you to step off the safe and narrow path.

If I hadn't dreamed about a creature in the woods; if I hadn't married the wrong man; if I hadn't believed that I had the power to change people's lives with my words.

I shivered when I finally stopped and pulled out my iPhone to shoot some photos of the misty forest. Then I turned in a slow circle, video camera on, seeking any movement in the bushes. Nothing. It was all white transparent shadows and layers of pale green, shapes that hung solid, unmoving.

Could that creature in the woods have been a chupacabras?

Maybe there was a nest nearby, or a cave, a den where the creatures lived. Maybe there were babies that the flying beast had been trying to protect.

I thought of Tucker, my stern warning for him to stay inside with all the windows and doors locked, Samwise there with him. I'd do anything to protect my boy. Was that the motivation behind these creatures? The primal instinct to protect their flock? I stopped, pulled a small notebook from my pocket and started jotting down ideas.

Just then the wind shifted, lifting my hair. It spun the fog around me, hissed through the treetops and stirred the leaves that lay on the ground. A small pile of leaves turned into a miniature dust devil at my feet, swirling, moving.

I glanced up. Then froze.

There, at the side of the path, the fog and the leaves had been brushed aside, revealing a shoe and part of a leg, sticking out from beneath a shallow mound of leaves. And over there, poking out from the leaves was another shoe.

Just off the path there lay a body, stiff and unmoving.

Dead.

Chapter 28

Secret Message

Ash:

The Legend howled through the wood, leaked through the cracks in the walls and the crevices in between the windows. It called my name, so insistent and loud that I found it hard to concentrate. Meanwhile, a soft knock sounded on my sitting-room door, a sylvan voice on the other side, begging entrance, speaking smooth words of repentance. Sienna. She wanted in. Ross stiffened and stared at the door but didn't move.

I raised a hand of assurance. "She won't harm you," I told him.

"Ash," Sienna's velvet voice called from the hallway, "I didn't mean to frighten your human. I just—I just couldn't help myself."

Ross took a step backward, closer to the window.

"I would never take anything that belongs to you. I didn't know he was yours." Another soft knock. Rhythmic, part of a song. "Let me in. Please."

I walked toward the door, felt Ross retreating inside himself, building walls and digging trenches, laying out an assortment of grenades, painting his skin in camouflage black and green.

"She's lying," Ross said.

I paused at the door, laid one hand on the wood, listened for the vibrations that were always present, knowing there was a secret message between her words.

"We're blood cousins." Her siren voice called to me, sweet and tempting. "But you don't have to open the door if you don't want to—"

The drumming of knuckle against wood continued, beating hypnotic and pure. I could feel myself being lulled into an enchantment, but suddenly I didn't care. I wanted to believe; I knew that even now her face had shifted. *The voice, the face.* It couldn't be, but I felt that it might be and that was almost enough.

Lily, my dead wife, was on the other side of the door.

"No, Ash, don't!" Ross said. "Don't let her in—"

But the pain and the longing fell on my shoulders, sparks and the fragrance of a meadow at dawn. It *might* be Lily, risen from the dead, back from the Land of Dreams.

One hand on the doorknob.

I turned and pulled.

Hoping.

Chapter 29

Chameleon Skin

Thane:

The back door opened, just far enough for River and me to slip through. Wearing the chameleon skin of fog and bark, we dashed away from the Driscoll mansion, both of us knowing that we wouldn't have much time. At best, Sienna would be able to distract Ash for a few minutes. Hopefully, that would be long enough for us to sneak back into the woods and dispose of the body.

"You should have done this last night," I snarled as we circled around the side of the house. "Before you met me at the edge of the forest."

"Hindsight and wishes don't bring dinner," River answered, his mood sullen.

I kept low to the ground, running rather than flying, changing my body into that of a mottled gray fox. River loped at my side, now wearing the skin of a ring-tailed cat. As soon as we had both crossed the road and passed the crowd of teenage boys, we made a patchwork quilt of our animal bodies, adding wings and horns and claws. Then we flew through the wood.

That's when the scent grew stronger—the stench of that human carcass blooming clear and ripe. It was nearby, sure enough, just a little bit farther.

We zipped through the forest, knowing that what we sought was up ahead, just around the next bend. I dropped my animal skin as I flew, replaced it with the garments of home. Gray flesh, wings of taut vellum membrane stretched wide.

Then I cast a Veil—knit from years of study and training, not a haphazard, shapeless creation like those made by the Blackmoors. My side of the family, the Underwoods, were the true craftsmen. We might not have been as good as the Blackmoors at casting enchantments, but we far exceeded them when it came to hammering Veils.

Before long, my handiwork glittered around us, strong and sturdy enough to provide shelter and privacy for what we had to do next.

Chapter 30

Monsters

Maddie:

The fog swept closer, the trees towered overhead and the forest filled with menacing shadows. Somewhere in the distance a bird took flight and my stomach wrenched at the unexpected sound. I fought a scream, pressed a knuckled fist to my mouth. With a quick glance, I scanned the surrounding area, checking to see if there was anyone else around.

Like whoever had killed the man who now lay on the ground.

The woods were empty, so I switched on my video, then took a cautious step closer to the body, leaning down to pick up a long stick with my free hand. Using the stick, I tapped the legs, checking to see if maybe, hopefully, the person lying on the ground was just asleep. He didn't move. With a flick of my wrist, I started brushing the leaves away, uncovering the body.

I saw two legs and a torso.

Strange.

The body looked flat. Like all the life had somehow been

drained out. I'd never seen anything like it. And there—at the neck—were two bloody puncture wounds, some sort of bite.

It hit me then, the whiff of death, the realization that this truly was a dead body.

My stomach lurched and I turned aside and retched.

Then I wiped my mouth and lifted my head.

At that moment, a rushing wind surged through the forest, but it didn't move the branches or stir the leaves. I dropped the stick and stepped away from the body. Whatever this noise was, it was heading straight for me, getting louder, increasing in pitch. I spun on my heel, headed back toward the cabin and that was when I saw it—an almost invisible cloud of fog and bark, flying toward me through the trees. It grew blacker and more menacing as it approached—a thick gloom that blocked out the sun, turning the forest mists into thunderclouds.

Recognizable shapes began to emerge from the clouds: massive wings that soared to the sky, charcoal shadows that melted and turned into bodies, backs and chests covered with gray skin and leathery muscles, wild faces with sharp features and feral eyes and sharp, crooked teeth.

I screamed.

Then I ran as fast as I could, feet slipping on leaves, hands grasping at branches, all the while lunging forward.

"Help!" I screamed again.

But they were coming at me from two directions. I was surrounded by a heavy darkness that obscured everything, overshadowing both sky and earth.

Monsters.

Two of them.

I wasn't going to get away.

I couldn't see past the reach of my own arms. Still I ran, feet pounding dirt, faster and faster. My legs grew weary and my chest ached, but the landscape around me never changed.

I wasn't moving.

Meanwhile, the shadowy creatures pressed closer. I tried to scream, but this time I couldn't. I couldn't move, couldn't even cry out.

It was just like a nightmare.

Whatever these monsters were, they had me pinned in; they now blocked off the path back to the cabin and the trail that led up to the rocky cliffs.

Let me go, you're not real, you can't be—

As soon as I thought that, the creatures suddenly fluttered and a white hole shattered through their black skin. For a moment, I surged forward, felt my feet gain purchase on the wood-chip trail and I spun a foot further away. The darkness around me faded, a small hole appeared right in front of me—just large enough for me to crawl through. I dropped to my knees and I scurried toward it.

Just then, one of the beasts snapped forward, leaped upon me with a snarl, teeth glittering. I fought him, beat fists against his chest, kicked against his legs. All the while, I could sense him sifting through my thoughts, as if reading my mind. Then I saw his eyes flash, bright and yellow, and I knew exactly what he was doing.

He was trying to fashion a nightmare from my secret fears.

"No!" I growled, baring my teeth.

They are my dreams, my visions, my hopes; not one of them belongs to you, nor ever shall. I will fight with all I have within me—

"Nay, you will not escape me, my love," the beast said.

He pushed me to the ground with a strong hand and then followed with a feathery incantation of his own, though I noticed that his words and chant were spoken too quickly and the rhythm wasn't quite right. I knew then that he didn't have the strength for this kind of battle.

Words were my kingdom, not his. I would find a way to break through his poetry, write my own song and spit the words in his face.

But even as I thought that I could feel myself growing sleepy.

Chapter 31

Words of Warning

Ash:

Sunlight cascaded through the windows, dampened only by velvet panels. The golden-white light set dust motes spinning about me, made me feel as if I had been trapped in one of my own enchantments. I swung the door to my suite open, all reason gone, all memory of the past and the future gone. All that mattered was this moment. Lily could be on the other side of the door. Somewhere, on the edge of the human universe, Ross talked and pleaded with me, spoke words of warning. But it was a foreign language.

Lily could be here. Miracles do happen. Dreams do come true.

Shadows from the hallway spilled into the room, a Darkling female stood on the threshold. Beautiful as a handful of starlight, she was almost too bright to look upon. I couldn't see her features clearly.

"Ash. Let me in." It was her voice.

Lily.

"No!" Ross yelled. Ross, my one human friend.

But humans were the enemy, the spoils of conquest, the

fields ripe for harvest. No need to listen to the faithful pet. Not now.

I reached out a hand, ready to pull my wife closer, to bring her into the room and invite her inside. She leaned toward me, eager.

That was when I knew. Her scent was wrong.

It wasn't her. The dead don't come back. They stay in the cold grave, turn into stardust, blow away on the wind. They vanish into the unknown, the place of the forever gone and forever mourned.

I grabbed on to her flesh, this not-Lily creature and dug my claws deep into her neck, pressing so hard that her blood started to flow. She screamed, her visage melted; she fought and tried to get away, tried to make her flesh burn mine, flames erupting where my hand had reached across the threshold and into the hallway. My fangs grew and I wanted to lunge out, to bite her, to rip her arm from her body.

Imposter. Evil. Beast.

Then her disguise fell away.

Sienna screamed again, pleading with me to release her. I growled, considered tightening my grip on her throat until all life vanished, until she joined my dead wife.

"Give Lily a message for me," I said, my words like fire, ready to kill.

"Life—and—limb." Her words came out one at a time in a wet, choking whisper. Sienna begged for her life, tried to remind me of our code, to never kill, not human and not Darkling.

"Must preserve life. Must," she said.

"Ash! Let her go! Listen—" Ross was at the window, staring toward the forest.

Just then a woman's scream echoed from the woods, followed by the flapping of great wings and the folding of reality. And after it came another sound, like all the rules in the world were being broken at once, breaking branches, howling wind.

One of my humans was being hunted.

I tossed my cousin to the ground, where she lay gasping, one of her hands attempting to stop the flow of blood from her neck. With a snarl, I dropped my human skin and folded reality, then swept across the room to the window and threw it open. In an instant, I was flying toward the forest—past the human boys who had gathered by the side of the road—toward the throbbing black hole where a Darkling fought against a human.

Somewhere in the forest deep, shrouded in murky fog.

Another human was being harvested. And this time I knew who was to blame. 'Twas none other than my own dear cousins, Thane and River.

I flashed my wings wide, tensed my muscles, blended the color of my skin to match the mottled blue-and-gray sky. Leaning into the wind, I scanned the wood for movement. I saw something then, a haze that hung over a section of the wood like a misshapen bubble—a Veil of cloud. I measured the beginning and the end of the anomaly, knowing that once I got closer it would be near impossible to see the sharp edges.

Then I called my sister, Sage, to join me in the hunt.

Like an electric shock, my cry sparked through the trees, snapped and buzzed and sang. I felt it strike her in the center of her forehead.

Come!
Take the northern edge of the Veil, then move upstream.

I heard the whisper of her wings as she answered, taking flight almost instantly.

That was when I reached the Veil, felt it brush against my skin like the ruffling of feathers. I hovered at the top of the forest, until I got my bearings, then sank to the ground, watching as the treetops gave way to thick trunks and finally to a mass of ferns and bramble bushes. Meanwhile, heavy fog twined through the wood, tendrils erasing and changing the landscape as they drifted past.

I dared not believe what I saw.

Instead, I battled against this foul magic with song—an Evenquest sonnet, words that overlapped one another, fourteen lines of iambic pentameter that rang strong as a blade. My enchantment fought the Veil, one form of magic against another, until at last, the false landscape began to fade. Then I heard another song echo through the thicket, one with sweet, high notes, cadence strong as a warrior's drum. It came from the creek, somewhere upstream.

Sage.

Together we would break through.

The Veil hung between the trees like razor wire now, biting my flesh. Still, I continued to sing, like a man leaning into a blizzard, hunching my shoulders, squinting my eyes, a low chant warming my chest as I walked with my head tucked down. I ignored the many cuts that slivered my flesh, my poems raising the temperature, making the earth hiss. With a lungful of damp air, I lifted my voice, louder and then louder still.

I wasn't going to give up, no matter how long it took me to break through. For I knew now that it was Maddie who had been captured in my cousin's Veil. I heard her voice slip through as she fought Thane, verse against verse. Then the clouds rolled thick and heavy across the path.

And after that, no more sounds escaped.

Chapter 32

Gnarled Fingers

Thane:

Fog drifted around us, a thick, black haze with gnarled fingers. It teased the trees and blocked out blue sky, turned the forest into a nightmarish vista. She fought me, this woman named Maddie that I had followed through the wood only last night, and as she did, I could see why my cousin had been so intrigued by her. Bits of poems and snippets of stories dripped from her lips, sweet as honey wine, each one of them more lovely than the one before. Meanwhile, my concentration was failing. This human woman was slicing through my Veil and confusing me with her own magic incantations. Then with a mere whisper of words, she knocked me on my back, drove the wind from my lungs, her poem strong as a warrior's blow.

I rolled away from her and she bounded to her feet, ready to run away.

"No!" I bellowed, then I leaped, tackled her and drove her to the ground again. River chanted at my side the whole while, holding the Veil fast, for my strength was waning. "Sleep, my love, rest now," I said, my voice soft and soothing.

Her limbs relaxed and her eyelids fluttered.

I slid one arm beneath her neck, pulled her to my chest. This human was not meant for a quick glutted death; she carried the dreams of a lifetime and should be kept in a cage, given robes of velvet. She could keep an entire village alive with her dreams.

With a swipe of rough tongue against her forearm, I claimed her with my mark.

Promising death to any who took her from this moment on.

Then I sang to her, the words so quick that she couldn't understand them, and I began to sift through her dreams, rooting about like a child through a chest of toys. Webbed fingers spread wide, yellow claws gleaming, I stirred them and watched: First I saw an image of her son falling in love; then another of her grandchildren playing in the yard; then a vision of someone standing beside her—a man, her true love, though his features were masked in shadow.

And finally, I saw a picture of her dog, Samwise. He was running through the house, chasing a black-winged beast, another Darkling, and suddenly, in an instant, he changed, grew until he was as large as the room itself with wings of his own—

'Twas a werebeast she was dreaming about.

Terrified, I sat back on my haunches. *No, couldn't be real.*

Then, somehow, Maddie found the magic beat that sang in the silent spaces between the letters. She rose up from the ground and forced words to the surface in one final scream.

"Samwise!" she shouted. "Come!"

River and I clamped our hands over her mouth, pushed her back to the ground, but we both knew that it was already too late. We could feel it. Reality was shifting, something horrid was being summoned by this human, something we couldn't stop.

A shiver raced over me and I heard it beginning; far away a dog pawed frantically at a front door, until finally, someone opened it. But the door swung open too fast and the dog slipped away.

Now it was running. I could hear it, galloping through the forest toward me, blood pumping through its body. New blood with a new purpose soared through the dog's limbs like fire, tangled through every organ and changed the beast with every beat of its heart. It was running faster than ever before; it was bigger than the sky and darker than the night, a shadow with teeth and claws, taller than the trees—

"The woman has summoned a werebeast," I said, astonished and afraid.

"Run!" River cried and he spread his wings.

At that moment I saw Cousin Sage, rising up out of the river, one hand raised, ready to cast an enchantment. But even she was too late.

For the ground thundered and the valley echoed with an unholy growl. A mythic beast was charging up the trail, shredding the Veil that should have protected us. I could hear the Veil ripping, the sound shocking through the fog. A werebeast would be here in a moment and the monster would have the power to kill all three of us with a single blow.

Chapter 33

Wild Thundering

Thane:

The trees cracked and thrashed, branches were breaking and the beast was coming toward us on the trail. I was still holding Maddie in my arms when the werebeast appeared, towering above the treetops, part dog, part monster; it skidded to a halt beside me, ripped down two fifty-foot pines with its front paws. Before I could move, it swung a meaty paw and knocked my brother on the chin, sent him bleeding and tumbling into the bramble.

It glared down at me, jaws spread wide, revealing a guillotine of teeth.

I held Maddie tighter, thought about flying away. It would take but a moment to soar above this beast, though carrying her would surely slow me down.

Then the werebeast dropped its head below the treetops, catching me in its silver gaze. It lunged closer, swiped at my head. I dodged to the left, almost dropped the woman.

It growled again, sniffed the woman, tested the air with its tongue.

It was after the woman.

"Nay, beast, you cannot have her," I growled.

As soon as I spoke, the hairy beast roared and shook the ground with a stamp of its rear paw. I almost fell, but forced myself to cling to her. I crouched low, ready to fly.

At that very moment, the dog's front paws morphed into nightmarish ape hands, giant and misshapen. It swung and caught me, wrapped massive fingers about my torso, pressed the air from my lungs, wrinkled and tore my wings. I would have cried out, but it had squeezed the air from my lungs. With its other ape hand, the beast grabbed my arm, twisting until my bone broke and my flesh shredded, forcing me to drop the woman.

I finally pulled in a full lung of air and I screamed, a wail that echoed from valley deep to mountain peak.

Then—while River lay dazed and bleeding on the ground, while Cousin Sage hid behind a thick oak—the werebeast lifted me high above its head. It pitched me into the sky, sent me tumbling, end over end, back toward the valley, until I was so far away from them that I was surrounded by heavy fog.

Still flying, out of control, I was just barely clearing the treetops.

Rage filled my veins, turned my blood hot. At last, I managed to right myself; I spun around and headed back.

I would not lose this battle. Not today.

Chapter 34

Foq and Shadow

Maddie:

The forest rushed past, a wildwood trail of briar and bramble. All the birds and woodland creatures scampered away as soon we approached. It was a dream, it had to be, a dream larger than the world. Some creature taller than the trees held me against its furry chest; it was a misshapen beast, all fur and claws and teeth, like a cross between a wolf and a dragon, and it galloped on two legs through stands of towering pine. Green branches danced beside us, the creek glistened between the trees.

Finally, the beast that carried me slowed down. It carefully lowered me to the ground; it licked me on the face, as if trying to wake me.

Then the cocoon of sleep that had surrounded me faded away. I felt gritty earth and twigs beneath me, saw a flicker of blue sky above, saw the movement of gray fog drifting between me and heaven. And I heard a dog barking, frantic, as it circled around me; it stopped to lick me on the face, then barked and ran around me again.

It was Samwise, but then again, it wasn't.

"Stop barking," I mumbled.

A heavy dream was shattering, all around me the forest began to poke through, and then, a faint, familiar voice called in the distance. *Mom*, someone was calling me, *Mom. Tucker.*

I sat up, blinked my eyes open, tried to make sense of where I was and how I had gotten here, but couldn't. Beside me, Samwise yipped and stopped running, he poked a wet nose against my cheek, licked me over and over, nudged his nose against my shoulder and tried to get me to move, to get up.

"Mom!" Tucker called. I heard him running, closer now, feet pounding dirt. Then he fell to his knees beside me. "Mom, what happened? Are you hurt? Did you fall?"

I stood up awkwardly, wincing. The wind had been driven out of my chest, and my legs hurt, as if they had been pinned beneath me for a long time. "I'm okay," I said. But the ground seemed to tilt to the left and my thoughts scattered.

Then, as my lungs filled with clear mountain air, my thoughts cleared.

And suddenly, I remembered what I had seen in the woods, the dead body and the shadowy creatures that had tried to hold me. Something foul and dreadful had been loosed in the wood this afternoon. We had to get out of here, quickly. I grabbed my son by the hand.

"Run, Tucker!" I said. "Back to the cabin."

He frowned, puzzled.

"Hurry, we have to get out of here!"

Then all three of us were running down the trail back toward the cottage, Samwise leading the way. The dog continually turned around to make sure we were behind him, as we reached the clearing. Then he stood at the edge of the wood, guarding the exit, until we were safe inside the house.

Chapter 35

Bending Reality

Ash:

A loud thunderclap shook the sky, followed by a meaty roar. The ground trembled and in the near distance, something uprooted trees, cracked their trunks like kindling. At the same moment, the Veil shattered and the true landscape was revealed—the wood was once again shrouded in milky fog. The stench of toadstools and cobwebs filled the copse and I knew that someone had just flown overhead. *Thane.* We each have our own masked scent, unique as a human fingerprint, and this was the scent my cousin wore. I squinted. I could see him now through the haze, a leathery silhouette, soaring above the trees. Something about his flight path, crooked and careening, said that he had been recently wounded.

But who had he been fighting?

I bristled. Wings spread wide, I thumped above the tree line. There, I saw Sage tumble into the distant treetops, her face bruised, her body bleeding. River crouched at her side, fists studded with bone, hands clasped together and ready to swing again.

And now, just a wingspan away from my sister, was the beast that is my cousin, Thane, ready and eager to join the fight.

I swooped through mist and shadow, wings spread, mouth open wide, long fangs and claws bared. I latched onto Thane with iron fists, stopped his flight, and then swung him around until he slammed against a sixty-foot pine. He snarled and spit, gnawed at my hands. Then together, we rolled and tumbled through the branches and trunks, smashed against an oak and then a white fir, shattering the trees and breaking branches, until needles fell from nearby trees in a dark green rain.

Finally, I grabbed Thane by the throat and tossed him into the creek, a good seventy feet below us.

Sage hovered above the tree line, one side of her beautiful face swollen and bleeding. It was evidence enough for me, though it wouldn't hold up in court. Fortunately, I knew exactly what would.

My cousins had broken the rules, sure enough.

"I warned you, cousins," I growled. "My invitation stated the rules, plain and clear—"

"We didn't take a thing," River cried when I approached, his country accent bleeding through. For all his pretending he was nothing but a scavenger and a pauper. "We never harmed any of your humans."

"You were both trying to harvest before the Hunt, I heard you—"

Then Thane flew up to meet us. He coughed and spit, water soaking his clothes and hair. "He tells the truth, cousin. I swear it."

Meanwhile, a foul stench rose from the forest floor, somewhere beneath us.

"On top of that, you dared to strike my sister?" I asked, my voice like thunder now. I kneed River in the gut, then slammed my fist across his brow.

"She called your werebeast down upon us with a spell," River gasped. "We couldn't defend ourselves—"

"I told you it wasn't my beast!" Sage growled.

"Then how do you explain its silver eyes? Only your clan has that distinction and you know it—"

"We have no claims on that beast," I said.

"Conjured up by one of your own enchantments, sure enough," Thane said. He narrowed his eyes.

I spun and slammed a fist in his side to quiet him. My cousin had always been a troublemaker back home, most likely this was all his idea. The blow fell close to Thane's left arm, causing him to curl over with a moan. At that same moment my sister lashed out at River, sliced talons, left ribbons of blood on his chest. River howled in pain and shrank away.

Sage and River parted, then hung in the air, panting, glaring at each other.

Again, closer now, the wind swept through branches, shimmered leaves, stirred an unclean stench of decaying human flesh. Somewhere nearby.

"You have broken the rules, I know it. The human woman you attacked may well have escaped, but there was another," I said. "I can smell a carcass somewhere below us."

I grabbed Thane's left arm, surprised to discover a strange throbbing mash of broken bone and flesh in the midst of healing. When my hold tightened, he wailed and struggled to get away. In retaliation he swung a wild blow with his other arm.

He dug a fist into the hole in my side—into the wound that would never heal.

I couldn't breathe, couldn't think. I bellowed, hot searing torment twisting through my gut. Still, I tightened my grip on him, forced him to withdraw his fist. I had to pretend that this blow had not injured me, couldn't let either of them know that Thane had accidentally discovered my one weakness.

He watched me, a low hiss escaping from gritted teeth as he slowly pulled his knuckled hand away.

"I'll endure no more of this! The Hunt is off! Take your

party and leave Ticonderoga Falls." I gripped Thane about the throat, threatened to press the life from him. "Immediately."

"Nay. We will not leave," he choked out. "You cannot make us—"

"You *will* leave, cousin. You and your clan," I said as I tossed him into a lattice of evergreen boughs. "Or by Darkling law, you will be banished. You'll never hunt again."

"You wouldn't do that," River said, trembling. His gaze darted toward Thane, then back to me again.

"Aye, we would." Sage flew closer until she hovered beside me. "Two votes is all it takes to have you and your entire clan banished from this earth. By court law, we cannot touch you until a full hour passes. But you must be gone by then, or I myself will sign the warrant against you."

Thane met her stare evenly. "So be it, then."

"You have one hour, no more. Find Sienna and take her with you," I said, my brow lowered, my words ending in a low growl.

Thane gave me a brusque nod of assent. Then with a huff, both he and River threw their shoulders back, cast their wings wide and set off through fog-veiled skies. They flew in the flight pattern of the hunt, less than a handspan apart as they headed back toward the Driscoll mansion, not bothering to conceal themselves. Sienna would be waiting for them there, then together the three of them could go anywhere.

As long as it wasn't here.

Once my cousins were out of sight, I glanced down. There it was, just beneath us. The stench of death rising from the forest floor, strong and dangerous. Human flesh, rotting. I saw the body then, plain and clear, legs sticking out from a haphazard pile of leaves, barely concealed from any human that might happen to wander down the trail.

This alone was enough to call attention to us, to bring the humans after us, just like Ross had warned. It was enough to make us the hunted instead of the hunters.

Part 3

*The best way to make your dreams
come true is to wake up.*
—Paul Valery

Chapter 36

δ Great Hairy Beast

Maddie:

A few lamps cast light about the small living room, though not enough to quench the darkness that seeped in every window. I leaned against the cabin door, my heart hammering. A scratching noise sounded outside, followed by a whimper. I held up my hand, motioning for Tucker to hold still. Then I cracked the door open. Samwise bounded in, a blur of black-and-tan fur, sometimes dog, sometimes something else.

I locked the door, then slid to the ground.

A dead body still lay back in the woods. Despite everything that had just happened, I had to let the authorities know.

One hand instinctively reached to my pocket and pulled out my iPhone. I couldn't even remember putting it back, thought I must have dropped it somewhere back in the woods, when I'd been fighting—

What the hell had I been fighting?

I shuddered, felt something crawling around inside my skin, in my mind. Something oily and dark and rancid was trying to figure out where I was.

That beast is inside me.

I dropped the phone with a clatter and pulled up my jacket sleeve. A six-inch ragged scrape ran down the inside of my left forearm. Blood and bits of torn flesh and something like speckles of silver. That monster had marked me with a rough swipe of its long tongue.

"No!"

My jacket fell to the floor and I ripped off my shirt as I ran to the bathroom.

"Mom, what is it? What's wrong?" Tucker jogged after me, the dog at his side.

I glanced back at the two of them. Didn't he see it? Couldn't my son see that Samwise wasn't a dog anymore? Even now I saw the hackles on the dog grow as his back hunched up and his chest widened. It looked like he was preparing to go into battle.

With a twist of my wrist, I turned on the hot water, let it run in the sink, grabbed the soap and started scrubbing my arm, wincing when the water got too hot.

"Tucker, look in the medicine cabinet. Quick! See if we brought any disinfectant or rubbing alcohol or anything—"

He climbed on the toilet, awkwardly reached over me, rummaged through the few items in the cabinet that we had brought with us. He pulled them out one by one. I lifted my arm out of the water, doused it with mouthwash, then hydrogen peroxide. My arm was bleeding, the peroxide foaming up, turning a sickly shade of green.

Tucker ran into the other room and left me alone with the dog.

We stared at each other. His tail wagging, his mouth opened in a grin.

A memory came back: a nightmarish monster that had pawed through my every hope and dream. A great hairy beast had come lumbering through the forest, taller than the sky; it had swept the shadow monsters away. Then it had taken me in one hand and carried me back up the trail—

Samwise.

"It was you, boy. Wasn't it?" I asked, kneeling down. He padded closer, nuzzled my free hand, pushed it open and licked it. I pulled his big head next to my face, then kissed him on the nose. "Good boy," I whispered.

He licked me on the mouth and I laughed.

Tucker ran back into the room then, his hands full. He poured his loot on the bathroom counter: aloe vera and Neosporin and gauze bandages. And my iPhone.

"Someone's talking," he said as I spread a thick layer of Neosporin over the scratch.

I pressed my ear against the phone while he held it up. I didn't remember dialing any numbers but I must have.

"This is nine-one-one. What is your emergency—"

The patrol car arrived sooner than I expected. San Bernardino County Sheriff's Department. Lights flashing outside. Someone pounding on my door. When I opened it, I found myself face-to-face with 250 pounds of backwoodsman-in-khaki.

"Evening, ma'am." He touched his hat with a hand. "I'm Sheriff Brandon Kyle."

Was it evening? I peered around him, wondered how long I had been down in the woods. The fog had settled in the lowlands and it had started snowing. Still, I could see patches of dusky blue sky and a full moon that cast the Driscoll mansion in an eerie silhouette. A group of trick-or-treaters shuffled along the main road, clutching paper sacks that would soon be filled with candy.

"You reported a dead body in the woods?" He shuffled from one foot to the other, as if eager to get down to business.

"Yes. I did. It's on the Ponderosa Trail." I pointed toward the gap between the trees, where a wood-chip tongue and a throaty trail led down into a dangerous black chasm—like a hungry mouth. A shiver worked its way up my arms to my neck, but I fought it. Gauze bandages laced my arm, covering the wound that I had scrubbed until raw and bleeding. It tingled now at the thought of what might be down in the forest, waiting for me.

Were those creatures still down there?

"What happened?" The officer gestured toward my arm.

"I—uh—I must have scraped my arm in the bushes. I don't remember. Think I panicked when I saw that body." *Oh, yeah, and by the way, there are monsters down there.*

His stare said he didn't believe me.

I shrugged. "I'm clumsy."

"She is." Tucker joined me at the door, nodding. "Really. She tripped and fell down the stairs back home last year—"

"Okay, sweetheart." I put an arm around my son. "They don't need to know what a klutz I am."

"I'm going to need you to show me where you saw the body, Mrs. MacFaddin—"

"Miss, not Mrs. Miss MacFaddin."

He glanced down at his clipboard. "Right. Sorry. My deputy can stay with your boy." A woman in uniform, almost as tall and broad as Mr. Backwoodsman himself, appeared on the porch.

"Deputy Rodriguez," she introduced herself. "Think your dog will mind if I come in?"

I glanced down at Samwise, standing beside Tucker. Well, Rodriguez wasn't a mailman, so it should be all right. I knelt beside the dog, "Stay with Tucker. Stay." The dog stared at me with inquisitive brown eyes, tilted his head to the side as if trying to read between the lines. *Don't follow me and don't even think about turning into a werewolf while I'm gone.* I had no idea if he could read my mind, but it was worth a try.

Then I cautiously opened the screen door, watching the dog to see how he acted. With a wag of the tail and a lick on the hand, he proved that he could be good.

If he had to.

Chapter 37

a Haze of Flies

Maddie:

The moon slid behind the tree line. A breeze followed the creek, over mossy banks, past a swinging bridge. A light snow drifted down and mixed with the fog, settling in clumps between tree trunks, drifting and stretching, now a vaporous cobweb. Wet, damp, cold. It filled my lungs as I led Sheriff Kyle down into the mazelike wilderness. We carried hefty flashlights and brandished them like weapons against the thick, steamy darkness.

I wasn't used to being so far away from the neon-city glare, from the white noise that speaks even at night. Here, the sky was so black it didn't seem real. The moon was full tonight, but at the edge of this wood-chip trail the darkness sang, heavy and deep. It whispered and sighed, told stories I wasn't sure I wanted to hear.

Stories about monsters with shadowy wings. Creatures that wanted to steal your dreams. Creatures that apparently only I could see.

My fingers tightened around the barrel of my flashlight. Both of our beams of light swung to the right now; they crossed each other, searching the empty pockets where trees refused to grow. A small figure darted through the woodland gloom, a charcoal silhouette against forest green. A fox or a rabbit, visible only for a moment, a flash of red eyes, and then gone.

"You were hiking down here by yourself?" Kyle asked.

"Yes. Stupid idea." The moon stared down at us through black filigree branches. I saw his shoulders rise in a brief shrug. "You think I imagined the body?"

We passed a berry briar and the scent of wild raspberries swirled around us.

"No, ma'am, it's just—"

He hesitated. One hand tumbled through the air as he searched for the right words.

"—visitors don't always understand what it's like out here. Kinda surprised me too, when I first transferred from L.A. The locals claim that this place is a sanctuary, protected from things like that." He continued as we tramped through autumn leaves. "I can't remember the last time anybody got murdered, either in town or in the woods. Haven't had any problems with coyotes or bears either, not like they do up in Lake Arrowhead or Big Bear. It's like there's something out here that watches over folks."

I gave him a sidelong glance. Welcome to Mayberry. "What about your local legends? Somebody at the vet's office told me he'd seen a chupacabras."

"Chupacabras, huh?" He let out a short laugh. "You must have been talking to Joe Wimbledon. His family's been seeing and talking about those damn things for almost a hundred years."

"I thought chupacabras have only been around for about twenty years."

"The Wimbledons used to call 'em something else." He focused a white-hot shaft of light across the thicket, through trees that wavered and shadows that danced. "Can't remember what. Not vampires or werewolves—"

"Shape-shifters?"

He scratched his chin, inadvertently tossing the light into the branches above us, making it look like we were in a cavern of interlocking branches. "Yeah. That's it."

"But nobody else has ever seen one."

He grinned. Even in the darkness I could feel it. "You mean besides you? Every couple of years somebody claims they see something 'funny' in the woods or outside their house. Pretty standard for a mountain community surrounded by thousands of acres of forest. Usually happens about this time of year. Right around Halloween, when everybody's already looking for ghosts and goblins. But nobody's ever gotten hurt. I take it back—there was that time when a group of Joe's poker buddies decided to play a practical joke on him, so they tied a big bat-like dummy outside his bedroom window. Joe's wife nearly had a heart attack when she saw it. But that's the only time. Honest. It's possible your guy fell and hit his head, then died from exposure."

"Yeah, and then a steamroller ran over him."

I stopped, swung my light over the ground. There, to the left of the trail was a lumpy, misshapen pile of leaves, dusted with snow. I bent down, picked up a long stick, maybe even the same one I had used before, then swept it through the leaves.

A haze of flies and gnats rose up.

I froze. This was it, I was sure of it. A quick flash of light revealed all the landmarks I remembered.

But it couldn't be the right place.

Because the body was gone.

Chapter 38

Skin Like Chameleons

Ash:

I watched Thane and River spin through October skies until they finally landed on the lawn before the Driscoll mansion. They would be gone soon, though not soon enough. Pain surged through my gut, stubborn and incessant, horrid beyond bearing.

"We must hide the dead human," Sage warned.

At least, I thought she said something like that. I wasn't sure. The knife blade had gone in a hundred years ago, but the pain had never left. My wings curled in spasms of agony.

I tried to latch one hand around a nearby tree trunk, but failed.

"Ash!" my sister cried.

One feeble gasp and then, suddenly I was tumbling to the ground, weakly grasping at branches as I fell, a rustling thunder of pine needles and leaves, and the cracking of bone against wood. Sage tried to catch me, tried to soar faster than my descent, but couldn't reach me in time.

The forest walls became a rushing tunnel of pain. I instinctively tucked my wings around myself, but couldn't stop the jagged rips or brutal blows, each delivered with purpose and intent.

I could feel it—even the forest was angry with me.

With a wicked thump that echoed and reverberated, I hit the ground. Crumpled in a ball. Spine striking earth. A cloud of dirt and fallen leaves exploded around me.

For a second, I thought I might never breathe again.

Then oxygen came rushing back and with it, every pain and every blow the forest had given. Still, the worst was the ache in my side, that damnable hole that would never heal. I masked it with a Veil when around other Darklings, I couldn't have them know how easily I could be defeated in battle.

And yet, somehow Thane had found it.

The world around me wavered and faded, turned into a ghost horizon.

My sister was holding me in her arms, but she was as transparent as the fog.

"Can't have them run away," I murmured. "The humans always run away when they see my wound—"

"Lie still," Sage said. "Your old wound is ripped and torn."

Leaves and evergreen needles still fell in a rain, blanketing me, burying me just like the dead human who lay a mere wingspan away. I tried to straighten my limbs. Unable to stand, unable to move, and yet, through it all, I could hear the song of the moon, somewhere overhead, a song like ambrosia—fragrant, healing, powerful. But not strong enough.

"Drink this."

I shuddered, then realized that my eyes had opened and Sage had lifted a vial to my lips. A thick, rich liquid flowed down my throat—a fresh harvest. I could taste the tang of wild berry and russet leaves, could hear the song of summer wind through green branches. Could feel strength returning to weak limbs.

Already I was growing stronger, muscles sleek, flesh glowing. The distilled dreams of a hundred Sleepers warmed my belly through the elixir that Sage had poured down my unwilling throat. The Nectar of the Hunt stirred the old hunger within. For the first time in almost a century, my desire for the old dreams vanished.

My sister had won. She had lured me back into the Land of the Living.

"Did Thane hurt her?" I asked, my voice weak. My cousin had been hunting Maddie, I knew it.

"No." Sage paused, some unwilling bit of news on her tongue. "But he marked her."

I sighed and glanced away.

Then Sage placed a firm hand on my wrist. "We must hide the dead body. Quickly. The sun has departed. They will come stumbling through the wood soon, with their bright lights and their weapons of sulfur and steel." She lifted her head, caught a scent on the wind. "One of them is here already, a man who wears the stench of oil and death."

We stood at opposite ends of the dead human, lifted him gently, ceremoniously, both chanting a holy requiem poem. Then, wings flapping, we carried the body into star-spun skies, shifted our skin like chameleons, and we sailed to the boundary of Ticonderoga Falls.

But the Legend followed me, even there. When the moon rose in the heavens, and we mourned the human's death, joining the hymn offered by the birds—at that very same moment, the Legend sang in my ear. Maybe a mother was telling her children a story as she tucked them into bed. Or maybe one teenager was daring another to walk through the shadowed wood.

The curse descended and his human disguise cracked and fell away, it seared and turned black. Because of it, he is no longer a beautiful mythical creature in a wooded glen. He is now a monster who slinks through darkened corridors, someone who haunts your dreams . . .

Chapter 39

A Wintery Nightmare

Elspeth:

I woke and shook off a wintry nightmare, bits of it still glowing around me as I opened my eyes. In my dream, light had spattered through silver trees and fragrant blue snow filled the fields—I had been standing barefoot in a snowdrift, toes burning and tingling from unbearable cold. But now, the dream melted and changed back into my father's room. Armoire in the corner, carved chest against the wall, a massive four-poster bed where I now stretched.

It felt strange to be on this side of a dream. Disoriented, groggy, still remembering snippets of another landscape and the disjointed story that went with it.

I shivered, then realized that a stiff, cold wind was blowing in from the open door to the widow's walk. My mouth was dry and my limbs stiff. I sat up slowly, then glanced down at the bandage on my arm, remembering the previous evening and my encounter with that dog. With a flick of my thumb, I peeled off the gauze.

The wound had healed, completely.

I flexed my muscles, felt a slight twinge.

Voices outside, laughing and joking, stole my attention. I crossed the room, padded out onto the small balcony, then peered down. Just across the road stood a small herd of humans—young boys. Most of them were younger than me, but at least two looked like they could be my age.

Just then one of them turned, glanced up in my direction.

I immediately shrank back into the shadows. But in my mind, I studied what I had seen—their clothes, their hairstyles, the shade of their skin—and then within a few moments, I made a new skin for myself. I didn't look exactly like they did; I knew I had to change a few details or they would grow suspicious.

You can't show up at a party looking exactly like the host.

I kept my long black hair, but lightened my skin, rimmed my eyes with black, put on tight blue pants, red plaid sneakers, a black sweater and a short black leather jacket. For a finishing touch, I added a tattoo on my left hand.

Then I retreated back inside the mansion, opened the door to the hallway and peeked out. A heavy silence claimed the house. Head cocked, I picked up on a heartbeat—in the room down the hallway, Driscoll's room. I could feel him, crouched and silent, hiding, probably hoping that we would all leave soon.

The door swung closed behind me with a soft whoosh as I crept down the stairs toward the foyer. All the adults were gone. They had left for the Hunt without me. For a moment, I felt a pang of regret, I had really wanted to hunt at my father's side this year. Maybe I could still catch up with him later tonight.

But right now, more than anything I wanted to go outside and play.

With the humans.

Chapter 40

Indulgences

Driscoll:

The sky darkened, the air sizzled with electricity and carried a stench like burned hair. They were folding reality. Breaking reality was probably more accurate. I huddled in the bed, my back to the wall, a pillow on my lap. Sometimes I buried my face, trying to block out the sounds and the images in my head. From where I sat I could see both the door and the window, so none of them would be able to sneak up on me.

Not this time.

Compared to the rest of the house, this room was stark, with bare wooden floors, an iron bed and one chair in the corner. The only indulgences I had allowed myself were the paintings that covered the walls—oils done by my father, watercolors of my own, most mounted in gilt-edged frames, although a few simply hung by tacks. I followed the paintings around the room, my gaze lingering on each for a few moments, allowing myself to remember.

The most beautiful one hung directly across from me. Done by my father at the age of fifteen, it didn't have the ex-

ecution he would achieve later in life, but the subject matter
was unique.

It was Lily. In the forest, pretending to be a faery.

She hovered over a patch of northern shooting star, their
slender stems bending beneath the weight of delicate lavender flowers. The background deepened to a wall of coulter
pine and incense cedar, sprinkled with weathered rocks and
juniper moss. But the most lovely part of the painting was
Lily, herself. Pale skin, a halo around her face, her wings
iridescent and translucent. If you stared at the picture long
enough, you could almost see her wings move, blurring in
the afternoon shadows.

Whenever I looked at this image, I could understand how
my father had been so easily enchanted. I found myself
wishing that she had been the one to keep me here, that hers
was the curse.

It was my own private faery tale, the one that kept me
grappling at the edge of sanity.

But then my gaze drifted, as it always did, and I saw the
rest of the paintings. All induced by the Darklings: that
odd muse-like quality they had, leaving traces of inspiration behind like dusty fingerprints after they had stolen your
dreams. I had counted the paintings once. Not including the
one of Lily, there were somewhere around forty total—all of
the same subject and yet all different.

They were all of Ash, the Great Beast, wearing a vari-
ety of skins throughout the past century. Most showed the
Darkling with spine erect, shoulders back, chin tilted with
an arrogant gaze—as if he dared the viewer to see past his
façade. But a few of the paintings captured his torment,
bowed stance, gaze lowered, expression unreadable, as if he
were trying to remember exactly what he had lost, where it
might be, so he could recover it somehow. All the skin tones
were different, and the hair as well, sometimes curly, sometimes straight. Still, the look in his eyes always remained
the same.

A guarded expression.

And an unquenchable hunger.

I wondered if he looked at everyone that way, or if he saved that particular gaze for his prey.

I walked to the window and glanced down. A small crowd of teenagers huddled at the end of that woman's driveway, that Madeline MacFaddin. Like they were waiting for her. I wondered why.

She was going to be my distraction. I knew it already, could feel it thumping through the floor when I saw how Ash had stared at her when she returned for her credit card earlier.

It was the same look he'd had when he gazed at Elspeth's mother.

I should have warned her. I sighed. But whenever I had tried to say anything, Ash would freeze my vocal cords. Still there might have been a way. Too late now.

Too late for her.

Not too late for me.

I lifted the bedspread, peeked beneath the bed, just to make sure it was still there, that I hadn't imagined it. Another long sigh, then I sank back and sat on the floor.

My suitcase, all packed. Ready and waiting. Gas in the car. A pocketful of cash.

As soon as they were all distracted, I was going to escape.

Chapter 41

ᴀ Ravenoᴜs Glare

Thane:

The Driscoll mansion grew larger as I approached, until it consumed the horizon, six gables and towering turret, mullioned windows and wraparound porch. It
was a dark, faceless silhouette, all features erased by the
fast-approaching night—all save the yellow glow, warm as
a fire on a winter night, that came from an open window
upstairs, Ash's bedroom.

The room where Elspeth slept.

Anger and humiliation shivered across my skin as I
crossed the threshold, as I shook the short flight out of my
wings with a hasty snap. River at my side, we both paused in
the lobby, lifted our heads to sniff the air.

I was supposed to leave—some swaggering threat of ban-
ishment that my father would fight and lose in the twisted
Darkling court, another dark stain on my family crest that
would be traced back to me. We were all supposed to leave,
but I couldn't—not when the Hunt was so near, when the
moon hung in the sky like a temptress, demanding obeisance. I glanced out one of the floor-to-ceiling windows that
lined the cavernous room.

At that moment, the moon wooed me with a dark song of harvest, wrapped about me with smoky tendrils, enveloped me with an ache that sank all the way to my marrow.

As always, she was perfect, mesmerizing, demanding.

"Sienna!" I called. The syllables of her name echoed, touched every corner of the massive Queen Anne like probing fingers. A soft sound, almost like a kiss, answered, followed by heavy silence.

My sister was here, feeding, trying to mask herself.

With a thunderous flap of wings, I soared to the upper stair landing, then pulled my wings tight against my back as I stalked down the hallway. Head tilted back, nostrils flared, I drank in the scents that drifted through the massive house. Coffee from this morning, shoe polish in a cupboard, wild peony on the dining-room table, starch on a laundered shirt, sweat dripping from a brow, lavender soap on the kitchen counter—

I stopped.

Sweat. Human sweat.

A nearby door stood almost closed, open a mere hand's breadth. I peered inside. Something moved, a flash of arm and legs and then I caught the sweet fragrance of harvest, of fresh dreams. For half a second I closed my eyes, analyzed the flavor.

"Bad dreams," River whispered at my side.

"Aye," I answered.

We could both see her then, standing in the slivered opening—Sienna, almost drunk from harvest, her mouth still wet.

"Go away," she said, her voice low as a growl, a territorial glimmer turning her golden eyes dark.

"We've been banished," I told her.

"Because of what you and River did," she answered. "I'm *not* leaving." Without moving, with just a whispered chant, the door slammed shut.

"She's got the human that belongs to Ash in there, that doctor with the nightmares," River said.

"Aye, she does."

River flinched when I started to laugh, a thick booming sound that ricocheted down the hallway, that bled down the stairs and made the windows rattle. Then I cast a ravenous glare at him. "I'm not leaving either! What do you say we have a light meal?"

River answered with a snicker and an eager nod.

Then the two of us headed down the hallway, toward Driscoll's room.

Chapter 42

Bittersweet

Ash:

There in a grotto laced with the song of black-chinned sparrows, we placed the body. I sang the funeral poems, head bowed, hands crossed on my chest, wings tight against my back, my voice in braided harmony with the voice of my sister. But even as I sang I could hear the empty melody, the missing notes.

The harmony that belonged to Lily.

Death always brought her back. The days after her murder had been the worst. Once the sun rose, it had baked the sky, sent white-hot shards of light to sizzle the ground. It was never the fact that I couldn't walk in the light.

It was that I was alone.

Measured in meaningless hours, this human eternity had dripped past, heartbeat by heartbeat, and the green shelter of the forest always seemed too far away. There in the dark spaces between the tree trunks, I could sometimes find peace—though not often. I would stand on the craggy hill, always leaving space for her beside me; I would speak as if waiting for her to finish my sentences, would wait longing for the full moon. And then when it finally came, I would realize that even the perfect, magic night would not bring her back.

My own curse held me here.

My revenge.

Not sweet, not even bittersweet.

And then one night of blinding moon promise, I had stumbled into another bedroom, discovered a human woman with dreams like milk and honey. This one could not see the world—her eyes had never looked upon green fields or blue skies—so she never really saw me as the beast I was. I would kneel beside her bed while she slept, clinging to the visions she brought, harvesting each of them with gentle care, never taking too much, always leaving enough for her.

So we could both have hope.

But then, like a moth, I had flown too close to the flame.

A year after I began visiting this woman, Elspeth was born, a child of two worlds, a child with wings singed by my sin. I couldn't leave my babe to be discovered by the other humans. She was too young to mask her Darkling features. The humans would have killed the child and persecuted the mother.

So I stole the babe and gave it to my sister, Sage.

Then the mother had withdrawn from me, barring her windows and doors. I didn't know how the loss of the child had tormented her, or I would have broken every rule, would have forced my way inside. I never expected that she would take her own life a few weeks later.

I would have found a way to rescue her—that is the story that I tell myself, over and over.

After that, I vowed that I would never let a closed door or window stand in my way again.

Chapter 43

The Boy with the Music

Elspeth:

Wearing blue jeans, black leather and human skin, I sauntered up the road toward the herd of boys. A slight apprehension slipped across my shoulders and down my neck. I felt naked and exposed without my wings, like I wouldn't be able to get away quick enough if I had to. Out of instinct, I tried to sort out their hierarchy, tried to figure out which one was the pack leader—that was the one I needed to be wary of.

Pack leaders often made wrong decisions. But it didn't matter. Followers would still follow.

Two of them stood almost a head taller than the others. One slouched against a tree and his clothes carried the stench of smoke and alcohol. The other stood a little apart from the group, quiet. I could almost hear poetry in the rhythm of his breathing. As I drew nearer I noticed that he tapped the side of his leg with his fingers. A song. He could hear a song in his mind.

Just then they all swiveled and turned to look at me. One of them must have said something.

I stopped, cautious.

The one with the song in his fingers gave me a shy grin. "Hey," he said. Pale eyes the color of the sky after a storm, bronze skin, hair bleached almost white blond.

"Why are you all standing here?" I asked.

The leader moved, catlike, away from his position by the tree. Dark hair and dark eyes and skin the color of milk. He was lovely and dangerous. And I was sure that most of his dreams would be about himself. "We're waitin' for Mad Mac," he said, his words slurring a bit.

The taint of alcohol grew stronger as he approached.

"Who?" I asked.

One of the younger boys sidled up next to me, russet hair and sandy-brown eyes. "She wrote the Nemesis series."

Another child frowned. "And the Shadowland series. You always forget that. Nick and Pinch used to drag children into the Land of Nightmares—"

"Dude, I didn't forget. That series gave me the creeps when I was little."

The boy with the music stared at me with a pensive gaze. I wanted to know his name. Almost immediately he held out his hand. "I'm Jake."

I glanced at his hand, not sure what to do. "I—my name is Elspeth."

Jake shrugged, put his hand back in his pocket.

The leader laughed, then pushed his way closer. "You can call me Hunter. Hey, I like your accent, where you from?"

I shuffled, uncomfortable.

"Don't hassle her—" Jake said.

"It's okay." I tossed him a smile and heard the soft drumming of his heart speed up. "My family's from Western Europe, someplace in the Carpathian Mountains of Romania or Hungary."

"Wicked! Vampire country," Hunter said, laughing again. This time the three younger boys laughed too, a bit nervously.

My gaze focused on Jake. He hadn't joined in the laughter.

With a quiet rebellion, he was challenging the leader. I could smell the stain of the forest on his skin, like he had been lying in the grass. "Do you all live in Ticonderoga Falls?" I asked.

"Unfortunately," Hunter answered.

Then the three younger boys chimed in, words tumbling over each other.

"The Falls. It's the edge of the universe."

"Yeah, nothin' ever happens here."

"Except fires and mud slides and global warming."

"What's global warming?" I asked.

They all stared at me with blank expressions. Finally Jake said, "My dad says it's all a myth. That everybody's reading all the data wrong and makin' a big deal out of nothin'."

"But what do you think?" I asked.

At that moment, everything and everyone around us seemed to fade away. All I could smell was his breath, all I could hear was the music of his heartbeat. I wanted to peel him back, layer by layer, and find out what was underneath.

"I think it's like every other myth. Based on truth, when you look deep enough." He paused. "Like the Legend of Ticonderoga Falls, 'bout the shape-shifters that come here once a year to harvest."

I froze. Unable to speak.

The humans know about our clan?

"You're scaring her," one of the younger boys said.

"No, I—it's just—where I come from, we have legends about shape-shifters too." I stammered my way through what I hoped was a plausible explanation. "But I've never heard of a harvest. Who—what do they eat?"

"You're shivering," Jake said. "Maybe we shouldn't talk about—"

Hunter moved closer, slid an arm around my shoulder. "Honey, our shape-shifters eat humans," he said in a low dramatic voice.

"And goats," the little boy with sandy-brown eyes said.

"And babies—"

"Stupid, babies is the same as humans," Hunter chided the kid with a swipe on the arm.

I pulled away from him. "Your shape-shifters eat people?"

"I told you guys, drop the subject." Jake's voice was firmer now. Ice crystals shimmered in the air around him. Like magic. Everybody held still for a moment and I almost thought that he had cast a Veil.

Then I realized what it really was.

The first snow of the year. Tiny perfect flakes drifted down, swirled in patterns around him. A few of them landed on his shoulders and clung for a second before his body heat melted them. For now, the subject of carnivorous shape-shifters was gone.

Everyone was captivated by the bewitching snow. Even me.

Until someone finally broke the spell.

"Hey, we can't all stand around and freeze to death," Hunter said, stamping his feet in the cold. I wished Jake had spoken first, that he would have proven that he truly was the leader of this pack. "It's time to go trick-or-treating!"

"Come with us, Elspeth," one of the younger boys pleaded.

"Yeah, come with."

Jake didn't say anything, but I could see it in his eyes. He wanted me to come too. I had no idea what trick-or-treating was, but I wanted to spend more time with him. Maybe if I could get him alone, I'd be able to harvest his dreams. I'd be more careful this time, keep my scent under control. I stole a quick glance at him again, hunger in my eyes this time. I couldn't hide it anymore.

And then I saw something almost as magical as the snow that continued to drift down.

When his eyes met mine, I realized that he carried a secret hunger too.

Chapter 44

Strange Costumes

Thane:

Paintings of Cousin Ash and his dead wife covered the walls; this room was a mausoleum, a temple, a place where a tormented human begged for release. I pulled away from Driscoll, even before the dream was finished, then sat back on my haunches. The meal wasn't what I had expected. It lacked effervescence, it lay in my gut, flat and stale. I stroked one long taloned finger across my chin, thinking about the many nights last winter when I had shivered beneath a pale moon, crouched low in snow banks at the edge of the Belovezhskaya Pushcha Forest, waiting and hoping that a human would wander off the path, that an unexpected and sudden feast might be laid at my feet.

Such were the dreams of a Darkling who doesn't own land. Dreams of food and harvest. Even now, I could still taste the foul, twitching dreams of the rabbits and squirrels, remembered how the furry creatures had fought to be set free, then fell still. Before I was finished with them, even their flesh, ripped and raw, had been devoured.

My stomach and my soul had ached for weeks after each woodland creature died.

Until even the forbidden flesh of my brothers began to look winsome and whole.

I stood up and rubbed my arm, still aching from that horrid werebeast.

One good meal, maybe two, and my wound would be healed. After that my strength would grow. If I only could find a way inside the little homes of Ticonderoga Falls, if I could find a way to get a quick succession of meals—

Just then a knock sounded on the downstairs door.

I peeked out the window. From this angle I could see a portion of the downstairs wraparound porch. A small crowd of children gathered there, all dressed in strange costumes, holding bags.

With a grin, I left my brother to finish his bland meal, and I changed my skin as I walked down the stairs. By the time I reached the front door I looked exactly like Cousin Ash. Except for the fact that my feet curled up a bit on the ends.

But none of the children noticed that small detail.

Chapter 45

Like a Beacon

Maddie:

For two hours we roamed the woods, flashlights dividing the night into black and white. Sheriff Kyle taped off the area where the body had been, made vague comments—Maybe the guy was drunk or maybe some kids had been partying in the woods and they'd decided to play a practical joke. So far no one had been reported missing. Ticonderoga Falls was a small town, we would know if someone was missing—

"Not if that someone was from out of town," I said. "Like me."

"True," he answered me with a slow nod.

But I could tell he was humoring me. He didn't think there was a body out here, despite the effort he was making. No body meant no crime and therefore no paperwork or investigation. Once reality set in, I could feel the tension between my shoulder blades return.

Hands on my hips, I stopped. This was what he had been waiting for—me to give up. "There really was a body," I said.

He nodded. Quiet. Then we both turned and headed back down the trail toward my cabin.

"I'll call the search-and-rescue team," he said. "They'll come over in the morning and comb the woods. We might have been looking in the wrong spot. These trails all start to look the same after a while—"

I could see the cabin then, flickering like a beacon through the forest deep, peeking through a fine netting of black branches. The path steepened here at the edge of the wood. Somewhere up ahead, in one of the cottages that dotted the Driscoll property, someone was baking. The scent of apples and cinnamon wafted through the trees, reminded me that I hadn't eaten lunch or dinner.

"I'm not imagining this, any of it," I said, half to myself. "I don't care what Dr. Madera says about hallucinations from deadly nightshade."

Sheriff Kyle pushed his hat back on his head, then stared at me quizzically. "Deadly nightshade? What's that? Sounds like a horror movie or a kid's book."

We were walking up the steps and I could see the inside of the cabin through the screen door. There were three silhouettes inside—and Samwise, paws up on the windowsill; the dog stared out at me with a big grin. I temporarily lost interest in what the sheriff was saying when I realized that someone was talking to my son.

Someone I hadn't invited inside.

Chapter 46

Trick or Treat

Thane:

The door swung open, a gust of autumn wind swirled into the foyer, and with it, a chorus of voices chanted, "Trick or treat!" My heartbeat slowed to a deliberate, calculated rhythm as I scanned the crowd of costumed children standing before me. Bedecked in plastic masks and fluorescent fabrics, faces painted in garish colors, skin glittering with sparkle dust, hair tucked beneath heavy wigs, they each held arms outstretched with open bags. I grinned, opened the door wider for them to enter, one word pressing against my tongue, though I dared not say it aloud.

Delicious.

Instead, I chatted in a cheery tone, one hand poised with palm up as the other gestured toward a table that rested against a near wall. Some of them may have noticed the glittering enchantment that hung in the air, almost as lovely as the light snow that swirled outside. But even if they did, it only added to the magic of the evening.

"Come in," I said, speaking in my most soothing voice. "Help yourselves to the candy in the bowl. Take as much as you want. Only, please, wait until all of you are inside and I can close the door to the chill wind."

"We can have as much as we want?" One little boy gazed at the bowl, eyes wide.

"Of course. Inside now, all of you." I nodded to the two adults who chaperoned the bunch. "You too. You need a tiny reward for watching over these wild ghouls and goblins."

A hearty laugh resounded through the group, all of them pleased that their efforts to appear macabre had been successful.

I guarded the door, counting as they shuffled inside.

Six, seven, eight—

Already the children were lining up in front of the bowl, staring down into untold treasures of chocolate and caramel and licorice.

Eleven, twelve, thirteen—

I closed the door behind the last adult, gave the signal for the trick-or-treaters to help themselves. Then amidst the clatter and the chatter, when no one was paying attention to me anymore, I locked the door.

Finally, with a theatrical flair, I raised both arms above my head, almost like the conductor of a great opera. I then lowered them with mercurial speed, casting a spell with a single word at the same time.

"Sleep."

Chapter 47

Below the Surface

Maddie:

From the moment I walked onto the porch, a delicious heat beckoned from inside the cottage. And when I crossed the threshold, I almost thought that the room glittered, like there were sparkles floating through the air; I even imagined that I heard a song, but as quickly as it came, it vanished. I felt like I had been interrupted mid-thought, awkward and disoriented.

He spoke first and the silence broke like a bubble on the surface of a rushing stream.

"Are you all right?"

It was Ash. I was surprisingly glad to see him, especially since he had helped us find our way home last night. I remembered how comfortable I had felt with him at my side as we walked through the wood. Up until now, every time a new man wandered into my life I would get an uneasy feeling in my stomach. Sooner or later, I was going to have to learn to trust men again. Right now, I was hoping it was sooner.

I could feel myself blushing as I stared at him. It felt like the temperature in the room had ratcheted up about ten degrees.

"I saw the patrol car and wanted to make sure everything was okay. I hope you didn't get hurt in the woods." His words came out all smooth and soothing, a sincere concern rippling below the surface. There was much below the surface here, I realized. He took a step closer and again, I noticed how incredibly handsome he was, that he had the slender, broad-shouldered build of a swimmer or a gymnast, as if every muscle was poised and ready for flight.

"I'm fine," I answered, hoping that no one else in the room noticed how long it had taken me to answer. When he leaned even nearer I realized that he smelled like the forest—pine needles and cedar chips and crumbling leaves.

He glanced at my arm and I saw a sudden suspicion in his eyes. "What happened?"

Did he know about the creatures in the woods? "Something in the forest bit me," I said.

"May I see it?" He gently took my arm in his hand.

I carefully pulled away the gauze bandage, just far enough to reveal part of the wound.

"Oh, that's a nasty scrape," Deputy Rodriguez said, beside me now in what might have been a protective stance, though I wasn't sure. "You should have Doc Weatherby look at it."

"Yeah." Kyle leaned in, agreeing.

"Yes, you should," Ash said. "Meanwhile, put ice on it and keep your arm elevated so it doesn't swell. But it looks like you did a good job disinfecting the wound. Most people don't think to do that—" He paused and glanced at the sheriff, as if he had said too much. Then he took a step backward.

Tucker pushed his way through the adults until he could see my arm.

"It kinda looks like the mark on that guy's arm, the one back in the grocery store," he said. "Remember?"

I shook my head. "What guy?"

"Miss MacFaddin, you and your son might want to stay indoors tonight," Sheriff Kyle said.

"But it's Halloween," Tucker said, with a defiant thrust of his jaw. It was the first time I realized that he had put together a makeshift costume while I was gone, some cross between a rapper and a cowboy.

"I'm not sure why we would need to stay home," I said. "We never found the dead body and you were pretty confident there was no foul play—" I paused, remembering something. "Wait a minute." I headed toward the bathroom.

"Dead body? You saw a body in the woods?" Ash frowned, glanced from me to the sheriff as if we had been withholding information. "Where?"

I ignored him, scooped my iPhone off the bathroom counter and started scrolling through the applications. "There's a video in here somewhere," I mumbled. The video of the dead body would prove I hadn't imagined everything. There might even be footage here of those two creatures that had attacked me in the woods.

Everyone followed me and stood in the door to the bathroom, staring at me.

"You took a video of it?" Tucker asked. "I wanna see. Jeremy's never gonna believe we found a dead body up in the mountains! Can I e-mail it to him?"

But I couldn't find it. All of my settings were mixed up, like somebody had been messing around with my phone. I kept searching, from one icon to the next, until finally I just leaned against the counter, limp. I wanted to throw the phone across the room and watch it break into a hundred pieces, but I didn't. Instead I just set it down and crossed my arms.

"Something wrong with your phone, ma'am?" Sheriff Kyle asked.

Ash watched me, a veiled expression on his face. He turned his head away before I could look into his eyes.

"Yes, there's something wrong with my phone," I answered, my voice cool. "All of my videos have been erased."

Chapter 48

Mountain Empire

Thane:

They all collapsed on the floor, a colorful tumble of rag dolls, arms limp, masks and costumes askew. I walked in their midst, careful to not to tread on any tiny hands or feet, a sense of awe rushing through me. I'd never had so many humans at one time, and certainly never so many children.

I remembered the stories back home of how Ash and Lily had been lured to this territory by a small boy. One child, only nine years old, had changed their lives, had given them a harvest that made the entire Blackmoor clan wealthy.

And here on the floor lay a herd of nine-year-old boys and girls.

Already I could smell the intoxicating aroma of their dreams, bubbling to the surface like a rich caramel sauce. I longed to sink to my knees in their midst, to dine at my leisure for days, not even stopping to rest. But in that instant I realized that this was only a portion of what I could have. Suddenly I could see a vision of the future—and each step that it would take to achieve it.

I forced myself to look away, to walk to the foot of the stairs. There I called my sister and brother, both loath to leave the meal set before them.

Finally, with the right tone and the proper enchantment, I lured them both downstairs, where they saw the treasure, my treasure, sprawled across gleaming quartersawn oak floors.

I watched, grinning. Sienna stared at the assortment of children as if they were a platter of decadent pastries. She couldn't speak. Tears welled in her eyes. She glanced at me, suspicious for a moment, as if waiting for the trickery to be exposed.

I admitted it to myself. I had been cruel to both of them.

Like a proper trained dog, River froze at the foot of the stairs, not moving. From time to time, he glanced at the children, his gaze flicking across them as if afraid to stare too long. But always his attention returned to me. He was waiting for permission. Sure enough, he had learned his lesson yesterday.

Now it was time to make them acknowledge me as leader. When they both stared at me, completely obedient, I gave a small nod.

"Feast," I said.

And they did.

Chapter 49

almost Blinded

Maddie:

I stood at the screen door longer than I should have. The October cold bled into the cabin, while snow flurries darted across a dark horizon. Lights beckoned up the road, from every house that tried to hide behind thick hedges and towering pines. A steady stream of trick-or-treaters flowed up and down the main road, each cluster lit up with lanterns, flashlights and glow strips. I could almost smell the peppermint and chocolate that filled every bag.

Behind me, Tucker was putting the last touches on his costume, spiking his hair with my mousse, layering strands of my costume jewelry around his neck.

Meanwhile, I was waiting for the police car to leave.

I told the sheriff that I didn't need him to stay any longer. He could come over in the morning and prowl the woods if he wanted, but right now I needed some space. Ash and Kyle stood in front of the Chevy Tahoe, talking about something. Rodriguez waited inside the vehicle, headlights cutting through the blinding darkness, white beams like tunnels of daylight washing the side of the cabin.

Kyle got in the car, put it in reverse, then started to back out of the driveway.

But Ash didn't leave. My heart sped up when I saw him jogging back toward the house. I wasn't sure if I was ready for this, whatever these feelings were that I had for him. Some part of me felt like I'd known him a lot longer than a few days.

Wasn't that what my mother had said about my father? She fell for him over a weekend. And look how great that all turned out.

He was coming up the stairs now, head tucked down as the wind began to blow. It caught his hair and twisted it to the side, revealing chiseled cheekbones and a strong jaw. Every part of him looked like he had just walked off a movie set. I was glad he couldn't see the hopeful expression in my eyes. That was the last thing I wanted him to know right now—that I was glad he had decided to come back.

Just then, when he was on the top step—lifting his head to meet my gaze—a wild gust of wind latched onto his coat and blew it to the side. At that same moment, Kyle's headlights caught him in full silhouette.

I was almost blinded for a second. Then I saw something. A beam of light, about the size of my fist, shone right through Ash's waist.

I caught my breath.

He was one of them. He had to be. No human could have a hole like that in their side.

Then I couldn't move. In an instant, I was sorting through all of my memories of him. Somehow Ash had turned up each time right after I had seen one of those creatures in the woods. Today, he was here when I came back with the sheriff. Yesterday, he had found Tucker and me when we were lost in the forest. And what about last night? Something had come into my room, something that smelled just like he did.

He was standing in front of the screen door, staring at me.

Meanwhile, the sheriff's car pulled out onto Main Street and the sudden breeze was gone.

"I'm not sure it's a good idea for the two of you to be alone tonight," he said. He waited on the other side of the threshold, a faceless silhouette.

I took a half step away from the door, unable to speak.

I realized that he could have worn any face, that he probably had a whole trunk full of disguises and this was only one of many. The light fell across his features then, revealed that he was as tall and dark and handsome as a human dared to be. Even more attractive than he had been a few minutes ago. But there was something else, something quiet and deadly that pulsed beneath the surface.

I nervously glanced back to make sure Tucker was still in the other room.

"I told Sheriff Kyle that I could stay and keep an eye on you," Ash said.

"No," I answered, forcing a smile. A moment earlier, I couldn't wait for him to come back. Now, more than anything, I wanted him to leave. "Thanks, really, but we're going out in a few minutes and I need to get ready." I remembered last night, when I had left the window open and two creatures had crept into my house. Had he been one of them? I needed to check the doors and windows again before I left, make sure they were all still locked. "But maybe you could answer a question." I paused, stiffened my shoulders, forced a courage that I didn't feel. "What were those creatures that attacked me down in the woods?" I asked.

Silence was my only answer, uncomfortable and dangerous. It felt like shadows were melting, reality was folding and the world was changing into something unrecognizable. I took another half step away from him.

"I don't know," he said, finally, his voice different now, rough and raw.

"I think you're lying."

He started to lift his hand, palm up, and I remembered

the sparkling lights—in my living room, in the forest, back in the bed and breakfast when I went back to get my credit card.

Years ago, when I woke up in the forest and the caretaker had found me.

It all came together in a flash of insight.

Ash was going to cast an enchantment.

I slammed the door shut. Then I leaned against it, terrified that I was going mad. What was I doing? For the first time in years, I finally met a nice, attractive man, someone with no Hollywood or publishing connections. I mean, here was someone who might actually be a decent guy, but no, I'm convinced he's one of the monsters in the woods. And it wasn't even as if I had any evidence that the monsters in the woods were real. Maybe I really had stumbled through deadly nightshade, like the vet said. My eyes closed and I still refused to move. I stayed right there, leaning against the door, praying that I would hear Ash's footsteps thudding down the stairs as he walked away.

And at the same time, I wished that he would never leave.

For a long, frightening moment I didn't hear anything. Then finally something moved on the porch, the boards creaked.

"Stay indoors, Madeline," he said from the other side of the door. "Promise me one thing, then I will leave."

"What?" I asked.

"If anything happens, promise that you will call for me."

The wind surged against the door, strong and screaming, all the trees scratched against the sky, and a howl raced around the outside of the house.

And then, complete silence.

I opened the door a fraction of an inch.

Ash was gone.

I curled in a bedroom chair, the door closed, a blanket over my lap. Tucker was still in the kitchen, finishing up his dinner. So far he hadn't noticed that I was acting strangely.

"I feel like I'm going crazy," I said in a low voice, phone pressed against my ear. "First there was a dead body in the woods and then there wasn't. Monsters sneak into my house at night, then they attack me in the woods, and I don't think I even told you this part—Samwise turned into a werewolf, or something—"

"Samwise? Your dog?" my younger sister, Kate, asked.

"Yeah, and he rescued me from the chupacabras—"

"What's a chupa—chupa-whatever you said?"

"Just another monster, I guess."

"How's Tucker?" Kate asked.

"Fine. He's dressed for Halloween. But I don't think we're going out—"

"Other than this whole 'the monsters are out to get me' thing, how are you?"

I paused. Reflected for a long moment. "Good, actually."

"No more depression or crying?"

"No."

A long quiet followed. Kate must have been thinking. She was always the logical one, the person I turned to whenever my world unraveled. Kate came to stay with Tucker and me when my divorce proceedings started, when there were camera crews and reporters lurking outside my front door every day for weeks. It certainly hadn't helped that my husband worked in the entertainment industry, or that he had run off with my best friend—the woman who had been a collaborator on my last two books.

"Wasn't there a part about some hallucinogen and a doctor who said that you might have accidentally ingested some?" Kate said.

"Yeah."

"How long has it been since you've seen anything—anything strange?"

"It was about an hour ago, maybe longer," I answered,

remembering the headlights that had blinded me, that hole in Ash's side. I wrapped the blanket around my feet, then glanced out the window. The snow was coming down harder now, in big clumps. It was sticking to the ground and the trees, turning the landscape white.

"And the first time was when?"

"Last night, wait, yesterday late in the day, when I was in the woods. Um, about four o'clock, I guess. It was starting to get dark."

Another long pause while Kate digested all the information.

"I think you probably did get some of that nightshade stuff in your system. But it's been more than twenty-four hours, so I think it's worked its way out. I don't know for sure, maybe you should go see a doctor, but Maddie," Kate took a deep breath before continuing, "I really don't think there's anything up there for you to worry about. Did Tucker ever see the creatures?"

"No."

"And the videos you took are gone?"

"All my videos are gone."

"I know, honey. But you might have tried to take a video, under the influence, and accidentally erased all of them by mistake."

"So, you think I'm making everything up," I said, running my fingers over the edge of the blanket, not sure whether I liked this answer.

"I didn't say that you were making anything up. Some wild animal, maybe a raccoon or a squirrel, probably did break into your house, and you must have scraped your arm in the woods. Maddie, you've got to admit, you have a pretty active imagination. Combine your imagination, the stress you've been under, and some unknown hallucinogenic plant, and I think you've got the perfect recipe for shadowy monsters with big wings. Sheesh. You've almost got me seeing them now."

Kate laughed. I joined in, a bit nervously, wishing that she were here.

"You think I should stay home?"

"Not unless you think you're not safe to drive," Kate answered. "How's your vision? Any slurred speech?"

"My vision and speech are fine. And I've already driven today, no problems."

"Well, you don't have to drive to go trick-or-treating. Just go to a few houses in your neighborhood. Take a flashlight—"

"Yes, Mom."

Kate laughed again. "And don't stay out late. You're probably exhausted from all this."

"You really are a lot like Mom, you know it? I miss her."

"Me, too, sweetie. Are you okay now?"

"Yeah."

"Look, just promise me one thing," Kate said. "Promise me you'll call if you need anything."

"Weird. That's exactly what Ash said."

"Yeah, well, he was probably worried about you. Just like me. Maybe he knows what can happen when people get that plant in them. And I think you mentioned that somebody warned you to stay off that trail—"

"I'm hanging up now. Thanks, really. I love you—"

"I love you too—"

I hung up the phone and listened to the wind. It took a wild circuitous route, began down by the creek, then rushed up through the trees, and finally raced around the cabin, all the while singing in a pale, fragile howl. I glanced up, saw Tucker standing in my bedroom door, all nine years of him pretending to be someone street tough and ultra cool.

"I'm ready, Mom. Let's go," he said, flashing a dazzling rapper grin. He had fashioned a fake tooth, trimmed with gold and a rhinestone in the center.

This was my boy, from skin to bone to soul, the best thing in my world and the reason why I was going to beat that demon writer's block. No way my ex-husband was going to get custody, even though our divorce settlement had left me broke, even though his dalliance with my best friend had stolen my confidence.

All I needed was one more best seller.

And I knew exactly what I was going to write about now. The monsters who lived in Ticonderoga Falls.

Chapter 50

Moon Song

Ash:

The wind whisked through the forest hollows, stronger, meaner, more self-possessed than usual. It spoke with a voice tonight, like a whistling moan, like it mourned the dying of autumn. I huddled against the far end of the cottage porch, invisible, my skin the same color as the moon-shifting shadows. Sage hovered at my side. I sensed the eagerness within her, a buoyancy that couldn't be bridled. I could feel it too—an ache at the base of my wings and in the back of my throat, all the colors around me turning pale.

Overhead, the moon sang.

The cloud cover pulled back from time to time, like a beast that longed to show its teeth; the snow had frosted the passing humans, making them look candy-coated. Still, through all of this, the moon called.

It wasn't truly a song, more of a hum actually. A vibration that surged from sky to sinew, reverberated inside me and all of my people—a single low, holy note that drove us to feast, sifting through humans and dreams until we each found the perfect one.

To have and to cherish. To memorize and immortalize. To tell and retell around the flickering fires of home. During long winter nights, dreams were our only food; we continually retold the tales harvested during summer. Human dreams built every home and cultivated every field, they fueled every teacher and inspired every child.

Meanwhile, the harvest itself left behind a trail of moon dust and inspiration that would drive the host to greater dreams.

It was a symbiotic dance, unknowable, unbelievable, unthinkable. And perfect.

And now the moon sent spidery tendrils that wrapped around my ankles, tugging ever so slightly, keeping me off balance.

But I couldn't leave.

Not yet.

I had to see her again.

Madeline, the writer. The human who had been marked by my cousin.

I knew now that I should have been watching her more closely. From the moment I first saw her, I had been able to smell her, had almost been able to taste her dreams. I should have been at her side, protecting her from the very danger I had invited.

I should be with her tonight when the moon sang, strong and sweet and insistent. When she came back to the cabin and lay in her bed, eyes closed, vision focused on another world.

But she had slammed the door closed before I could convince her to invite me in. And now I hugged the wall outside her door, like the wretched beast I truly was, ashamed of the desire that sang through my veins. Ashamed because I knew now it wasn't all about the harvest.

I wondered what it would be like to hold her in my arms, to kiss her. Humans were so different from Darklings. My own kind were all muscle and bone, every inch of flesh lean from hours of flight, from the physical demands of transforming from one beast to another, from the constant movement, since we never slept.

But human women were soft and pliant, their flesh inviting—almost demanding—that you pull them closer.

At that moment, the door swung open.

As always, when Maddie stepped outside, the world around her suddenly turned submissive. The wind shivered through the trees with a softer note, the snow flurries cleared a path, etched with paisley patterns. Even the moon herself peeked through sullen clouds and cast a path of silvery light.

If ever there was a magical creature, it was her.

A sigh echoed through my chest, came out in a gentle puff of frost.

She glanced in my direction, though I crouched hidden and invisible in velvet blue shadows. I longed to reach out and pull her into the Land of Dreams, to hold her in my arms and kiss her as she fell asleep.

But of course, she didn't see me. I was invisible after all.

And even if she had, she wouldn't have come to me willingly.

I was a monster, a nightmare; the stuff of legend and myth.

And she was formed from mortal flesh and blood.

Behind me, Sage shivered in the cold pocket of human architecture, no shelter from the wind. I could tell that her every fiber and muscle longed to spring from this cursed porch and shout through snow-drifted skies. She wanted to soar over rooftops, listening for the right timbre and cadence, for the human so filled with poetry that even his dreams would be lyrical.

She wanted to hunt. Now.

But I couldn't leave, I clung to the cottage wall like a lovesick suitor. We both knew that this certainly wasn't the first time I'd taken a fancy to a human woman. Elspeth was evidence of that. A part of me knew that I needed to remember these were the fields of harvest, there were no mates hidden here.

There were no more Lilies waiting for me.

"We must leave, brother," my sister whispered when the clouds rolled across the sky, hiding the sweet moon and muffling her song. Now my muscles were beginning to ache.

"Soon," I growled in response.

Human language becomes difficult when the full moon sits upon her throne—circle of heavenly light, surrounded tonight by a blue halo.

Already Maddie was shuffling down the walk with her boy and dog, claiming all the moonlight for herself, calling it to follow her like a wayward child.

"Even Elspeth has left for the Hunt," Sage said as she spread her wings, then shook the snow from their folds.

I glanced at her with raised brow. "She's not sleeping?"

"No. The house is empty, save Driscoll, who lies tangled in his own dreams."

"Where is she?" I lifted my head, thankfully distracted from Maddie, and took a long sip of crisp, cold air.

"Your daughter changed her scent, some mingling of crushed rose petals and clover."

I spread my wings, pushed away from the porch and sailed into the low sky, still drinking in the flavors of night. Finally I nodded. "I found her scent," I said. "A few streets away. Surrounded by humans, I think."

Sage was at my side then, wings eager to push past me. Still she forced herself to stay. "Aye. She has a right to hunt, you know."

Silver eyes watched me, a challenge in their depths.

"She's of the age and you must allow her this, brother."

"It doesn't mean that I have to enjoy it," I answered.

We were passing Maddie and her boy, flying high above them. She glanced up at us, seemed to search the sky for our shapes, unable to discern the difference between wing and cloud. Together Sage and I continued on our journey, over the rooftops, above the trees, always looking down at the humans that drifted in small huddles over snowy sidewalks, leaving a trail of prints in the soft white powder. They would be so easy to track tonight, so easy to hunt.

"Remember the cold," I warned Sage as we hovered above Elspeth and the crowd she traveled with. "Humans can't be out in it too long. If you harvest someone outside you must shelter them with a Veil and then make sure they are awake and moving before you leave them."

"I know." She smiled.

"You're sure Thane and his clan are gone?" I asked.

She was just about to depart. The moon's song latched about her limbs, pulling her. Meanwhile, music wafted from a nearby hilltop, and I could tell it was making it hard for her to concentrate. My sister had always loved musicians.

"Sage?"

She glanced at me. "Aye. Sienna, River, Thane. I searched the village for their scents while you were in that human's cottage. All three are gone. I'm certain."

"Go," I said then, remembering the many hunts we had shared before I came to Ticonderoga Falls. "Hunt 'til you be full! I will see you on the morrow."

"And I will see you. May your harvest be both rich and deep."

Then we parted ways.

But even when she flew away, something nagged at me, gentle and soft, like the pull of a toddler on my cloak. Some strange fragrance was circling through the town that I hadn't noticed before, an odor of smoke and wet cut wood. Those two smells didn't go together. Most likely it was some game or activity the humans were engaged in, some part of their holiday celebration.

Wet wood doesn't burn. Only humans would be that foolish.

Chapter 51

To Be Human

Elspeth:

A mask clung to my face, held in place by a thin rubber string that stretched around the back of my head. I peered through almond-shaped openings, every breath stained with the heavy stench of plastic and my own sweat. Jake took my arm as I climbed the stairs. My balance, my sense of smell, my vision, everything was off.

But I was having so much fun.

Somewhere along the way, we had merged with another group, all younger children, all dressed as comic-book heroes, and now we converged on a long, narrow porch.

Waiting for the door to open.

This is what it's like, I thought. To be human. You never sneak into someone's home or trick them into inviting you inside. You stand outside and politely knock until they answer. And then—no enchantments involved—if they want to, they might let you inside. Although tonight was different. Tonight, if the homeowners didn't open the door and offer candy, which I had already discovered was sinfully delicious, then they might have to pay a price.

Earlier, Jake and I and two of the younger boys had strung toilet paper through the branches of the trees when a homeowner refused to open his door. Now the paper hung like soggy garlands, ripping in places where the snow had fallen.

"Open your bag," Jake reminded me, giving me a gentle nudge toward the door. It stood open now, revealing an elderly woman with bowed stance. She raked withered fingers through a basket that crinkled with colorful bits of cellophane. "It's Miss Ballard. She gives out homemade fudge. See if you can get two pieces."

I stumbled forward. I could smell the unanswered dreams of a lifetime wafting from the woman—the husband and children that she never had, the holidays spent alone, the cat that died two months ago from feline leukemia. Tabby.

Sorrow poured from the woman as she reached into her basket and pulled out a carefully wrapped piece of candy, then dropped it into my bag. At that moment, I lowered my mask, leaned forward and touched her hand.

"I'm sorry about Tabby," I whispered.

Tears formed in Miss Ballard's eyes. She nodded. "Me too." Then she reached into the basket and slipped a second piece of candy in my bag.

"No, I don't—"

"Maybe you don't want it, but he does," the old woman said, looking at Jake with a grin. "He always tries to get more. Every year since he was four years old."

"Now, Miss Ballard, don't go making fun of me," Jake said. "You know you make the best fudge in the world."

"In the universe," she corrected him with a wag of her finger. "Here." She handed him two squares, neatly wrapped in pink cellophane. "And don't you forget our deal."

"I won't." He peeled back the plastic and took a bite as we shuffled down the stairs behind a steady line of trick-or-treaters.

"What's your deal?" I asked as I stuffed my hands in my

pockets, pretending that I needed to stay warm. His first piece of fudge was already gone.

"She gives me two pieces of fudge and I shovel her walk 'til spring."

"Is it a good trade?"

"For sure." He glanced at the rest of their group. Hunter was showing off for some teenage girls, taking sips from a flask he kept tucked inside his coat. "By the way, you need to fix your tattoo before we get to the next house."

A small wave of panic thundered in my gut. "What do you mean?"

He leaned nearer so no one else could hear. "It's supposed to be on your left hand, but when you just held your bag open, it was on your right hand. I don't think anyone else noticed—"

"That's—that's just silly. Tattoos don't move."

"I know." He was staring into my eyes now, making it hard for me to concentrate. "So either put it back where it was or here." He pulled a pair of gloves from his pocket and handed them to me. "Put these on and it won't matter. I shouldn't have brought it up."

I took the gloves and slid them on. He was right, I had accidentally switched the tattoo from one hand to the other. I swallowed nervously, then glanced over at Hunter. He was turning mean now, shoving another boy and swearing.

"He didn't see anything," Jake said.

"Didn't see what?" Hunter staggered back toward us then, a roguish look in his eyes.

I wanted to cast a Veil and escape, but at the same time, I didn't want to leave Jake. No boy back home had ever walked this close to me before or talked to me like he did.

"This," Jake said then and he leaned down and kissed me on the cheek.

"Oh, ho! So that's how it is!" Hunter said.

I flushed and lost control of my disguise. I could feel my skin darkening, heat spreading down my body. The snow around us began to melt and Jake's eyes widened slightly—but only a tiny bit. It was as if he already knew what I was.

"I've never seen anyone blush like that before," he told me in a dusky whisper.

"Why, you little weasel," Hunter said then as he clapped Jake on the shoulder. "Hooking up with my girl when my back was turned." His words slurred and a grin curved his cheek, then he turned back to the rest of the crowd. "Apparently I'm free for the evening. Now which one of you ladies would like an escort?"

Three teenage girls giggled.

Hunter slid his arm around the waist of the prettiest one. "Come on," he said. "It's time we got this party started. Who thinks it's time for some Halloween mischief?"

A chorus of cheers and hoots rang around us.

Meanwhile, a sliver of fear ran through me as I wondered how quickly I would be able to get away. If the rest of them somehow realized who and what I was. If they suddenly turned and attacked.

Chapter 52

Honey Wine and Starlight

Joe Wimbledon:

I climbed out of my Toyota Sequoia, then reclaimed a bag of groceries from the backseat, all the while thinking about Rachel, my wife. She had left yesterday to stay with her sister in Bakersfield, couldn't bear to be here for another hunt. She'd endured twenty-one, total, since we'd gotten married and I'd convinced her to move to Ticonderoga Falls. As far as she was concerned, that was twenty-one too many. I remembered grinning indulgently as she packed up the Subaru Outback in a hurry, as if the full moon was a boogeyman that had crept up on her when her back was turned.

I understood.

But I always missed her when she was out of town. Our double bed was too big, the house was too cold, even my clothes didn't seem to fit right when she was gone. And now the snow was drifting down, settling in the low places, turning the back mountain roads slick and dangerous. Rachel wouldn't want to come home until the snow melted.

I had a feeling this snow was going to stick.

Meanwhile, the Hunt was beginning sooner than I had expected. I could already hear the Legend overhead, chittering through the treetops, scratching holes in the sky, folding reality. It circled above me, stronger than usual, words that seemed to drop from the sky, mixing with the snowflakes: *poison, trickery, death.* I could feel the Darklings coming closer—everything felt different this year. More dangerous. I sensed something in the air, serpentine and thorny. I limped up the wooden stairs, leaves tumbling from trees, whispers and chants ringing in the chill wind, breeze slicing me with frost. I jumbled a handful of keys, tried to slide the right one in the lock and missed, just as something black slipped from the bushes on the side of the porch. From the corner of my eye, I saw a long shadow, heard a moan. I jostled the groceries from one arm to the other, refused to look behind me.

"I got the mark," I said. "Can't take another."

"Yes, you can." A voice spoke behind me, silver and silken, as the shadow took form and substance. I heard the porch creak beneath its weight.

"No." I still fumbled with my keys. "'Sides, you're not invited in. Just run along and play with somebody else now."

"I'd rather stay here." It was a female, her scent like honey wine and starlight.

"Already told ya, no. Got me a deal with Mr. Ash, so you just go 'way. Right now. Scat."

"I'll go if you sing it. Let me hear you sing."

My key was in the lock and I shoved the door open with my shoulder.

"I don't need ta sing to no one. Move along. Get." I didn't look back, just thrust my body in the door, swung it shut behind me in a fluid movement and latched it. Then I rushed from window to window, latching each and every one, finishing off with the basement door. No way I was going down there now, not with the moon already full and bright in the sky. I should have gone down earlier. If my ferret hadn't gotten sick and needed to go the vet, I would have. Would have locked the outside cellar door too, and all those narrow basement windows that no human could ever slide through.

They could slide through, though. If they were invited.

I opened the fridge, pulled out a Coors, popped the cap and took a deep slug.

Then I hitched my way into the back parlor and tossed some logs and kindling in the fireplace, scratched a match, watched the whole mess turn into flame. The heat didn't seem to penetrate, couldn't thaw the chill that poured in every glass orifice that faced the outer world. I thought about the groceries still sitting on the kitchen table, the sandwich that I had Agnes over at the Steak & Ale make me special. But my appetite was gone now. All I wanted was another beer.

It was going to be a long night.

Chapter 53

All Alone

Thane:

River and I crouched in a tangle of greenery, our bellies full and the both of us still wanting more. Sienna had sauntered off on her own not long ago, weary of our company. So my brother and I were at the edge of town now, hunkered down outside the Steak & Ale. We watched a human woman through the windows as she wiped a wet bar cloth across a counter, mopping up spilled beer and gravy—she was all alone now. Her last customer had walked out almost an hour ago and the pub was empty, save pockets of shadows and the cold wind that whistled whenever she got too close to the windows.

She lugged the last dirty dishes off to the kitchen. Meanwhile, the wind moaned through the poplars that stood like sentinels around the building. Their shadows bled in the windows, tossing and tumbling in the breeze.

She paused in the kitchen doorway, looking toward the bank of windows. I listened to her thoughts, grinning.

She could tell something felt different tonight, but of course, she couldn't figure out what. Right now all she

*wanted was a soak in a hot tub, followed by a glass of wine
and that new novel she'd picked up yesterday. She shrugged
on her jacket. Snow flurries had caked the roads with white,
slippery powder. She wasn't looking forward to the drive
home.*

So my brother and I stayed hidden in silver shadows. We
left the poplars that lined the building, flew up into the high
branches of a ponderosa pine. Even from here we could
smell her—ripe and plump and as ready for harvest as she
would ever get. Another year and her dreams would evapo-
rate, but tonight they were still effervescent and childlike.

As always, River waited for my signal.

Together we stared at the front door.

Then it swung open and the woman—Agnes Miller, that
was her name, sure enough—stepped outside. She pulled the
door closed behind her, stuck a key in the lock, ready to bolt
it shut.

But she never did.

Because at that moment, we swooped down from the sky,
each of us grabbing one of her arms. Then we flew off with
her, her screams burrowing through the fog-drenched sky
and finally ending somewhere in the ever deep forest.

I loomed over the cringing human, let my shape grow and
darken until I was nearly twice her size. Then I growled,
teeth glittering in the midnight gloom. Fear seeped from her
pores like stale sweat and urine. She tried to run, but I just
laughed; then I tossed out a small Veil like a lasso and used
it to pull her back. Her protests came in a flurry of incom-
prehensible words. Meanwhile, River watched the two of us
from the shadows, every inch of him submissive, just as he
should be. He backed away, a step at a time, giving me room
as I needed it, all the while not daring to take his eyes off me.

He knew that soon I would tire of this game and the feeding would begin.

Finally an oppressive hush fell over the forest as the
human submitted, lying down in forest gloom. She glanced

at the two of us, then lowered her head, as if she didn't want to know what was going to happen next.

"Sleep," I said.

Her eyes closed. Then, taking turns, River and I both ate our fill. It wasn't until much later—when the woman curled in a fetal position on the forest floor, when her limbs were frozen and her thoughts were growing more cloudy with each shallow breath—that River pulled away with great reluctance.

And he allowed me to take the kill that was rightfully mine.

We stepped from the woodland copse, masking the rotted sour stench of death that clung to our hands and mouths. This kill had gone better than the last. No sound had leaked out. I made sure of it this time. Now, a human vessel of steel and glass lumbered over a hill toward us, engine rolling into gear with a deep bear-like growl. Narrow beams of light shot toward me and I instinctively raised one arm to shield the glare.

The lights flashed, pain-bright waves of heat. I closed my eyes as the beams steadily approached, growing stronger.

Even the darkness has been corrupted by these humans.

Then I felt something moving through silken-black shadow, faceless. It wore a mask, but I could smell it.

Ash was somewhere among the humans back in the village, hunting Madeline MacFaddin, the woman that bore my mark.

Fair and square, she would be mine again before this night ended.

I gripped a nearby sapling and gave a little shrug, shaking my human skin back into place—stretching out the folds that had tangled while climbing up that last bramble-covered hill, mending the tear that hung loose on my hip. I gulped a mouthful of fresh mountain air, clear and sweet. Just a little bit stronger and then I'd be able to steal all of Ash's humans, whether they wore his mark or not.

I chuckled.

Cousin Ash had been too weak today; he hadn't been able to break through my Veil.

He wasn't near as strong as he used to be. The stories from home had painted him almost invincible, but that wasn't true. I'd seen and felt his wound for myself, knew exactly where it was. Wouldn't take much to fight him. All I needed was a proper Veil or just the right enchantment. One well-placed blow. He'd fall then, crash and burn like only a Darkling can. Sizzle all the way across the night sky, a streak of meteor light. A bright bit of flotsam in the sunless heavens.

Then, at that moment, I would take the deed to Ticonderoga Falls.

I'd steal it before anyone else could claim it.

Chapter 54

A Perfect Home

Thane:

The village of Ticonderoga Falls spread before me now, street after street of wooden houses, all with lights glowing and doors open. A new journey led me from house to house. I grinned behind the mask that hid my face, the taste of the forest lingering in my throat, the remnants of that gluttonous feast back at the Driscoll mansion still surging through my belly. I ran testy fingers over my arm, wounded by the werebeast not that long ago. Now, it was completely healed.

Together River and I clambered up the steps to a screened-in porch. There we knocked and huddled, shivering in the wind. We were posing as a pair of six-year-old boys. All alone. Much too young to be out on a night like this without a chaperone.

The door swung open and a young man stood silhouetted in the doorway.

I lifted my head, then sniffed. What I wanted was inside. I chattered my teeth together as I stammered a weak, "Trick or treat." Then I followed it with a sneeze.

A young woman appeared on the porch, shaking her head.

"It's too cold to let those boys stand outside, Hank. Bring them in the house. Would you two like some hot cocoa?"

"Yes, ma'am," River answered with a smile. He clapped his hands together, as if trying to keep them warm.

"Come in." The young man held the door open for both of us.

This was the seventh home River and I had approached since our feast in the wood. With each meal, my plan had grown until now I was certain it would succeed.

Just a few more houses like this one and then everything would be set in place.

River sat on a vintage horsehair sofa, sipping hot chocolate, always keeping one eye fixed on me. Just like he should. An old clock ticked on the mantel, a hypnotic rhythm, pendulum swinging back and forth inside a polished case of wood and glass. Everything inside the home sparkled—the wood floors, the silver teaspoons, the chandeliers.

It was a perfect home.

But one dream remained unanswered here, flitting about like a butterfly too fragile to grasp. This young couple had always wanted a child of their own, but so far—

I nodded at River, granting him permission to do as he wished. Then I walked toward the kitchen, where the human woman was frosting cookies. I heard the sizzle of a Veil as soon as I turned my back, knew that River was already leaning over the young man and conjuring up a dream.

But dreams come and go, I mused as I stared at the woman, who stood with her back to me. I changed my shape to imitate that of her sleeping husband, altered it only slightly— broadened his shoulders, deepened the blue of his eyes, erased the scar on his cheek. Then I put one hand gently on the woman's waist and pulled her to me, kissing her neck.

She giggled and leaned into my embrace, whispered, "Hank, what about the boys in the next room?"

"They just left."

"Really? I didn't hear them leave." She turned to face me, her eyes widening for a second, then her gaze ran over my body. She grinned.

"Quiet as little mice. I think it was your cocoa." I slid my arms around her, untied her apron. Then I kissed her shoulder, her neck, her lips, my desire growing. I took her hand in mine, gave her a shy smile.

"Come on." I tugged her hand ever so gently, leading her toward the bedroom.

She followed me with nary an enchantment.

Dreams come and go, I thought as I ran my tongue over her salty skin. But this was the dream of a lifetime. If it turned out the way I hoped, then it would grant me everything I had ever wished for—an empire of my own, just like the one Cousin Ash had. In fact, it was no longer just my cousin's empire that I longed to possess.

To that end, I was building myself an army tonight as I journeyed from bedroom to bedroom, an army of half-breeds just like Elspeth, who could walk through doors and windows without an invitation.

With this newborn army at my side, I could claim any village. In fact, I could take every city on this entire mountain if I wanted.

Chapter 55

Cavern of Light

Maddie:

I waited with the other parents at the curb. An occasional car swiveled past on slippery streets, washing us in brief splashes of light, almost like a freeze-action strobe. Each time, my eyes would readjust to the darkness and I would search the near horizon of stair, porch and open door until I recognized the small shape of my son, outlined in the dim silver moonlight, walking back to me.

Flashlight in hand, I carved the darkness, forged the path from one house to the next. Along the way I lost count of the houses, couldn't remember if we had visited six or sixteen or sixty, my toes numb from the cold, frost curling around my face with each breath. Meanwhile, Tucker couldn't hold in his excitement. He practiced his rap imitation of "trick or treat," repeated it over and over as we tramped through the slushy snow, until his words echoed in my ears.

He stood fifty yards away now. Bathed in the yellow light of an open door.

Samwise pressed against me as if he wanted to keep me warm, staring after Tucker with longing eyes. The dog would yip whenever my son went inside a house, would pull at the leash each time the boy dipped out of sight.

"Good boy," I said, leaning down to stroke Samwise on the head.

The snow eddied around us in mesmerizing patterns, sticking to my eyelashes and my hood. Strange weather. I couldn't remember the last time it had snowed this early in the mountains.

Maybe they caused it, those shape-shifting chupacabras.

I glanced quickly at the woman standing beside me, wondering for a second if I had accidentally spoken out loud. The woman just stared straight ahead, arms bundled in a small blanket.

Okay, maybe they did cause the snow. But why?

The door opened then, revealing a cavern of light and bowls of candy that lured the children closer. Black papier-mâché cats and a row of glowing pumpkins and cutout ghosts that stuck to the windows. A faery tale come to life.

All the children disappeared inside the tiny cottage with green shutters and picket fence. Samwise tugged at the leash, whining, straining for the house—

They could be inside, they could want my boy.

I suddenly dropped the leash, let the dog gallop up the path. I trotted behind him, remembering images of that dead body in the woods, the two strange puncture wounds in the neck, looking like all the life had been mysteriously drained out. My hood flopped down and my left foot slid as I ran, but Samwise was already up the stairs, barreling across the small porch, heading for the open door.

Let Tucker be okay, let all this be my imagination, I can handle that, I just can't have anything happen to him, he's all I have left—

Samwise was through the door now, his deep bark sounding inside the house.

A middle-aged woman appeared in the rectangle of yellow light, a startled look on her face. I was taking the stairs two at a time, hoping I didn't fall. A chorus of laughter, of children, all the notes high and clear and happy, met me at the door.

Inside, Samwise was chasing the children around the living room, bounding and laughing with them, big smile on his face, probably because he had found his boy.

My boy. He was leading the pack, around and around, giggling and screaming on a Halloween sugar high, all of them trying to escape from the "wolf" that had just burst through the front door. The little girls were holding their bags of candy high, as if these were the most precious things in the world and obviously what the dog was after.

I sagged against the door frame, ashamed and relieved.

"I'm sorry," I said.

The homeowner tried to smile while watching the dog, making sure he didn't break the chintz porcelain that decorated every table and shelf.

"Come, Samwise," I said, holding out my hand. The dog padded over to me reluctantly. "I'm sorry, really," I repeated, even though I wasn't.

Tucker was safe and that was all I really cared about.

"New game plan," I said as I clutched Tucker's hand. We were blocks away from the house where I had embarrassed myself. We were now separated from that last group of skeletons, Harry Potters and princesses, and trudged along on our own path. I couldn't help glancing behind us from time to time, wondering if someone was following us. But I never saw anyone.

Meanwhile, heat seemed to radiate down from the sky, just enough to keep me from shivering. I noted that I now wore my jacket open and the hood down. Part of me kept thinking about Ash, standing on the porch, demanding a promise.

Surely, Kate was right. He had just wanted to make sure we were safe.

I wished I knew more about him, more about the creatures in the woods.

I walked Tucker to the door of the next house, pulled my iPhone out of a pocket while he did a rapper spiel for the homeowners. I scrolled through my e-mails: spam, overdue credit card bill, message from Kate, more spam, invitation to speak, endorsement request, message from my agent, overdue car payment—

I paused, flicked open the message from my agent. Like all his correspondence, it was brief.

> Fantastic! I need more, ASAP. Talked with three editors today. Showed them what you sent. One of them is offering a three-book deal. How soon can you get us the first fifty pages? We're thinking a novel this time, not graphic. She's talking six figures for all three books, based on your previous sales figures, but we need it like yesterday so she can squeeze the first one into next year's lineup—

My heart skipped a beat.
Six figures.
A couple of years ago I wouldn't have gotten excited over that amount, but everything was different now.
Now I needed it. Desperately. Immediately.

Chapter 56

Moon Magic

Ash:

Fog licked the edges of the forest, met the drifting snow, merged with the villagescape, reminding me of the mountains in Europe, two hundred years ago. I missed the Old World—when humans had whispered legends about me, telling their children dark faery tales just before they drifted off to sleep.

It had been the time of dreams.

And now the scent of moss and juniper sharpened in the frost-filled air. Wearing a skin of dappled shadow and snow, I followed Maddie down a narrow street. I was nearly invisible. If she happened to turn around, I would have looked like a blank spot in the landscape.

A blank spot. How appropriate.

I shouldn't have been following her. She bore the mark of another. But Thane had been exiled and it certainly wouldn't be the first time I had broken the rules. Nor the last.

The snow crunched beneath her feet and a cloud of frost surrounded her. The boy and the dog frolicked at Maddie's side, distracted by the promise of adventure and bite-sized treasures neatly wrapped in plastic.

None of them could see what I saw.

Madeline was encompassed by transparent cogs and circles, every one of them spinning and sparking, an organic legion of ideas that blossomed from the mists. All of her thoughts were being built and fashioned from the ether, fog swirling in tempestuous roiling eddies, patterns that morphed and growled, a womb of cloud and idea that was giving birth as she walked. White spirals, curling tendrils, fog merging with the canvas of imagination—

I drew even closer, watching in awe.

The moon cast down silver beams, touching her, setting the machinery that surrounded her on fire, making it luminescent. It even transformed her skin, making her glow as if filled with stardust. Every move of her hands, every word from her lips caused the great sprockets to turn and twirl and twist.

Moon magic.

On a night like this, anything could happen.

Chapter 57

Shadow-Cast Landscape

Elspeth:

The snow layered in drifts along the edges of the houses and against the cars. Leaves, soggy and heavy, muddled to the ground, broken mementos of the narrow bridge between summer and winter. I pretended that the cold bothered me, like it did the other girls. I stamped my feet, made my nose and cheeks turn red, and kept my hands inside the gloves Jake had given me. So far we had spray painted a barn, let the air out of several car tires and filled mailboxes with gravel.

And now we were playing hide-and-seek in the village cemetery, jumping out and scaring other children that scurried past, all clasping precious bags of candy with white-knuckled fists. Hunter tried to get our group to steal candy from the passing kids, but Jake refused. It was the only time he stood up to Hunter and I wasn't sure what was going to happen.

Hunter backed down.

I crouched beside Jake now, snow turning his pale hair a frosty white.

The sky shifted above us, black and gray and blue, twisting patterns of cloud and moon. And song.

No, not song. Something else.

I closed my eyes, tried to focus on this new sound that drifted through the night sky. "Do you hear that?" I asked, keeping my voice low.

"What?"

I lifted my head, certain I could hear someone calling my name, far away. It was my name, certainly it was, soft as the snow, but growing stronger.

"What do you hear?" Jake asked again.

Then I realized what it was and why he couldn't hear it. None of the humans could hear it. It was the Legend, rippling through the heavens, twisting its way between the branches, circling ever downward toward the earth. But it was suddenly different tonight.

For the first time I could hear my own name in its midst.

A wrought-iron fence guarded the tiny cemetery, corralled all the tombstones and withered flowers, kept them safe from the gnarled oaks that grew on the perimeter, twisted branches weaving in the October wind, casting shadows that traveled across crypt and tomb. Hunter left his hiding place, sauntered forward to the center of the old churchyard like a vengeful ghost. Flask raised above his head, he called out to his followers.

"Time for a contest," he announced. The others gathered around him, though Jake and I stood at a distance. "Split up into teams, see how many kids you can get to join your group. Then we'll all meet over at the old junkyard in an hour for a bonfire."

Some of the younger kids cheered at this point. The older ones kept silent. They seemed to knew what was coming.

"The winner will be the one with the most followers. He'll get to choose this year's dare. Better get goin'!" His gaze met Jake's. "And you know I plan to win this year, so be ready."

The crowd broke up into clusters, all whispering and excited.

I didn't want to leave. Not yet. I meandered through the shadow-cast landscape of weathered stone and tarnished angels, searching. Jake watched me silently for a few moments, then he pulled out a flashlight and handed it to me. Together we walked, side by side, fog curling between the gravestones as I swept the light across the names carved in marble. Finally, I paused to run my fingers along the top of one of the tombstones.

The name cut through black granite—*Audrey Meissner*—but it felt like it was cutting through my flesh.

"My mother's grave," I said, my voice soft.

"I didn't know," Jake said. "I'm sorry."

I stared at the stone, my feet resting on the grave. This was as close as I had ever been to my mother. "I was just a baby when she died."

He nodded. There were no words for this. Only feelings. Only the cold wind gnawing at me and the moon, that ghastly orb, making me crave things, making me want to turn and pull his dreams from him when no one else was around. Where was my human side? Was I only a beast with wings and claws or did I actually have a soul?

"Sometimes, when I come here, it feels like my mother's here too," I confessed. "Like she can hear me and see me. Like I'm the one who's a ghost and we accidentally traded places. That's weird, huh?"

Jake took my hand in his, his skin warm, refreshing.

"No," he answered, a strange sound in his voice. "I used to come here all the time, after my grandma died."

"You were close to her?"

He nodded, head lowered. Then he lifted his gaze until he was staring into my eyes. One hand rested on my shoulder. "I won't tell anyone your secret, Elspeth. You're safe with me."

Then he leaned closer, his scent overwhelming, his thoughts like the wind through the leaves, a wild rushing, his skin like the embrace of the forest. His lips touched mine and I slid my arms around his waist, leaning in to the kiss, suddenly wanting more. I wanted to cast an enchantment, to lead him into sleep, to harvest his dreams. Wanted to walk into a dream with him, to see the hidden world on the other side of his eyelids. Wanted to know everything about him.

The kiss had only just begun and already I wanted another.

His arms were around me then, and the winter chill disappeared. In its place, fire crackled through my limbs, from my fingertips to my feet.

I could see it then, the world inside him. Tender and gentle as a spring morning, the shadows of night lingering at the edge of the wood, a handful of stars scattered across a pale sky. I never knew that humans could be filled with so much magic.

It was my first hunt and I had chosen my prey wisely.

We pulled away from each other with reluctance.

Then he took my hand in his.

"We should go," he said, his voice husky. "Can't let Hunter win the contest."

Chapter 58

The Beating of Wings

Driscoll:

I crept down the stairs, suitcase in hand, down two landings until I finally reached the first floor. It felt like I was in another world, another time, as if this gigantic Victorian house with the towering turret was a great woolly mammoth, frozen in the sudden snowstorm. Electric lights gleamed overhead, as if only yesterday the stairway had been lit by flickering gas jets, pristine Persian rugs had covered the polished floors and intricate wallpaper had glittered with metallic inks.

Time passes. Some things change, some things die.

The Driscoll mansion creaked and moaned as I walked toward the foyer. Every movement caused a welcome response from this aged beauty, as if it didn't want to see me go. My fingers trailed the polished wainscoting, moonlight flickered through a wall of stained glass, lace curtains drifted as I passed. If there were ghosts inside these walls, they would be glad to see me. They would nod as I moved through midnight gloom toward destiny.

They would be glad to see me free, at last.

The front door opened and I stood on the threshold.

The wind whistled and howled outside the mansion, carried the beating of wings and the chanting of a thousand voices. A carrion stench filled the air, as if a foul predator had just been loosed, as if it now stalked the perimeter of Ticonderoga Falls. The trees wavered in the strong wind and bent to the side, branches snapping and twigs flying through the sky.

I stumbled backward, waiting for the magic, waiting for the world to shift, for one of the monsters to come sweeping down from the sky.

But nothing happened.

Instead, the October wind whipped leaves and branches and black sky, swept through the doorway with screeching and howling, shook the windows in the dining room and slammed a door shut in the kitchen.

My legs trembled and I clutched the suitcase to my chest like a shield.

"They're gone," I mumbled, pushing myself forward. "They're all in the village, flitting from house to house." Snow stung my face with little bites of cold and I almost slipped on the last porch step.

But I didn't stop. I couldn't.

I headed toward the carriage house and the car nestled safe inside.

Toward freedom.

Chapter 59

ɑlmost Magical

Maddie:

We weren't alone anymore. Black sky glimmered overhead, low clouds framed a tempestuous moon. I was trying to work out a rough plot outline in my head, only partially aware of the real world as Tucker and I ventured from one glowing jack-o'-lantern to the next, Samwise panting along at my side. I didn't even realize that we had been swallowed up by another group of trick-or-treaters, some of the kids taller than I was. It wasn't until I stood on the doorstep of yet another candy-doling bungalow that one of the kids got the courage to talk to me.

"You're Mad Mac, aren't you?" he asked, words whistling slightly through the space where his front teeth used to be.

I nodded with a smile.

"We was at your cabin earlier," another confessed.

This happened often, especially when I was trying to work on a story. Whether I hunkered down with a laptop in the local Starbucks or scribbled on a yellow legal pad in a Barnes and Noble, I would eventually find myself surrounded by kids and young adults—those who thrived on my stories. It was almost as if they could sense that another tale was about to be created and they would arrive at my doorstep, hungry. Ready to devour my children before they were even born.

Right now the snow spiraled around all of us in sparkles of white light. It mixed with the fragrance of popcorn balls and caramel apples, combined with the mystery of prepubescent faces concealed behind masks and painted skin. It was as if the children were all hiding from me, yet eager to be found.

Just like my characters. They hid from me too.

Until finally one day—after weeks of puzzling through my plot—I'd be tromping from my office to the kitchen for another cup of espresso, when all of sudden, I'd see one of them. Sometimes crouching in the shadow by the stairs, sometimes lounging on the sofa, sometimes lurking in a doorway. As if they had been following me all along, just waiting while I mused over the story. Waiting until I knew too much about them for them to resist me anymore.

Waiting for me to tell their story.

I had always figured that it was just my imagination.

But now I wondered if I had been wrong. Maybe they'd been real all along.

An exhilarating mood flowed through the streets of Ticonderoga Falls tonight, almost magical, like the current of an underground river. Part of it surged through the ethereal mountain forest. Part of it eddied around the quirky residents. Part of it sprinkled down with the white crystalline snow that continued to drift from the heavens.

Just then, while the kids were bantering about which house to go to next and how long they had before they should meet for the bonfire, I thought I saw someone familiar emerge from the mists that surrounded us. Outlined in white and silver shadow, his body transparent, he hulked alongside the children, as if they were the best of friends, as if they'd known one another for years. Dangerous, mischievous, the grin of an imp on his face, he lurked behind one of the older boys.

This can't be happening.

It was Pinch. One of the characters from my Shadowland series.

And there at his side, forming from the mists, was Nick. His dark-skinned partner in legendary crimes.

The two transparent rascals glanced at me; one even gave me a wink.

Then Nick took a swing at the hat one child was wearing, knocked it off his head. At the same time, Pinch shoved another boy.

"Hey! Why'd you do that?" the first boy cried as he fished his hat from the gutter, soggy now from melted snow.

"What'd you shove *me* for? I didn't do nothin'," the second boy answered.

Almost instantly, the two boys were pushing each other.

Meanwhile, Nick and Pinch laughed. Nick tickled a girl dressed as Uhura, who then elbowed a Wolverine-clad boy beside her in retaliation.

"Stop it!" Uhura said.

Wolverine got ready to push her back.

"Enough, you two!" I said, suddenly feeling like an errant mother. I glared at Nick and Pinch.

They both cowered, as if ashamed.

In fact, all the kids looked at me with a mixed expression of surprise and fear. All of them except Tucker. He just gave me a quizzical stare.

"But Mom, it's only Nick and Pinch. They always act like that," he said.

I should have been astonished. Up until this point, my characters had always stayed inside my head, where they belonged. At least, that was what I thought. But right now I was either suffering from another side effect of that deadly nightshade—or there was definitely something strange and mystical about this town.

Samwise trotted alongside Tucker. Snow fell, cold bits of sky; it clung to his fur, sloshed wet on his paws. All around us children were laughing and running, wearing strange clothes. He stopped and sniffed the white-sprinkled sky, as if listening. Then the dog cocked his head, yipped.

"What is it, boy?" I asked.

Suddenly the dog strained at his leash, dragging me through slippery snow. He seemed to want something across the street. For a moment, it almost looked as if the house on the corner were glowing, as if it were thrumming and humming with words. I thought I saw words drifting down from the sky, like smoke flowing into the house.

"What is it?" I asked again as I stared at the bungalow that sat on the corner, fenced in by neatly trimmed hedges, flanked by a matching pair of sugar pines. No pumpkins lined the porch, no paper skeletons danced in the breeze. All the shutters were pulled closed and heavy curtains shrouded the front picture window.

But light peeked out from every crevice and smoke curled from the chimney.

And now I could feel it too, some unseen force pulling me toward the house, like it had suddenly become the center of the universe.

"I don't think they want trick-or-treaters," I said, trying to convince myself not to cross the street.

"That's Joe Wimbledon's house," one of the children told me.

"He loves to tell stories," another ventured.

Joe Wimbledon. The man in the vet's office. The guy Sheriff Kyle told me about.

"What kind of stories?" I asked, teetering on the edge of the curb. Samwise was already halfway into the street. I hoped a car didn't come around the corner, this dog was out of control.

"Creepy stories, about ghosts and shape-shifters and chupacabras." It was the little boy with the missing front teeth talking.

"Hey, we gotta go to the bonfire or Hunter will start without us," a teenage girl dressed like a green-skinned pixie warned. "We're already late!"

Suddenly the whole crowd of children pulled away from us, all heading in another direction, half jogging, half running. Tucker stared after them.

"Mom, let's go with them. I wanna see the bonfire too," he said.

"Not yet," I answered, as if we saw bonfires every day. "We're going to one more house first." Then I grabbed his hand, just in time, because at that moment Samwise lunged with an almost supernatural strength, his chest and back widening, his fur bristling.

Like a magical sled dog, he pulled all three of us across the street and up the steps.

Until we all stood right in front of Joe Wimbledon's front door.

Part 4

*Those who dream by day are cognizant
of many things that escape
those who dream only at night.*
—Edgar Allan Poe

Chapter 60

Fire and Smoke

Thane:

A chaos of children jostled their way down the street, voices tumbling over one another, all fighting for prominence. Masks and costumes askew, bags brimming with candy, a high level of excitement charged through them. The evening should have been winding down, they should have been heading home soon, but they weren't. Instead, they veered away from the main streets and ambled toward the edge of town.

I slumped in a doorway, made sure my scent was still that of wet wood and smoke, then I folded my shape back to what it had been before—a towheaded six-year-old boy. I watched the crowd of children approach, my steady gaze running through their ranks, studying them. I was getting particular now, only wanted a certain type of dream, something heady and strong with dark stormy edges. Meanwhile, River stumbled and sang along the sidewalk. Drunk from feeding too fast, he was now having trouble keeping his disguise focused. He repeatedly slipped from a six-year-old boy to a seventeen-year-old girl.

It would have been funny except, at that exact moment, I suddenly realized something wonderful was strolling in my direction.

A young man led the group of approaching children, snickering and boasting—my favorite kind of human, self-possessed and arrogant. I could smell fire and smoke inside the teenager, who carried danger like an explosive weapon.

I thrilled at the possibilities.

I held up a hand to silence my brother. "Hold your skin steady," I muttered.

"Trying. I am trying." Then River laughed and his hair spiraled in luminescent tangles.

"Freeze your shape and do it quick—"

River's eyes shrank to dark spots but his visage still wavered.

I grabbed him by the arm, then yanked him back into the shadows. "I don't need these humans to feast, you know. I could siphon the dreams right out of you. I could slow down all those children with a Veil and take my time bleeding you dry—"

"You wouldn't do that, I'm your blood brother, sure enough—"

"Wouldn't I? You almost cost me everything yesterday, *brother*." I held him with a strong hand, pressed him against a wall, then watched him for a long, dreadful moment. Finally, I gave River one last warning, "Hold your shape steady and do it quick or I'll drag you off someplace private and feast on *your* dreams."

"That's sacrilege," he answered, a whining tone in his voice.

"You think I care about Darkling law now that I've had a taste of freedom? Do you? Either hold your skin straight or go off into the shadows and stay there until the moon sets—"

My brother closed his eyes, then gave his skin a fierce shake. For a second he was no more than a blur of color. I glanced over my shoulder at the humans, a mere wingspan away. Fortunately, they were distracted, chattering and laughing amongst themselves. None of them even looked in our direction.

"I've got it, I do," River said.

I checked him over, from head to toe. He was an innocent six-year-old boy again, no wavering or distortion or blasts of bright light.

"See that you keep it, then," I said as I gave him one last toss against the wall, knocking the wind out of him.

Meanwhile, the company of adolescents rumbled past, all sparks and glitter and squeals of laughter. I turned with a grin and fell into step behind the last child, listening now to their confident boasts of winning a prize, all the while focusing on the dark-haired beauty that led them like the Pied Piper away from the village.

Hunter. That was his name. I could smell fire and smoke wafting from his clothes. Danger thudded through the crowd.

And fortunately, I was the only one who could hear it.

Chapter 61

Dark Magic

Joe:

I peeked out a side window, watched another group of trick-or-treaters drift down the street like wanton revelers, shouting, laughing, occasionally tossing a rock at a parked car, lacing windshields with spiderweb cracks. They were heading toward the outskirts of town, to the old junkyard for their traditional Halloween bonfire. But there was something different about this year. I could feel it charging through the air, electric and sharp.

I almost thought about stepping outside and calling out a warning.

But three things stopped me. One, they wouldn't care what I said, nobody listened to me in this town; Two, I didn't want to take a chance on accidentally inviting a Darkling inside; and Three, a woman, a boy and a dog had just scrambled up my front steps.

They hadn't knocked on the door yet. But they would. Soon. Meanwhile, the Legend whirled overhead, a tornado of words, tumultuous and quicksilver. It was changing. All legends change as time passes, as the story gets passed from one person to the next, but for the first time I heard a chorus of new voices and names.

And the ending was wrong. Dreadfully wrong.

Ash was outside, somewhere nearby. He always stopped by on Halloween, it had become a ritual. I would nurse another beer, fire raging, Ash would come inside—all the doors and windows opened for him, this was his village, his flock, it all belonged to him—and we would spend an hour or two together, me retelling the Legend, while Ash leaned back in a chair, nodding at all the right places, raising an eyebrow if any detail was missed. He sheltered us from the wild Darklings that prowled Big Bear and Lake Arrowhead and all the other little towns in between.

The curse had been our protection, though neither Driscoll nor Ash saw it that way.

From Blueridge Mount to the Ticonderoga Waterfall, from Castle Rock to Cedarpine Peak, an invisible hedge of protection wrapped around Ticonderoga Falls and it had from the day Lily died. The curse had protected us as well as the fluorescent lights protected the inhabitants of L.A.

Here, in the mountain crevices, there was room for dark magic and moonlit nights. Here, the Darklings practiced the fine art of harvest and interpretation and inspiration. And as a result, Ticonderoga Falls was brimming with artists, musicians, writers, craftsmen and inventors. From the turn-of-the-century plein air painters to the twenty-first-century rapper who lived in the hills to that war-poet who had just sold a screenplay, artists were drawn here like slivers of steel to a magnet.

Kismet. Destiny.

I took another slug of beer, finished off the bottle and set the empty on a nearby table. I didn't want the Legend to change, but I had learned long ago that I was just a cog in the Darkling machinery.

Like the rest of the town.

My opinion didn't matter.

But I wished that it did, because an uncontrollable fear surged through me, so strong that even the alcohol couldn't numb it. Something was going to happen tonight, something dark and unexpected, and no one in Ticonderoga Falls—not even Ash himself—would be powerful enough to stop it.

Chapter 62

Shadowy Creatures

Maddie:

Fist clenched, my knuckles struck wood once, twice, three times, and the knock echoed with a dull thud. I glanced down at Tucker. He turned away from the door and stared back in the direction we had come, probably watching the crowd of trick-or-treaters as they disappeared around a distant corner.

Samwise stood at attention, ears forward, listening for movement on the other side of the door. Just then the dog cocked his head and looked up at the sky, as if he heard something.

I glanced back toward the sky too, still shrouded with cloud, moon peeking through, snow tumbling down. Sometimes the snow drifted up, as if it had changed its mind, white flotsam caught in an unseen eddy of wind. I hoped there wasn't something lurking out there—something I couldn't see.

Like another one of those shape-shifting chupacabras.

Standing on the porch, with all the other trick-or-treaters gone, I suddenly realized how vulnerable we were.

I should have stayed home like Ash suggested. I should have realized something was off-kilter in this Thomas Kinkade village.

A shadow drifted behind me, moved ever so gently, and when it did I saw the outline of a man in its midst—almost invisible except around the edges. The unnatural warmth returned and the snow around us began to melt. I instinctively draped one arm around Tucker's shoulders.

Would the dog attack if I told him to? I'd never tried anything like that before, but then he'd never been a werewolf-hybrid before either.

Would you turn into a werewolf if I told you to, boy?

Samwise gave me a piercing glance, then answered with a hearty, *"Wrrooof!"*

The door swung open just then, revealed a light-filled room and a tall man dressed in flannel shirt and jeans. Joe Wimbledon, an unopened bottle of beer in one hand. He glared outside, eyes hooded, head tilted down as if he didn't want to see what might be prowling beyond the edge of the porch.

Nobody said anything for a long moment, then Tucker started his trick-or-treat rap song.

"If you wanna trick or if you wanna treat,

I'm the one to folla 'cuz I can't be beat,

If you do your part an' give me somethin' sweet,

Then I'll leave you be an' move on up the street—"

He opened his bag right on cue and flashed a bling-studded grin.

But Joe just stared at me, a glimmer of recognition in his eyes.

"You're that woman from the vet's office today, the one that claimed chupacabras were in her house last night. But it was the wrong night, don't ya know. They don't come out 'til tonight. See"—he pointed to the sky, a black canvas where the clouds had pulled back to reveal a glorious moon—"full moon is tonight."

He retreated a step, hand on the doorknob as if he were

about to slam it closed. Just like I had done to Ash earlier.

"I think ya made the whole thing up," he said.

I knew I had about a second or less to convince him to let us in. I grabbed my coat sleeve, hitched it up to my elbow. Exposed bare flesh on my forearm and a six-inch jagged wound. "Did I make this up?"

He cursed, eyes narrowed.

Then he reluctantly widened the door for us to enter. "You better get inside," he said. "Whoever made that mark is probably lookin' for ya right now."

Chapter 63

The Darkness of His Soul

Ash:

The Hunt called, strong and sweet, just like it had for thousands of years. I crouched in a corner, behind a house, listening, trying to resist. I didn't want to take Maddie against her will, but she was fair game as long as she was out in the open. I could swoop down from a rooftop, cast a Veil, put the boy and the dog to sleep while I harvested. None of them would even remember.

But the Legend was too loud tonight, and the version that curled through the trees was wrong—it was painting me too dark, with brushstrokes too broad. All the nuances of love and torment had been erased, the paint had cracked and bits had fallen off. I was no longer a noble creature who had cursed the village for a horrid wrong, I was now an evil captor who kept his sheep from roaming free, who kept Driscoll prisoner.

It said that madness was the cup I had offered the Driscoll family on that night, that mercy and hope had died with Lily. And now, the darkness of my soul was spreading throughout the village, it leaked down alleys and streets like dark oil, contaminating everyone. They all walked with my stain on their brow, all marked for my pleasure.

But none of it was true. Not really.

The curse had bound *me* here—I was the prisoner. Unable to hunt anywhere else. Unable to return home.

I covered my ears, bowed my head, but I could still hear every footstep Maddie took and each one took her farther away from me. Yes, I might be able to seduce her, to enchant her for an evening.

But in a few days she would leave and go back to the world of humans, she would return to her place of prominence. I knew what she truly was—a master storyteller. In my world, she would have been royalty, she would have been the one to rule this village and I would have been the peasant, even lower than Thane.

If she knew what I had done, she would hate me. If she knew what I was . . .

I stood suddenly, with a snap of wings in the brittle cold, lifted my head.

I could feel *him* now, pulling on the tether that connected us—Driscoll, climbing in his car, tires grinding gravel, running away.

A sharp ache tugged at my chest like a grappling hook, pulling me unwillingly toward the fleeing human. I didn't want to go, but the curse had wearied me, burned down my resistance. I felt as if I had been dipped in wax, all senses deadened to the world everyone else inhabited.

I longed to follow Maddie—the storyteller—I wanted to see where she would go this last night when she walked through my world. Wanted to see every blade of frost-crusted grass that she touched. Wanted to drink the fragrance of her ideas trailing behind her like pale ghosts.

But I couldn't.

The curse demanded that I follow my prey.

And stop him from escaping.

Chapter 64

A Quiet Night

Sheriff Kyle:

I sat in my patrol car with Rodriguez, both of us eating the roast-beef sandwiches I had picked up over at the Steak & Ale about an hour and a half earlier. So far it seemed like a quiet night, unusually tame for a Halloween. Even the kids' pranks had been toned down this year. No animals locked in the garage or eggs splattered on new cars. A few complaints had sizzled through on the police radio: rocks in mailboxes, flattened tires, and apparently a spray-painted barn. But old Mr. Hudson had needed to paint that barn for years. Served him right for leaving an eyesore like that right on Main Street where everybody could see it.

The radio crackled to life again.

"Kyle, you there?"

I sighed.

"Here," I answered. No need to follow protocol when Alice was working dispatch.

"I just got a bunch of weird calls, Sarah Duncan over on Timberline, Jane Culpepper on Creek Wood, and the Walkers on Mountainview—that new couple that just moved to town, remember them?"

"I remember, Alice. What happened?"

"Oh, yeah, well, each of the women just walked into their living room and found their husbands asleep on the floor."

Deputy Rodriguez looked at me with raised eyebrows.

"Do they want us to go over and make sure everything's all right?"

"Well, you could, but then I got a call from Bob Miller. He says Agnes hasn't come home yet. Guess she's like clockwork, locks up the Steak & Ale at nine, drives home, in the door by nine fifteen. He tried calling the pub, but no answer. No answer on her cell either."

I glanced at my watch. 10:08 P.M. I set my sandwich on the seat and started the engine.

"Tell Bob we're on our way."

The streets were deserted, all the trick-or-treaters had either gone home or headed over to the annual bonfire. The patrol car fishtailed in the snow on the corner of Main and Running Springs Road. That was when I noticed the string of Buicks and Hondas and Mazdas with cracked windshields, all leading toward the junkyard.

The kids had taken it up a notch after all.

"We should stop at the bonfire after we're done with Agnes," I said. "See if we can figure who's been up to trouble."

"Good idea," Rodriguez said, then she stuffed the last bite of roast beef in her mouth.

I glanced at my own sandwich with longing, realized I probably wouldn't get to finish it. We drove slower through town, giving it a visual once-over just in case anything else was amiss. Saw a flurry of overturned trash cans, picket fences kicked in and a broken picture window on Charlie Mitchell's house.

"Kids have been busy," Rodriguez noted as we pulled into the Steak & Ale parking lot. One car waited for us, covered in snow.

Agnes's car.

I stepped into the cold, felt an uncharacteristic shiver

run over my back. I walked toward her car—a Honda Element. "Check the front door of the pub," I told Rodriguez. Meanwhile, I brushed the snow off the windshield, stared through the tinted glass. Empty, all doors locked. No purse or coat inside, just a few empty Diet Coke cans and a half-eaten package of donuts. "Agnes!" I called out, sweeping the nearby bushes with my flashlight. No footprints in the snow out here, no evidence that she'd been to her car recently. I paced around the lot, stared into the thickening gloom that had settled like glue amid the shrubbery.

"Hey, Kyle, you need to come see this!" Rodriguez shouted from the front of the pub.

You need to come see this. My least-favorite expression when investigating a crime. It never went well after somebody said that.

I reached the edge of the building, was just about to swing around the corner when Rodriguez grabbed my arm.

"No, stay where you are," she said. Her flashlight pooled on the ground right in front of the door. "Look at the marks in the snow."

A pair of footprints, probably Agnes's, faced the door. She must have been closing up because the key was still in the lock. But then the footprints slid backward, formed two solid lines, like somebody had dragged her away from the door halfway into the street.

But that was where they stopped, and there were no other footprints beside hers. It was almost as if something had swooped down from the sky and carried her off.

Chapter 65

Shapeshifters

Maddie:

Pine logs crackled and spit in the fireplace, filled the room with flickering light and woodsy fragrance. Family mementoes covered the walls and mantel, black-and-white photos mixed with sepia tones and turn-of-the-century tintypes. The Wimbledon resemblance ran strong—I thought I could pick out Joe's mother and grandmother, possibly a sister or two. Tucker sulked in an overstuffed chair, while Samwise paced the room curiously, lifting his head whenever Joe started to speak.

"I want to go to the bonfire—" Tucker said in that whine all children have perfected by the age of three.

"Later, sweetheart."

"But, Mom—" He dragged the word *Mom* out for three syllables.

"No."

Then Joe walked back in the room with two cups of hot chocolate and a bowl of water. In a minute, both Tucker and Samwise were slurping their respective drinks. I leaned forward on the sofa, elbows on my knees.

"What do you know about the local chupacabras?" I asked.

He shrugged, took a long sip of Coors. "Not much."

"Now I think *you're* lying. One of your shape-shifters got into my cabin last night and then today, two of them attacked me in the woods."

He bristled, then shook his head. "I don't know how you got that mark on your arm, but if two Darklings attacked you in the woods then you wouldn't be here tellin' me about it."

"Darklings, huh. I knew they had another name. Chupacabras never quite fit." I pulled a small pad of paper from my pocket and started taking notes. "I found a dead body in the woods today." I paused to see how he would react. So far, he was still acting like I was making everything up, just like Sheriff Kyle. "The body was almost completely flat—"

His eyes found mine, studied them.

"—and there were two holes, just like all the blood had been drained out."

"Not blood. They're not vampires. You really found a body?" He stood up and walked to the mantel, his back to me. "Where is it? How come Kyle hasn't called me?"

"Why would he call you? He acted like you were the local nutcase."

"Some folks think so." I noticed that he held a small picture frame in his hand when he turned to face me again. A young woman, maybe his wife. "But whenever things turn sour around here, everybody suddenly remembers what I been tellin' them over the years."

"What's that?"

"You're an outsider," he said. "Ain't no reason for me to tell ya the Legend."

At that point, Samwise lifted his head and barked, his body shifted and grew, fur got longer and thicker, his eyes turned silver, his chest and back expanded.

"Whoa! Cool," Tucker said. "Do you see what Samwise just did, Mom?"

Joe retreated behind a chair.

"He isn't going to hurt you," I said.

"What the hell is that thing? It's not a dog." Joe had backed into the corner now, his eyes wide, a look of terror on his face.

"My dog bit one of your precious Darklings," I explained. "What you see is the result."

Joe continued to stare at the dog, an expression of shock and horror on his face.

"Then it's a werebeast," he said. "But he told me they were just a fable, he'd never even seen one before—"

"Who told you that, Mr. Wimbledon? Where did you hear about werebeasts?" I asked.

Before either of us could speak again, the front door swung open and a river of cold air rushed in. Outside, the wind mourned through the trees; sagging limbs, twisting clouds, and all the colors were suddenly wrong. It felt like all the air had been sucked from the room.

Then a lone silhouette stood poised on the threshold. A tall, black shadow framed by swirling snow and moonlight.

Ash.

Unlike the other Darklings in Ticonderoga Falls, *he* didn't need to be invited inside.

Chapter 66

Footprints in the Mud

Sheriff Kyle:

We searched the Steak & Ale, but I already knew we weren't going to find Agnes inside. Most likely she was somewhere in the woods on the other side of the street; I could feel it gnawing in my gut. First Madeline had claimed that she saw a dead body in the woods and now this.

But people didn't just disappear in Ticonderoga Falls.

Something was wrong here. I had a strong desire to call Joe Wimbledon; as loony as the guy was, he still had a handle on the local folklore and customs.

I stood outside the pub, hands on my hips, staring into the bramble of Sierra currant and bush chinquapin and lodgepole pine across the highway. Right now the pines whispered, branches taunting and swaying—

You won't find her. You'll never find her.

I wasn't about to be spooked by a thirty-acre canyon covered with seventy-foot trees.

"I'm hiking in the woods," I told Rodriguez.

"Right behind you."

As soon as I got across the two-lane highway I saw a spot

where the shrubs had been pushed aside. Two sets of foot-prints in the mud and snow led down into the darkness of a steep ravine. "Here," I said pointing so she could see, then I led the way down the rugged path. Whoever had been down here hadn't tried to cover their tracks, almost as if they didn't care. Or maybe they wanted to be caught. Criminals did that sometimes, led a merry chase, secretly hoping someone would stop them and put an end to the madness.

We didn't get cases like this very often up here, but I'd seen plenty back in L.A. Bodies found in Dumpsters, babies in garbage bags, people tossed out like litter. That was the reason why I had moved up here. I had needed to reconnect, to stop seeing people as victims. Or murderers.

Meanwhile, the wind tossed the trees about, making them creak and moan as it swept through the canyon. Then it broke overhead in a long pitiful wail.

"Creepy," Rodriguez muttered. "Wish that awful wind would stop."

"Me too," I admitted.

The narrow path leading into the ravine turned at a sharp angle, then turned again. Neither of us could see what was up ahead, not through the wild tangle of branches and un-dergrowth; our flashlights transformed the black night into shades of violet and blue. The mist still clung to the lowlands and it began to roll toward us, billowy clouds that ate up the landscape, that stopped our beams from exposing anything until we were right on top of it. Rodriguez sensed it before I did. She laid a hand on my arm, held me still.

"You smell that?" she asked.

I nodded. I didn't want to admit it, but there was some-thing dead up ahead. A fresh kill. I'd done enough hunting to recognize the stench.

"Be careful," I said. There was a chance that whoever kidnapped Agnes might still be down here in the gulley. I gestured for us to spread out. Now our lights overlapped, crisscrossed.

"Agnes?" I called her name. "Agnes, you out here?"

My words echoed across the canyon, returned empty and hollow.

The smell of death got stronger as the trail leveled out onto an old dried-up riverbed. I heard something moving up ahead, scratching and snarling. I pulled out my weapon and motioned for Rodriguez to do the same.

"Agnes!" One last shout as we continued to move forward through the shifting white gloom, reality changing with every step. First a fallen log, then an outcropping of rock that jutted into the riverbed, finally a mound of leaves and twigs driven here by the recent rains.

Up ahead, something yipped and howled.

I flashed the light and it reflected back in four sets of glowing eyes.

Coyotes.

I fired a shot in the air.

Blood dripped from their jaws. The closest one stared at me, head lowered. Then it turned and loped away, revealing a small pack behind it. About six coyotes total. In a second, the pack scattered.

That was when we both saw a body, curled on its side in a nest of leaves and bramble.

It was Agnes. Dead. I approached, swept her from head to foot with the white light. Aside from the recent carnage by the coyotes, this was almost exactly what Madeline had described, back on the Ponderosa Trail. Agnes's body was flat.

Like all of her life had been mysteriously drained out.

Chapter 67

Outsiders

Maddie:

Joe Wimbledon's front door hung open, the tide of cold air unending and time seemed to hold still. Finally, Ash stepped into the room and the front door closed on its own. In an instant, the heat returned, the curtains fluttered and a soft sigh moved through the living room and into the hallway, as if the house itself was glad to have him here. I watched him, couldn't stop watching him. It was as if no one existed but him right now.

He sat in an overstuffed chair.

Maybe human. Maybe not.

Pale skin, chin-length unruly black hair. Ash—the name fit him perfectly. What didn't fit was the way my heart skipped a beat when he entered the room or the way I forgot to breathe until he looked at me.

"It's time for the Legend," he said, his voice both compelling and chimeral at the same time. Dark eyes reflected an even darker light.

I sat back, my muscles finally relaxed, and I realized that I was going to hear everything I needed to know. Everything about this village was going to be revealed. I glanced at Tucker, saw that he was leaning forward, eyes wide, eager for whatever was coming—both he and the dog had taken the same positions they always did when I told them bed-time stories. Samwise curled on the floor beside the fire, tail thumping with anticipation, eyes on the man who had just walked in.

"Tell them," Ash said with a glance at Joe.

Joe hesitated. "But Mr. Ash, they're outsiders—"

"Not anymore," he answered. "Start at the beginning and don't leave anything out."

Then sparkles drifted from the ceiling, almost like the snow outside. An enchantment had been cast, time was standing still, and we would have as much time as we needed to hear the whole story.

All tales begin somewhere.

This one started with a whispered mountain legend, nearly a century ago.

Chapter 68

The Best Legend Keeper

Ash:

The engine roared to life at the same moment that Joe started telling the Legend. The two events weren't connected and yet they would change the destiny of Ticonderoga Falls. I could feel a shift in reality, like summer wind on naked flesh.

Welcome and uncontrollable.

The story flowed from Joe's lips, caught in his rough mountain cadence and transformed into something almost holy. He was the best Legend Keeper of them all.

It was too bad really. This would be the last time he would tell the story.

I didn't know what was coming, still I could feel it like a tsunami, building someplace far, far away, one unseen event that would lead to another and then another. If I stopped the story at any point in time, then the ending would have remained the same.

Everything in this village would have remained the same. Almost forever.

And I would have remained alone.

She needed to hear all of it before she would believe.

In my mind, I could see images, pictures of Professor Eli Driscoll. But they were mere interruptions. Just more of Driscoll's incessant cry for freedom and peace.

All humans wanted it, didn't have any idea that they told their own horror stories in silence. I don't like to gaze inside their minds during the day, for all the darkness they carried. But during the night, that is an entirely different matter.

So I refused to react. Instead, I sat there, listening to the Legend, watching the expression on Maddie's face, while Driscoll cast out secret messages like a blackjack dealer tossing cards.

Chapter 69

Paintings of Lily

Driscoll:

I cringed. The car engine growled, a loud, steady rumble. Surely Ash could hear it and he would come flying through night skies at any moment, would pounce on the hood as soon as the car backed out of the carriage house. I waited for a long time, until finally, the motor settled to a soft purr, and the exhaust fumes cleared. Then I rolled down my window, hoping the cold air would invigorate me, give me courage and resolve. It didn't work. Instead the car filled with the smells of lumber, old tires and linseed oil. Moonlight poured in the open carriage doors, illuminating canvases stacked against the far wall, more evidence of my father's visitations over the years.

Paintings of Lily.

The most haunting one had managed to find its way to the top again, despite my efforts to keep it buried.

She stood posed as a turn-of-the-century little girl, her disguise perfect. The only way I could tell it was her was by the eyes: no human had eyes that color. She stood inside the mansion, surrounded by other children, though they all paled next to her in detail, in composition, in beauty.

It was the night of the birthday party. The night of the curse.

Of course, I hadn't been born yet—my own father had been just a boy—but I'd heard the tale so often that it was embedded in my DNA. It was my curse now.

But not if I could get away. All I had to do was cross over the border of the old Ticonderoga Falls purchase, the piece of land bought by my great-grandfather. As far as I was concerned, the map of the world suddenly shrank, all of the boundaries were now defined by this village called Ticonderoga Falls. It stood like an invisible cage that had held me too long.

One hand on the steering wheel, I looked over my shoulder, pressed my foot ever so gently against the gas pedal, and began backing the car out of the carriage house.

Inch by inch, heartbeat thundering louder than the howling wind, I ventured forth, every bit of me as excited and terrified as Magellan.

This was going to be my journey into the New World.

Chapter 70

Moon and Sky

Ash:

I could feel the rip, like an umbilical cord being sliced with a knife, as Driscoll embarked on his escape. As expected, the curse forced every dark emotion to the surface—revenge, hatred, guilt—and yet tonight, they were mysteriously quelled as I listened to the Legend. I studied Maddie's face—rapt with the story, the tale of my fall from grace, my exile in this backwoods town. I found myself surprised that she didn't see what a horrid creature I truly was. Some other emotion seemed to emanate from her.

But I couldn't tell whether it was empathy or pity.

Meanwhile, the story coiled about us, rich as music, all the notes in just the right order, all the chords dissonant and minor, as they should be.

Driscoll's car pulled onto the highway. He was running away. The grandson of the Great Murdering Beast was trying to escape.

Maddie glanced at me.

In the story Lily had just run into the library, had seen the men coming back into the room. My wife then lost her true disguise in the panic, unable to remember what skin she'd been wearing—it had happened to me before, I knew what a dreadful experience it could be.

To be exposed. To be vulnerable.

Driscoll's car roared, eager to tame the wild road. The forest rose and fell away; one hill after another rolled ever onward. Moon and sky. Black and white. The serpentine road buckled and skipped, as if alive. A thin layer of sweat beaded Professor Driscoll's forehead as he struggled to make sense of the curving black ribbon that tried to throw him off. He tried to hide his thoughts from the Beast. But it wasn't working.

Just like Lily hadn't been able to hide from the net that caught her.

Like I couldn't hide now from the gaze that Tucker cast at me, eyes tender, almost weeping. He looked so much like the boy who had lured Lily back at the train station, so many years ago.

Ever since the beginning of the curse, Driscoll and his family had been the cattle on the Beast's thousand hills.

I had been the Beast.

Driscoll could feel my presence now—though far away— probing his mind. Searching. Watching to see which way the car turned, how fast he was going. His fingers clamped the steering wheel, knuckles white.

I closed my eyes and tried to ignore Driscoll's frantic heartbeat. In the Legend I had just entered the Driscoll mansion. Too late to save her.

Day and night. Good and evil.

Moon in the heavens, full and commanding.

Driscoll pushed the gas pedal to the floor. He was near the edge of Ticonderoga Falls now, pressing against the silver woven net that spread like gossamer magic, created from my flesh and blood, from the wound in my side that would never heal, from the broken heart that would never mend—

Maddie stared at me, tears in her eyes. Listening. Heart thundering.

Maybe my heart could mend.

If I could only let go of the past.

Driscoll's car tore through the invisible barrier, borne into freedom in an instant, in that moment when I contemplated the possibility of falling in love again.

"No!" Joe stopped telling the story, he cried out.

I smiled. Joe knew what was happening and it was already too late to stop it.

Moon spinning overhead, hypnotic and impulsive. Driscoll fleeing down the mountainside like a dog with the backyard gate left open. Me suddenly crumpling to the floor, unable to speak, unable to move, just like the night Lily had died, wound in my side that matched hers. We had been so in love, so linked in soul and flesh, that the wound that killed her had almost killed me too.

And now a sound like the world being destroyed was rocketing overhead. It began somewhere deep in the valley, then traveled through the village, rushing toward the top of the mountain. An unbearable ripping sound surged through Ticonderoga Falls.

On the floor, I curled in agony, my wound made fresh again, my blood spilling in a red-black pool.

Chapter 71

Fabric of Reality

Maddie:

The room spun with enchantment and magic, then the Legend ended abruptly. It felt as if I'd been startled awake and, all around me, a dream was dissipating. The image of Lily's death faded, along with it the image of Ash flying to the rooftop and casting a curse on all of Ticonderoga Falls; the sparkles that had been hanging in the air faded, and the century-old vista that I had been staring into—the Victorian landscape of the nineteenth century—disappeared. In its stead I saw the bungalow living room, Tucker in a corner chair, and Samwise still curled before the fire. Just then Joe Wimbledon scrambled to his feet.

"No!" he cried out. "You can't let Driscoll go."

A horrific noise, almost like the world itself was being pulled apart, screeched overhead and rumbled beneath my feet. It even vibrated on my skin. I reached out to pull Tucker into my arms, shielding him in case the ceiling began to crumble down.

Then I saw Ash, slumped to the floor, a strange wound in his side and his blood flowing.

The wound in his side, that place where the light shined through, revealing that he wasn't human.

Ash was the Darkling in the Legend. And he was the creature who had protected me in the woods when I was a little girl. All of my feelings changed in an instant. I was no longer afraid or curious, I was no longer searching for a story.

A friend of mine was wounded, possibly dying, right in front of me.

I leaped from my chair to kneel beside him, pulling Tucker with me, making sure my son was still safe. Then I ripped Ash's shirt open so I could see the wound better.

"Get some bandages!" I cried to Joe. Meanwhile, I tried to stop the flow of blood with part of Ash's shirt.

"Don't let him go, Mr. Ash, please—" Joe said, shaking his head.

"Look, I don't know what you're babbling about," I said, "but he needs help. Now! Tucker run to the bathroom, grab a couple of clean towels!"

Tucker dashed off. I wadded the shirt fabric into a lumpy ball and pressed it against Ash's flesh, his pulse racing beneath my fingertips. A scorching heat poured from him, almost too hot to bear, but I forced myself to remain, despite blistering fingers.

"Don't you see, you just can't let Driscoll leave," Joe pleaded as he sank to a weary kneeling position beside Ash. "The magic's ripping apart, we won't have no more protection from the wild ones—"

"You can't stop it," Ash said with a rough gasp.

Then Tucker came back with an armful of towels. I pushed the linens against the wound, tried to stop the blood flow, but they just soaked it up, turned scarlet, fabric singeing at the edges, smoke mixing with the coppery smell of blood.

Ash moaned and writhed from the pain. He glanced up at me, eyes like those of a trapped animal. Then I saw something else in their depths. A hidden emotion, finally revealed. Something I hadn't seen in a man's eyes for so long that I almost didn't recognize it.

He turned his face aside and pushed himself to a sitting position, then leaned against one of the chairs, the flow from his wound finally slowing. He lifted his head and roared, his voice echoing through the treetops, soaring all the way to Cedarpine Peak and then falling off the precipice into the blue-black valley below.

"I release you!" he cried.

And a still emptiness echoed back, with just as much power as the magic. It slivered through the room, pierced every chest, made every one of us stop and be still.

At that same moment, the hole in Ash's side began to miraculously mend, knitting together, silver threads of light stitching the edges of flesh and bone in a hundred lightning-quick sutures. It must have been unbearable, for he cried out again, then gasped for air, his face contorted in pain. Finally, with a shudder, he fell into a heap on the floor.

Outside the clouds whirled about the moon and the heavens roiled.

And somehow I knew that yet another chapter in this dark mountain legend was about to unfold.

Chapter 72

Until Now

Elspeth:

Magic sizzled through the air. It bristled across my arms and made the base of my hidden wings ache. I held hands with Jake as we joined the rest of the trick-or-treaters, and the touch of his flesh made me light-headed. The laughter of a large crowd filled the junkyard as I shimmied through the broken gate. A chain-link fence surrounded the area, guarded by a few deserted buildings, windows boarded over, doors hanging limp on broken hinges. Everything was broken here and the trees were set back, so far away I could barely smell them. Part of me wanted to leave. I didn't like being separated from the woods. They'd always provided protection, a place to run and hide when I felt like I didn't fit in.

The way I'd felt my entire childhood.

Until now.

Jake smiled as he led me down the narrow path between yesterday's cast-offs: past towering heaps of fenders and hubcaps and the rusted-out shells of old battered cars, past wire box springs and a ripped-up sofa, past heaps of toasters and blenders and microwaves. And underneath it all cracked a broken sea of cement, tufts of wild grass peeking through.

I'd never been anyplace like this before. No dirt or water nearby. Even the wind seemed to have abandoned this corner of the universe. Still, there was one who never left me, whether I wanted her to or not.

The moon.

Slipping from behind thick clouds to taunt me, to whisper and remind me of the Hunt. As if I had forgotten, as if I could think about anything else when Jake walked so close, his leg brushing against mine as we continued to wind through the rubble, fire rushing through my limbs the longer I denied the call to harvest.

Finally, we found our way into a large open space.

Here, the area was painted with flickering flames and the smell of smoke hung in the air, everything and everyone now dressed in shades of red and yellow and orange. A large bonfire snapped and crackled in the center, devouring beams of old lumber and wooden pallets. Other young people milled about with masks hanging loose, some already dipping into their cache of Pixy Stix and Good & Plenty, jaws chewing slowly, mouths creased in sugary grins.

That was when I caught a glimpse of myself in a cracked mirror. I gasped, retreating into the shadows. My own mask had unintentionally slipped during the course of the evening. Now many of my Darkling features were more pronounced: slender pointed ears sticking out of long dark hair, my eyes reflecting the firelight with a silver glow. I turned away from the others, adjusted my appearance and hastily glanced back in the mirror. *Completely human again.*

Jake was staring at me.

"I liked the way you looked. Before," he said, his voice low.

"What do you mean?" I asked.

"It's Halloween," he said. "You can wear any disguise you want tonight."

I shook my head, trembling. No. I couldn't. It wasn't safe.

"I won't let anyone hurt you."

I looked into his eyes, wishing it were true. Wishing he were strong enough to protect me if anyone found out who I really was, if they turned on me.

Just then Hunter pushed his way to the center of the crowd. In one arm he carried a long stick with a human skull on top.

"Is that real?" I whispered to Jake, suddenly imagining my own head on a pike. That sort of brutality hadn't happened since the Middle Ages. But it was part of my tormented Darkling heritage. It could happen again. Anything could happen if the humans realized Darklings weren't myth.

"Of course, it's not real." Jake took my hand, pulled me close to him, then slid one arm around my waist. "It's just part of the game. Hunter does this every year."

"Game?" Suddenly I was intrigued. Like all Darklings, I loved games. Humans were so easy to trick, and if the game was played right I would win. That would be a tale worthy of boasting about around the fires of home.

If I ever went home again.

Chapter 73

Wet Wood and Smoke

Thane:

The press of so many humans crowded into one place was exhilarating. I drifted through the crowd, touching each of the warm bodies as I passed, feeding off their excitement and sugar high. My strength had grown throughout the evening. The broken arm had completely healed, and now I sauntered with a bravado I hadn't felt in moons, each footstep claiming this little village as mine. I no longer masked my scent or pretended that I liked the fragrance of wet wood and smoke.

River clumped along beside me, trying so hard to maintain his disguise that all of his movements had become wooden and unnatural. He had followed behind me and the rest of the trick-or-treaters for almost a mile before he finally caught up with us. But there was no bitterness between us now. It no longer mattered whether the lad held his disguise. In this flickering firelight few would notice. Together, we were stalking Hunter, taking our time, knowing that soon enough we'd be sharing another feast.

Just then I stopped and ran a gaze through the crowd.

I could smell the presence of another Darkling, not far away, trying to hide, the sizzle of reality folding, casting a familiar odor into the brisk night air.

Then I found her standing in the moonlight, surrounded by a pale silver outline. Wearing human skin, hanging on the arm of one of the teenage boys—Elspeth. Even dressed as a human, she was quite lovely. I could see the Darkling features through her disguise, the delicate bone structure, slender chin, high forehead, all attesting to her Blackmoor clan lineage. And I could sense her hunger, though she tried to quench it. It made all the colors around her a smidgen brighter, especially those in the young man who strode with a quiet confidence at her side.

That was the one she wanted.

I snickered. Let her hunt. She deserved to take whatever she wanted, her father had all but abandoned her over the years. And soon all of this, including that teenage human she favored, would belong to me.

I grinned, a smile too deep and decadent for the six-year-old child that I pretended to be. Maybe, when this was all over, I'd invite her into my clan. She was a few years younger than I was, but she'd be useful. She could help train my half-breed children once they were born.

And she'd make a good mate.

I inhaled deeply, let her new scent swirl through my head—crushed rose petals and clover—imagined her training my children—our children—how to fly and hunt, how to cast enchantments. Maybe I would take a whole flock of wives, like they used to in the old days. A few humans mixed into the bunch.

Then I remembered Madeline.

I would find her, as soon as I was done stalking this group of sumptuous children. I watched Hunter, drank in the lad's smell, smoke flowing from his skin in a shimmer of heat. Dangerous young man—his dreams would be dark and self-possessed and sensuous, a good addition to my stable. I longed to swoop down on Hunter now, mark him as my own.

Just at that moment, Hunter dragged a wooden crate into position, then climbed on top.

"Time for the tally and the dare," he announced in a loud voice.

All heads turned toward him and all voices hushed.

Chapter 74

Rumbling Quake

Ash:

I could feel it building in the distance with a wild fury, the Legend was getting ready to slash through this mountain village. Like a butcher's cleaver, it would separate bone from marrow, severing the protective shield that had become a part of the fabric of every building, every rock, every living creature in Ticonderoga Falls. In an instant, the glowing, almost invisible latticework would fall away. From the edge of Blueridge Mount to Cedarpine Peak, the village would be laid bare.

It began with a rumbling quake.

Already I could hear it sweeping down Main Street, rattling all the windows and shaking doors. It flipped several cars and it shred a furrow right down the center of the highway. Then it shocked outward with the force of a sonic boom, knocked a few people off their feet, and with a quirky twist, it shattered all the glass globes in the vintage-inspired street lights that lined the town square.

It would only be felt by those humans who happened to be in Ticonderoga Falls at the time. No outsiders would suspect a thing. But that didn't matter, because I knew that it would be heard by every Darkling, wild or tame, for a thousand miles. And they would all know exactly what it meant.

Ticonderoga Falls no longer had a guardian. The humans who lived here were now fair game.

Chapter 75

The Dare

Elspeth:

The ground trembled and shook beneath us. The fence around the junkyard bowed and flexed; in the near distance, the line of trees rippled and waved. Instinctively, I wrapped one arm around Jake and covered us both with a Veil. All about us broken things began to tumble to the ground, until the aisle that led to the exit was choked with clutter and debris. The longer the quake lasted, the farther I cast my enchantment until nearly all of the children were sheltered beneath my covering. Even Hunter. I managed to keep him standing upright despite the tossing and the turning, always focusing my attention on the ever bright, ever strong moon.

And throughout it all, I felt myself growing stronger.

A strange whisper burned in my ear. *It's different now.* I wished Father were here, I suddenly longed to see him, to know that he was safe.

Then as quickly as it had started, the quake passed.

Jake seemed to know what I had done. He smiled and held my hand, just as Hunter raised his arms, claiming his right to the dare.

"Every year we play a game," he said, his voice triumphant, as if he had defeated the rolling quake himself. "This year I choose the dare and, with it, I command that everyone reveal their true nature tonight—"

Even from this distance, I could see a mischievous gleam in his eyes.

"—So, to get this epic adventure started, I'm going to sing something that my grandmother used to sing to me. She called it an incantation of protection—"

"No," Jake said, shaking his head. He started pulling me toward the exit, climbing over the top of the rubble, trying to make it toward the hole in the fence. "We need to leave, Elspeth. Now!" I stumbled over toasters and microwaves, cut my arm on a broken mirror, all the while compelled to turn and listen to Hunter. "Close your ears, don't listen to him," Jake warned.

He continued to pull me along the top of the debris, one laborious step at a time. It would have been easier if we had just flown out, if I just dropped my disguise and carried him. It felt like I might be strong enough to fly a great distance right now, although I didn't want to leave. I kept stopping, turning around to face Hunter and staring at him, his words melting into a lyrical song, so like the songs of home that it made my skin flush and my shoulders ache from the hiding. I longed to cast off my mask.

"—you can no longer hide," Hunter sang then, his voice strong and clear, "from those who dwell in the world of humans—"

Jake grabbed me by the wrist and began pulling me even harder over the top of the rubble. The exit wasn't completely blocked off—I could see that now. But at the same time, a growl of rebellion was building in my chest. I wrenched free from his grasp, my eyes glowing.

"No!" I bellowed. "I want to stay!"

"—all you, who live in a perpetual state of pretend," Hunter sang, "all wearing gowns made of false flesh, gowns fashioned from the fabric of dreams—"

Now I *couldn't* move. My feet were fastened in place and my face was locked in position. I had to stare at Hunter, had to listen, had to obey the incantation that poured from his lips, sweet as sugar, lovely as the silver moon. Even though, for the first time, I finally realized the danger that was coming.

"—all you Darklings, near and far, must reveal yourselves now!"

At that moment, Hunter's incantation sparked upward, toward the heavens, brilliant as heat lightning. There, it carved the night sky into colors and it wrinkled the clouds, then it reached down to earth with hands of mist and fog. The dark magic searched the junkyard, looking for the familiar fragrance of folded reality.

It was looking for me.

Without even glancing down, I knew that my skin was cracking, peeling off and blowing in the wind like ashes. Bits of the mask I had been wearing spiraled about me, turned into a dust devil of bright color before sailing away. I could now see two others like me in the human crowd.

Thane and River.

Their countenance dissolved, like a pile of crumbling autumn leaves.

They were frozen in place too, just like me.

The last note faded from Hunter's song and I was released; my wings unfurled wide and I was compelled to soar overhead. That was when I finally knew the true purpose of this ancient spell—in a moment, all of the Darklings near and far would be revealed. And then, like me, they would all be pulled here in a great hurricane of flapping black wings.

As if this were a black hole that none of us could escape.

Chapter 76

Fingers of Ice and Fog

Ash:

I tasted primitive magic in the air, an age-old incantation spoken with a strange accent—the voice of the unpracticed. Enchantments take a lifetime to learn and this one was out of control. It snaked down streets and pushed open doors. It was looking for me.

But I didn't want to be found.

Not now. Not when Maddie was so near. I could feel her pulse, could smell her dreams. I laughed lightly. Humans were the ones with the true magic, though they didn't realize it. Sometimes a heavy emptiness had rushed through my veins when I envied humans their ability to sleep and forget, how they could rebuild their lives in a single evening. Those were the times when I realized how truly alone I was in this world. But right now, for the first time in a century, I felt as if I had just met a friend who could bring dreams to life.

And in a moment, it was all going to be ripped away.

I reached out, took Maddie's hand in mine, tried to hold back the heat that had blistered her skin earlier. Her lips parted as if she was going to speak but didn't know what to say. I gently turned her hand over and kissed her palm. Her hands had been burned and were now stained with my red-black blood. Just like Iris Wimbledon—Joe's grandmother, the woman who had nursed me back to health after my injury, after the curse. If it hadn't been for her, I would have surely died from that wound. Because of it, her hands had been scorched, my blood on her palms. The old woman with silver-white hair and tormented dreams had become my first Legend Keeper.

But now, everything was changing.

I wished that I could cast a Veil and stop time, prevent the inevitable.

Instead, I released Maddie's hand and braced myself.

Chapter 77

A Distant Song

Maddie:

Ash pressed his lips against my palm and a rush of heat flowed up my arm; it spread across my shoulders and then spilled down my back like a waterfall. His eyes met mine and time stood still. An instant turned into eternity, and I knew then, that despite his flaws, this creature was more noble than any man I had ever met.

Then the door burst open.

A distant song reached into the room, followed by ghostly fingers of ice and fog.

Ash's human skin cracked, fissures clicked and snapped along his jaw and his forehead. A thin black crevice snipped down his neck, branched into a thousand crackling tributaries, veins that circled from his chest to his back and then around again.

Then they all burst.

An explosion of color—a mock tornado—surrounded him, almost hid him from view. Now I could see through to his true skin, and I knew for sure that this truly was the creature that I had met in the forest, so many years ago . . .

dark gray flesh, broad black wings, teeth that sparkled and eyes of silver. And he was still more handsome than anyone I'd ever met. His true self had been revealed, and for the first time I could see what a beautiful creature he truly was.

"Ash."

It was all I could say.

The smoky mist wrapped possessive tendrils around him, lifted him off the ground.

"No!" Joe rocked to his feet, as if he only now became aware of what was happening. "Don't let them take you!" He lashed out at the supernatural cloud that roped about Ash's chest, that bound his arms and wings to his sides.

Then the song of incantation stopped. In a flash, the smoldering vapor yanked Ash out of the room and out of the house.

Both Joe and I ran to the door, watching helplessly as Ash soared down the street until he disappeared in the distant gloom.

"Get your coat," I called to Tucker, but he already had it on. No one needed to speak of what had just happened or what we planned to do. It was instinctive. It was part of the incantation, though none of us realized it at the time. We all rushed out the door after Ash, even the dog galloped down the street, feet scuffing up clods of snow and dirt.

We ran, slipped and jogged down snow-covered streets, not even bothering to take the sidewalk or to get into a car. And as we ran, we were joined by other villagers, some wearing coats and hats, some dressed in pajamas, bathrobes and slippers. All of us hurled ourselves down the street as if in a panic, as if our lives—our very existence—depended upon it.

And not one of us stopped, from the youngest to the eldest, until we all stood at the junkyard.

Chapter 78

That Awful Quiet

Sheriff Kyle:

The pristine chill evaporated, turned into a sweaty panic-throbbing heat. I got ready to hike back up the ravine for the fifth time, my coat open, hat pushed back. Flashing lights spilled through the woods and over the highway. Three more deputies combed the woods and the deputy coroner picked his way down toward the dried-up riverbed.

"Nicole's in labor," he said, explaining why it took him longer than expected to show up.

"'Bout time she had that baby," I answered, trying to smile but knowing that it hung wrong on my face. "Rodriguez is down there waiting for you." I gestured back toward the pool of light that glowed in the mists. "We saw some coyotes earlier."

"Lovely."

"I was just getting ready to head over to the junkyard," I said as we passed each other on the trail. "I want to check up on the kids. This might be our second body of the evening, and if it is . . ." I paused.

"You don't need to explain it to me." The deputy coroner

held up a hand and kept walking. "I'd rather the body count didn't get any higher. Do what you need to."

I braced myself for the wind that had been howling through the mountain pass, but when I climbed back out onto the road I was met with silence instead. The wind had died down.

It felt like that awful quiet right before a storm.

I wasn't sure why, but ever since we found Agnes's body I'd been worried about all the kids still out wandering the streets. The snow had slowed down. Only a stray snowflake fell as I jogged across the highway and got into my car. A quick glance to the locked rack between the two front seats gave me a surge of confidence.

My weapon of choice. A Ruger Mini–14 semiautomatic rifle.

I hoped whoever killed Agnes would cross my path sometime tonight. Because I was going to take him down, blow the legs right out from under him, knock him flat on his back.

Maybe I'd even blow the bastard's head off.

My SUV plowed through snow and slush, faster than I ought, still, not fast enough. My skin rippled with gooseflesh, the sort of thing that used to happen when someone told ghost stories when I was boy. I couldn't stop thinking about Agnes, all alone back there in the woods with no one to rescue her. Something swooping down from the hell-black sky to drag her off, screaming.

And then, sucking out her life, drop by drop.

Some evil beast was stalking this town and it was my job to catch it and kill it. Before it struck again.

I whipped around a corner, passed the line of cars with cracked windshields. Only a few more blocks and I'd be at the junkyard. Hopefully, all the kids were together. There was safety in numbers—though not much if they were trying to defend themselves against some unnatural demon.

That was when I heard it—an awful ripping and tearing,

as if the village itself were being torn asunder, from foundation to crowning sky. An explosive crack rumbled and a massive furrow bolted down the highway, dissecting the road in two. I glanced in the rearview mirror and saw that an earthquake had just missed me. A second earlier and my car would have been tossed into the flanking woods like a toy.

I pressed my foot against the gas pedal, leaned into the steering wheel, not daring to look behind me. Strange clouds were forming overhead. And a song began to wend through the air; tendrils of unearthly smoke snaking down the street, testing every window and door that they passed. Then one vaporous hand reared up alongside my car window, seemed to hover beside me as my vehicle raced down the street.

Don't look at it. It's not real.

Ghostly fingers tapped the glass.

"Go away!" I shouted.

Then it paused, seemed to nod at the other serpentine branches of mist, and it slithered on down the street. Hunting.

My Chevy Tahoe swiveled. Skidded to a sloppy halt.

I climbed out of the car, grabbed my rifle, made sure it was loaded and that the safety was off. I took a couple spare magazines and stuffed them into my jacket pockets. Then, clutching the weapon like a talisman, I strode through blackened brush and weeds.

Toward the junkyard and the town's children.

Toward any beast that might even think about harming them.

Chapter 79

A Thousand Yellow Eyes

Maddie:

The heavens seethed with a mass of black wings and sharp claws, they rocked with the bellowing cries of those trapped in their midst. I slid to a stop at the edge of a weathered field, just outside a battered, fenced-in enclosure—a junkyard. Right now, hordes of children were clambering out of its narrow exit, climbing over refuse, Halloween costumes ripping, masks cast aside, makeup running in tear-stained rivulets. I latched onto Tucker, kept him at my side, all the while staring up at the tumultuous sky, at the storm of Darklings that continued to grow.

The creatures poured in from surrounding communities, a murder of black wings that surged over distant hills until they all collided overhead. A thousand yellow eyes smoldered in the skies. A wild fury charged the air, forced a panic in my chest that made me want to run and hide.

But I couldn't.

The incantation held all of us in place. Darkling and human alike.

"Mom, I'm scared," Tucker whimpered beside me.

Me too, I wanted to say. "No one's going to hurt you,

Tuck. I promise." I kissed his forehead, lifted his chin until he gazed into my eyes. "My seal of protection, remember?"

He nodded.

At the same time Samwise bristled. The dog grew, his chest widened, his teeth got longer, sharper, and he braced himself in front of us. He was watching the sky. Ready to protect us from anything that might be foolish enough to try and attack.

Meanwhile, I sensed Ash somewhere in the darkness above. We were united now, bound by the red-black blood that stained my hands. I could hear his thoughts, disjointed, grief-stricken over what had happened.

Flee.

He was speaking to me through a darkened corridor of my mind. I saw him then, recognized his shape amongst the puzzle of black. He was tumbling, unstable as a babe.

No, I can't leave you, I whispered back, realizing what truly held me here. *Nor do I want to.*

At that moment, in the shadowed edge of town, a chill wind brushed against me.

I knew then that the century-old curse was gone. All it would take was one Darkling to realize how vulnerable we were, to launch down from whirlwind skies and claim the village with another curse. There would be no one to save us. Even Tucker and I would be prisoners here, bound.

I shivered beneath the wild black sky, remembering the two beasts that had cornered me earlier, and I tightened my grip around my son.

My kiss on his forehead. My vow to protect him, no matter what.

Then the crowd parted and I saw Sheriff Kyle standing akimbo, a short distance away. Rifle in one hand, he was staring up into the sky. He was getting ready to fire into the cloud of Darklings. But he couldn't—Ash was up there.

"No!" I shouted.

In that instant, before I could get Kyle's attention, the crowd closed around me and I couldn't move.

Chapter 80

Darkling-Filled Sky

Sheriff Kyle:

I hoisted my weapon and braced it against my shoulder, training it on the Darkling-filled sky with a well-practiced aim. The first shot landed square in the center of the vile flock that circled overhead. I grinned as I took a step back from the recoil. Years of hunting paid off, for I managed to hit two of the wild beasts with one strike; both creatures screamed and writhed in pain.

Both of them now fell from the sky.

They pitched forward in turbulent spirals, wings outstretched and thumping without strength, limbs seeking purchase though none was found. They scratched at sky and cloud as they fell, leaving behind a trail of sparks. Then a sea of grass and earth met them both. They crashed to the ground with a loud, sickening thud.

Their dead bodies were quickly surrounded by a mob of angry villagers.

I aimed the rifle, ready to shoot again when several other winged beasts managed to break away from the flock and soared toward the ground. At first I thought one of them was coming for me and that was fine.

I had the creature lined up in my sights when the beast suddenly changed direction. It swooped down and grabbed one of the teenage boys—Hunter Callahan. Then it charged back up into the sky, heading toward the woods.

Toward another uninterrupted feast, no doubt.

Just like what had happened to Agnes.

"Drop the boy, put him back!" I shouted.

The winged beast glanced down and laughed, a deep throaty cackle. It was flying too high now, taller than the treetops, almost as high as the clouds.

I wiped my brow, squinted to keep my focus on the beast as it whisked away from the junkyard. "Bring him back, safe, or I swear, I'll shoot you out of the sky!"

The creature hovered over the trees, at least eighty feet off the ground. Hunter screamed and flailed in his grasp. I could hear the lad begging for his life.

That was when the creature laughed again and looked right at me.

Then it flung the boy toward the lance-sharp field of forest and death.

At that instant—when the beast cast Hunter to the ground and a sharp gasp swept through the crowd—the sky cracked with my second round. The cartridge blasted straight through the monster's chest, stained the sky red with his blood.

And now the beast was tumbling to the ground too.

Then the black hurricane that had been churning overhead slowed and stopped as bits of wing and tooth began to fly off; one by one, each beast had finally found a way to break the spell.

They were all soaring down now, hungry and mad, toward the people that scattered, helpless, before them.

Despite my efforts, the feeding was about to begin.

Chapter 81

Evil for Good

Thane:

Evil for good. I had watched, helpless, when shots cracked through the night sky. When the music of a hundred Darklings had sparked around me, cutting through the incantation like knives. When my own brother, River, had broken free, wings bristling, his body straight as an arrow as he sailed to the ground, trying to steal the lad we both wanted. But then the sky had burned bright and red with his blood.

River on the ground. Dead.

And now the tumultuous, crowded sky began to break up into black splinters. I shot a quick glance to the distant earth, sprinkled with white snow, covered with humans all looking toward heaven. Soon the northern barbarians would swoop down and claim what was supposed to be mine.

Be damned, all of you.

I cast a Veil, stronger than any I'd ever woven; dome-shaped and invisible, it would open only for me. I set the shrine-like structure near the edge of the wood, then I sailed to the ground, toward the man who had just killed my blood brother.

Skin for skin.

I flew so fast that I was nothing but a rushing, screaming wind. All the humans startled as I zipped past.

Evil for good.

This night shall become good for me, though you meant it for evil.

Then, as I drew closer, I flipped end over end and landed feet first on the village sheriff's back. I kicked that primitive weapon out of the human's hands. Then I followed with a swift blow, using strength from my recent feeding frenzy, and I tossed the man in a wide arc, over the junkyard and away.

What's mine is mine and ever shall be.

There was one more thing that I needed to do, before it was too late, before all the other Darklings broke free from the incantation that still frittered through the skies. With a second burst of energy, I swung wide over the junkyard and the surrounding field, all of my attention now focused on Maddie. Like the other humans, she stood staring at the heavens, an expression of horror on her face—perhaps because of what I had just done to the sheriff. With arms outstretched, I flew toward her, my movements still so fast that no one had time to react, not even the dread werebeast that growled at her side. The dog-creature sniffed the air, tried to figure out where I was, but couldn't. Madeline was the only one who seemed able to sense my presence as I approached. She turned, frightened, and stared as if she recognized me, though I was only a blur of dark color, and in that half second she pushed her son behind her, to shield and protect him.

There, there, my love, no need to hide the child from me.

I seized them both, one under each arm, and then I shot across the field, just an arm's length above the humans. No one saw us. Only a vague disquiet stirred their gaze in our direction after we passed overhead, as if they each sensed that danger was near enough to touch. Through the sky, toward my lair, until we reached my hidden sanctuary. There, I dropped both Maddie and Tucker inside, where no one could hear or see them.

Then I went out.

Hunting for more.

Chapter 82

Tumult of Black Wings

Elspeth:

A tumult of black wings crashed for space, churning up clouds and blocking out the moon. Pulled by invisible strings, I sailed through low clouds, unable to break away. My wings beat a frantic rhythm as I struggled to stay upright and I glanced down at the crowd of children, so far away. Jake was down there, staring up at me, an expression of fear on his face. Only a few moments ago, the sheriff had shot two Darklings from the sky. Their bodies had littered the ground, alongside the rubbish that filled the area. Then my cousin River had broken free from the spell and now both he and Hunter were dead.

All the villagers had flocked to the junkyard and as one, they now flailed angry fists toward the skies.

Meanwhile, I tumbled straight for a thick knot of Darklings—all of them wild and yellow-eyed, their skin a strange shade of cool gray, like those from the northern provinces. *Barbarians.* These were the ones who often plundered the cities of home and stole what they wanted when their own supplies ran low. One of them turned and snarled, swiped at me with raking claws.

I spun out of his reach.

Down below, Jake was cupping his hands to his mouth and calling something, but I couldn't hear.

I wished I knew where Father was. He was in charge of this village and its magic, how had he let this happen? Then I saw him, tumbling through the skies just like I was, not that far away. The wound in his side was revealed for all to see now, silver light sparking inside. I flew to his side, wrapped one arm about him to steady his flight.

"Father! What happened?" I asked. "What's going on?"

He tried to smile, but I could tell that it took great effort. "I let Driscoll escape."

Then the curse was over. Ticonderoga Falls was without a ruler.

"Sing with me," I said. The enchantment still wrapped about our limbs like fibrous tendons. Together we began to chant a song of release, each verse of the poem slicing through the spell, layer by layer. Already many of the other Darklings had broken free and they were flying toward the ground, a fury of black wings and hunger.

A few more verses and we would be free.

I kept my gaze focused on Jake, hoping that he would be safe until I got there. Then I noticed that he was standing near Maddie and Tucker and the werebeast. But as soon as I had fixed my eyes upon them, they vanished. Maddie and Tucker were gone. Only the dog-beast was left behind.

"No!" Father cried.

Then we sang one final chant, the spell fell away like broken chains and together we sailed toward the ground.

Chapter 83

Gone

Ash:

Madeline disappeared. Like a ghost in a nightmare, she just vanished, and in her place, the air simmered with the odor of mushrooms and cobwebs. I thumped to the ground, knees buckling slightly as I landed. With a sweeping glance, I knew what had happened. Thane hadn't left Ticonderoga Falls. He was still here. Overhead the enchantment broke, causing an unnatural silence to fall upon the field. No birds, no wind, no sound of rushing water. Only the flutter of wings could be heard as the great cloud of Darklings descended and each began to cast his own spell, as all the children and a number of the adults sank to their knees in unison, then all collapsed supine on the snow-covered earth.

Maddie and her boy were gone.

Her dog whined and howled and he ran in circles, yipping and hunting for them. He pawed the ground and he sniffed the air. Relentless.

Meanwhile, my strength returned, borne of anger. My skin darkened, turned blacker than the sky, my wings thundered, and with a wild cry I lifted above the crowd, leaving Elspeth and the others behind. I circled the field and the junkyard, then headed toward the forest. There the wind whistled, the trees bent to the side to let me pass. All the other Darklings watched me with a cautious gaze, almost all of them feeding. Within a few minutes, the grassy meadow had been transformed. Now it resembled a vision from centuries past, like the wars that had continually ravaged Europe; the earth trodden by horses; the bodies left scattered and twisted over an unknown battlefield.

She would *not* be a casualty of this.

"Maddie!" I cried. "Tucker!"

But all I heard was a whispering in the midnight wind, a throaty song tangled in the willow branches, rolling over me like a silver river. Broken. Sad. Bits and pieces of the Legend were teasing me now, taunting my impotence.

I had lost her. Before she had ever truly been mine.

Chapter 84

The Rules of Harvest

Elspeth:

Almost as soon as our feet touched the ground, my father flew off in search of Maddie. Now I sailed over the field of harvest on a mission of my own. I needed to find Jake and make sure that he was safe. I didn't know if these wild barbarians knew the laws, whether they would even consider abiding by the rules of harvest. Just then, a child moaned as I passed overhead. Already the girl had grown pale and weak. I dropped from the sky, then delivered a swift kick to the feeding Darkling's jaw, knocking the beast aside.

"Let the girl go," I cried.

He whirled about to face me, assuming the stance of attack, his back hunched and his claws extended, a low growl in his throat.

I returned his growl and kicked him again, harder this time, knocking him on his backside. It was a gesture intended to humiliate him in front of his clan. A twitter of laughter and harsh jests circled around us.

"Life and limb," I said. "'Tis the law here, same as anywhere else."

"You're not in charge, child," he said through clenched teeth.

"This here is my rightful inheritance," I answered with a sweeping gesture. "'Twas the curse of my father that claimed this land in the first place."

The Darkling clambered to his feet, stood two hands taller than me and twice as wide. With a hastily whispered enchantment, I matched his size in an instant.

"And what if I were to claim it for myself, right now?" he asked, a challenge in his tone. The others around us had stopped feeding and were watching the banter, yellow eyes glowing in the dark.

"Then you'd have to fight me for it." Hands on my hips, I grew even taller, stronger. The moon was shining favor on me, adding muscle to my flesh, sturdy weight to my bones. This was no mere skin I had taken on, this was magic of the strongest kind.

Moon magic.

"And if you happen to defeat me—though your chances be slim at best," I said with a confident laugh, "then you'll have to fight our werebeast as well."

Samwise towered over both of us then, snarling, leaning toward the Darkling, drool dripping from his glittering teeth. In an instant, he had transformed himself from a dog that meandered through the field to a massive monster with claw-studded paws and glowing silver eyes. A low growl was building in his throat; it reverberated down into his chest and shook the ground beneath us all.

My adversary lowered his head with reluctance. "So be it, then. Take the girl. And the land. 'Tis not mine and I never wanted it." With a dramatic gesture, he unfurled his wings and gave a sturdy flap that lifted him off the ground. Then he flew away, over the trees and into the black distance.

Meanwhile the rest of his clan studied me with narrowed eyes, murmuring as I hefted the sleeping child over a shoulder and carried her a safe distance away, then awakened her. I could feel the tension all around us, sensed the helplessness of the few adults still awake who cowered and watched from the edges of the field, unable to enter or to help any of their children, knowing that they could easily become the next meal.

If this wild flock wasn't satiated soon, it might never be.

Chapter 85

Whispered Enchantment

Maddie:

I crouched on the ground, weary, limbs aching, fighting the brief whispered enchantment that continued to circle throughout the enclosure. Tucker and I were at the edge of the wood, trapped inside a transparent, smoky blue dome—some sort of magic. Already he had slipped to the snow-crusted grass, eyes closed, his breathing deep and steady. Meanwhile, I fought the compelling urge to sleep, forced myself back onto my feet, pretended that I had a deadline, that I had to finish one more thing before I could succumb.

With every step the ground called, sweet and melodious. Like a feather bed lined with velvet pillows, it beckoned. One knee gave in and I sank to a kneeling position.

No.

I glanced back at Tucker, tucked between fronds and ferns, the moon causing his skin to glitter like diamonds in the snow. So beautiful. Like he was carved out of ice—a flesh-and-blood sculpture brought to decorate this Darkling garden.

It would be so easy to give in. To curl beside him, wrap him in my arms and float away into ever-sweet dreams. Instead, I pulled myself back up, studied our surroundings, tried to remember what had happened and how we got here. I rubbed my eyes. Ignored Thane's ever-present chant that tickled and teased.

Sleep, my love. Just close your eyes.

Help. Somebody, somewhere, please help.

I could feel myself drifting into a strange land, somewhere between sleep and something much darker. The spell surrounded me, a fragrance like a meadow of wildflowers. I stared through to the outside, but it was like looking through a murky haze. In the distance, dark winged creatures swooped down from the heavens like fallen angels, grabbing people and dragging them off.

Feasting.

Chapter 86

A Black Shadow

Maddie:

Woven as delicate as strands of invisible hair, the barrier glittered and sparked whenever new captives tumbled inside. The wall curved in a wide arc around us; it almost glistened in the moonlight, taller than the trees. I studied the enclosure, ran a finger over the strange material.

It was a cage.

I slammed my fists against the wall, sent a percussive shower of sparks bouncing all around me.

"Help! We can't get out!"

But no one on the other side could hear or see me.

That was when a black shadow flew closer.

Thane.

I cringed when he stared in at me, when he grinned. Then, with a rough toss and another flurry of poetic words, two more children tumbled through the wall to join the crowd of sleeping captives that now littered the ground. As soon as they were inside, they collapsed on the snow-covered grass, asleep. Thane flew off, disappearing in the distance, nothing more than a blur of dark wings.

I couldn't let Tucker sleep, wasn't about to let that monster harvest him.

"Wake up." I jostled my son. "Don't sleep, not now!" His eyes fluttered open reluctantly and he moaned. I grabbed a handful of snow and rubbed it in his face.

"Mom! Stop it," he mumbled.

I glanced outside and saw Samwise far away. The dog's ears perked up when Tucker complained. I took another handful of snow and poured it down my son's collar.

"What's wrong with you?" He grimaced and pulled away. "That's not funny."

I was filling my hands with snow now, scooping it up and tossing it at him.

Tucker frowned. "You better not do that again, or I'll—"

Samwise was running toward us then, like a flash of black lightning, speeding across the field faster than any dog had ever run.

"Or you'll what?" I asked, teasing. I grabbed his shirt and dumped another handful of snow inside.

"That's it! I'm telling you—" But now Tucker was fully awake and he started to laugh, he began to chase me around the inside of the enclosure, his hands filled with snow. I stopped and let him throw a handful in my face, glad for the brisk cold.

And then like magic, Samwise appeared, bolting to a stop on the other side of the invisible fence, barking, trying to see us, sniffing, trying to smell us. He scratched at the ground but couldn't figure out how to get through.

"Dig boy, dig a hole right here," I called to the dog.

"Dig, Sam!" Tucker echoed, his fists still clenching snow.

The dog stared at us, unseeing. But he understood the command, nonetheless.

With a fury, paws and chest growing, he started to burrow, paws moving in a blur of speed. He began digging a tunnel that would go beneath the barrier. He was going to set us free.

I fought the enchantment that continued to circle overhead; I gently shook my son to keep him awake, I draped my coat around his shoulders and I called to the dog on the other side of the Veil.

But all of my attention was focused on escaping, and because of it, I didn't notice what was happening a few feet beyond, back in the junkyard.

Chapter 87

Ghost-Like Wraith

Thane:

I swung through the air, wings beating midnight, Veil slicing time into neat little quadrants. I flew, near invisible, a ghost-like wraith with a heart filled with vengeance and a belly that hungered. No one saw me as I swept through the field, grabbing humans and carrying them off. Not even the other Darklings were aware of my plunder, they were so engrossed in their own decadent revelry. They all gathered around the humans, feasting until one by one, the Darklings fell to the ground, drunk.

I slung two more children through my Veil, pausing for moment to admire my own reflection in the glimmering weave. It was the strongest I'd ever made, plaited from the silken thread that flows through dreams, that binds the human soul to its body.

Then I noticed movement on the other side—Madeline was wandering around inside the enclosure, fighting sleep.

I smiled.

Rest, my sweet. Save your dreams for me. For no one but me.

Then I soared away, close to the ground, listening to the

dreams that scorched the near sky, dreams being harvested as I flew, some of them brushing against my skin, tempting me.

I thought about Madeline, skin like starlight, pale sparks that glimmered around her face, that shot from her lips when she spoke. And just below the surface—behind the waking thoughts that cluttered her mind—were her dreams. Like a vast unguarded playground, swings moved in the breeze and Ferris wheels sprang to life, sweet as spun sugar and just as fragile. Likewise, her boy had all the magic of a summer sunrise, of a breeze as it blew across a field of nodding poppies.

My nostrils flared, and deep in my belly, hunger stirred.

They would make a delicious feast—an appetizer and the main course. All I needed was dessert, maybe the whimsical dreams found in a little girl. I scanned the field, searching for just the right addition to my table when something caught my attention.

Maddie's dog.

The beast stood at attention, ears up, staring back toward the line of distant trees. Listening. I glanced in the same direction, back toward my hidden enclosure, and suddenly I could hear it too, the boy was laughing and playing with Maddie. They were both awake.

A dull fear surged in my gut.

Then the dog was running, a black-and-tan streak across snowy field, one part dog, one part werebeast, feet pummeling earth faster than any animal alive.

I bristled. Now the dog was digging at the edge of the enclosure.

No! It was going to tunnel beneath the Veil and set them free.

I turned, cast wings to the heavens, ready to fight the beast, strength flowing through my limbs. I would win. Tonight I could defeat even a werebeast if I had to.

Then a mooncast shadow suddenly held me in place.

Fingers gripped me by the throat. A body appeared in front of me, materializing from the mists, Darkling flesh and broad shoulders, silver eyes that sparked like fire, wings spread wide as a midnight cloak. The fragrance of a forest and the rushing of wind through the leaves.

A growl rippled from my opponent's chest and his lips parted, revealing sharp dagger-like teeth. "You were ordered to leave," Ash said, his voice like a nightmare brought to life. Then with a claw-studded blow to the gut, the fight for Ticonderoga Falls and everything in it began.

Chapter 88

Half-Cast Enchantments

Ash:

We rolled and tumbled over icy ground, slammed against the edge of the junkyard fence, fists burrowing deep in flesh, claws leaving trails of blood. Half-cast enchantments sputtered from my lips, each stopped by yet another blow to the face. I rumbled with anger, a fierce heat radiating from my skin, scorching Thane with every blow.

Then the other Darklings began to surround us, attracted by the fight and by the high stakes. They left their humans asleep on the ground, then gathered in clusters to take bets, all of them drunk from the feeding. Twittering with coarse laughter, the crowd began to hedge us in, forming a circle of black wings, their crude enchantments glittering.

Time in the human world slowed down and the fight seemed unending. I felt like I was moving in slow motion, every punch, every kick exaggerated by the incongruent spells that were continually cast about.

And then, all the other Darklings began to dance and fly, chanting, singing, laughing, caught up in the wild fury. From time to time one of the northern barbarians would fly close enough to take a nip at one of us, then he or she would sail away.

Meanwhile, the fight continued.

I bit Thane in the shoulder and dragged him across the field. I tried to get away from the other Darklings but they refused to let us pass, hemming us in on every side. All the while, my adversary thrashed and screamed, sliced his talons through the air. Thane spun out of my grasp, shoulders and arms broadening for yet another attack. My cousin lunged forward, head down, kicking and swinging and screaming an ancient battle cry. The shriek of war then echoed around us, taken up by every accent and clan. Suddenly an unexpected punch caught me in the gut as Thane slammed his fist into the still-healing wound in my side.

I bellowed in pain.

Again, Thane had found my weakness—this time, no longer hidden by a Veil. He glared, opened his mouth in a wicked grin. He narrowed yellow eyes, tilted his head to the side as if studying me. I didn't move, save a shallow breathing.

Thane crouched, got ready to pounce.

Then he soared the short distance between us, pummeled a talon-studded fist into my wound, ignoring the heat that blistered his skin, digging deeper and deeper: sparks flew in a shower all around us, until Thane's knuckles shoved all the way through the hole and emerged on the other side.

A raucous cheer resounded. Now wings hid the sky, became a dome of black and gray leathery flesh that surrounded us.

I collapsed on the ground amidst the screaming and howling of rival clans, while other fights broke out like drunken brawls.

While my own blood stained the ground.

Chapter 89

Supernatural Power

Maddie:

Samwise, sometimes dog, sometimes monster, dug furiously at the edge of Thane's created stockade. He tunneled beneath the Veil, squirmed through dirt and leaves and twigs until he burst through to the other side.

And there, on the other side, Tucker hooted and howled, then grabbed the dog—for he was all dog now and nothing else—around the neck, kissed and hugged him, rejoicing as Thane's enchantment began to fade when exposed to fresh air. The dog frolicked around the perimeter of the enclosure, big sloppy grin on his face, mud caking his paws and chest.

He was the hero.

He had saved the day.

I laughed too, then fell to the ground almost exhausted from trying to stay awake. I braced my arms on both sides of the hole in the earth, took a lungful of sweet mountain air, and with it I suddenly sensed a tension, a danger brewing outside.

It felt ominous, like the air pressure had changed and a tornado was brewing; I sensed a storm on the other side. A storm of Darkling against Darkling, supernatural power sizzling through night sky.

I sat back on my haunches, oblivious now to the antics of boy and dog, to the awakening of the crowd Thane had corralled. I focused on the words and the firestorm just outside, then widened the hole in the ground with bare hands so I could slide through. I pushed my head down inside, the smell of wet earth surrounding me; I wriggled through, feeling stuck but not giving in.

I didn't see the appearance of two white transparent figures inside the enclosure, or how they each reached down to help the trapped humans scramble to their feet. I didn't know that Nick and Pinch, my two darkest and most dangerous characters, had been mysteriously summoned, or that they were already pulling pranks, elbowing a few people and then tripping them on their way toward the exit.

Despite this, my chimerical villains were listening to me. For no one had ever loved them as much as I did.

They were watching me.

Ever faithful. Ever ready.

Just like they had been from the moment I first created them. Listening even now, ready to do whatever I asked them to do.

Chapter 90

A Great Wall

Maddie:

I pushed my way through to the surface, mud in my hair, on my face, fingers wet and dark with it. The scent of the earth clung to my clothes and skin; I pulled myself out of the narrow hole, then climbed to my feet and brushed my hair away from my face.

A black cloud bristled in front of me. Wings darting, talons gleaming, Darkling bodies merged together to form a great wall of negative and positive shapes, ever moving, a turmoil of hellish arms and legs and teeth. Screams and laughter filled the night air and the ground trembled. Something horrid was happening on the other side of this wall of Darkling flesh. Then a voice called through the hallways of my mind. The red-black blood on my hands burned again, blisters reminding me.

Ash.

Stay back.

He was trying to warn me.

Take your boy and leave. Now. *Never come back.*

Foolish creature. Foolish as any man I had ever known.

As if I would leave now, knowing that he was in the midst of some vicious battle; after he had saved me, more than once. I glanced at the perimeter of the wall, saw three female Darklings trying to break through. One of them had tears running down her face as she repeatedly called out, "Father!"

Even they couldn't save him.

Then I smelled Thane's stench, spidery and moldy, like a creature you would find in an abandoned shed.

I'm not leaving, I told Ash in a silent voice.

A sigh circled overhead, wrapped itself around the field, seemed to caress me before it drifted off into the trees.

For a moment the moon turned bright, even brighter than the sun.

It smiled down. Narrow beams of light poured through misty clouds, glanced upon my skin and set it aglow. I felt suddenly stronger, like a surge of electric energy pulsed through my limbs, radiated from my fingertips. And behind me, though I didn't see it, the field began to fill with the people who had been set free from Thane's spell, all of them climbing through the hole, following the path I had forged. Nearly fifty people scampered through the narrow earthen tunnel, Tucker and Samwise at their heels. Until finally, they had all escaped and now stood behind me, poised and ready.

Among them were Nick and Pinch.

A transparent army of two.

Chapter 91

The Feast of Forbidden Dreams

Ash:

Incantations flew through the air, dangerous and heavy as weapons made of iron. One misstep and a jaw could be torn loose. *Stay back.* I knew that Elspeth, Sage and Sienna were trying to rescue me. I could feel their spells, delicate as a spring breeze, offering a light reprieve, just enough for me to open my eyes. *Leave this place. There are too many.*

Those I loved would get caught up in the melee—they could be killed—if their enchantments broke through the wall and they tried to enter, but this fight was my choice, not theirs. My battle.

My sacrifice.

Thane laughed, withdrew his bloodstained fist from my side, then struck me across the face. He towered over me, pinning me to the ground, foot on my chest as he cast another enchantment.

A spell of silence.

Suddenly I was all alone, separated from my clan, unable to communicate through word or thought. Thane barked a command to those who huddled nearby.

"Guard the perimeter of the fight, see that no one enters, not one of his clan," Thane said. "Not even the werebeast!"

The barbarians chittered and cackled, sent patrols to defend the ragged edges of the flock.

Thane leaned down, then whispered, "And now I shall take the dreams that should have been mine. I take from you all the hope, all the glory, all the life that you have stolen from others, I take it and claim it as my own."

He began the ceremony of sacrilege, an act that left the surrounding Darklings incensed and amazed. No one had performed this rite in hundreds of years.

He was going to break our most sacred rule.

"Give me your dreams!" Thane cried then, conjuring magic that had been nearly forgotten, a spell so old he could barely pronounce the words. His voice carried through the crowd to the forest and the returning echo nearly shook him off his feet.

Thus the Feast of Forbidden Dreams began.

I trembled as each dream was siphoned off, each one like another layer of skin being ripped away. I clenched my fists, trapped in silence, cut off from the fragrance of the forest deep, hidden from the healing light of the moon, betrayed by one of my own clansmen, one I myself had invited. I wished I could see Elspeth one last time, wished that I would have been able to break through the barrier of fear within Maddie, that I could have shown her another side of myself.

But humans can't accept Darklings—our worlds are too different. To them, I would always be a monster that needed to be destroyed.

My heartbeat slowed to the droning pace of a requiem poem. My blood thinned and my limbs grew cold.

I fought for a few moments more, holding on to that last dream, the one that had bloomed tonight in the midst of the Hunt—the dream that I could be forgiven for what I had done to the Driscolls. And that I might be able to love again. I hid this last dream deep in my heart, where the red-black blood still glittered and sparked, where a few beats still remained.

I would not give this last one up. I would keep it locked and hidden, no matter how fierce the battle with Thane, willing to take this one with me into the Land of Dreams.

When my soul was finally pried loose.

And that would be soon. Very soon.

Chapter 92

Red-Black Hands

Maddie:

I stood, bathed in silver light, head cocked to one side, listening to the battle, remembering the last bitter words spoken by Ash. A heavy silence now reigned. I couldn't hear him anymore, couldn't feel his heartbeat pulsing in my red-black hands, couldn't smell his fragrance seeping through the horde of Darkling wings that surrounded him.

No. This will not happen.

You will not take him from me.

I clenched my fists, then ran toward the crowd of black and gray flesh that separated me from Ash. I raced across the torn and muddy field, leaping over those humans who still slept, anger replacing any fear I might have had. I struck the Darklings on their leathery backs, surprised when sparks tumbled from every blow.

"Let me in!" I cried, though none of them moved aside.

Instead, one of the beasts turned his head and snarled. He swiveled around until he faced me, his mouth open wide to reveal dagger-sharp teeth. He snapped and growled with a sinister grin, threatened to bite my arm if I dared strike him again.

Then, suddenly, two ghost-white creatures came between us, they grabbed the menacing Darkling and cast him aside, sent him tumbling into the distant wood.

I stared at the hovering transparent beings, who in turn looked back at me in silence. They glowed from the silver light of the moon, as if made of fire. *Nick and Pinch.* They came nearer until they stood at my side; they each bowed a knee to me.

"Send us in," they said in unison, their voices rough as a winter storm. "All you need do is give us the word."

Ash's daughter was beside me, fists clenched, tears on her cheeks. She nodded.

Then I—Madeline MacFaddin, known to many as Mad Mac—turned and pointed toward the Darkling flock that would not move, that would not let me pass.

"Go!" I said.

It was such a simple command and yet both Nick and Pinch knew exactly what I wanted and were willing to do it. With hearts ablaze, my transparent creatures pushed their way through the growling horde.

And their magic was stronger than any the Darklings had ever seen.

Chapter 93

Smoke in the Wind

Ash:

My dreams continued to be peeled away, from skin to bone to marrow, and then finally to soul. With each passing second, I felt as if I was becoming a mere wisp of who I had once been. Cherished memories rose to the surface, only to disappear: my father teaching me how to hunt through the midnight streets of Amsterdam; Lily pausing during a harvest to kiss me, the wildness of it stealing my breath; Elspeth running and laughing as a child, delicate wings lifting her off the ground for her first flight. My memories were fading and with each one, my dreams were being stolen as well. Before long, I would be nothing but a wraith, exiled from this world forever. Still, I clung to that one last dream until it consumed me, until it became all that I was. Everything else had been burned off and destroyed.

All the dreams of revenge faded, turned into smoke in the wind.

All hope of being set free from the curse—of one day pledging Ticonderoga Falls to Elspeth as her birthright—vanished.

All the hunger and anger and disappointment evaporated—the serpentine veins that had laced through me and held me captive against my will for nearly a century crumbled and broke.

Until, finally, the only thing left was this fragile hope of love.

My body sagged against the earth, muscles weary from the battle, while the thunder of the outside world grew dim. The only thing I could hear now was my own meager heartbeat. Meanwhile, the final chapter of the Legend circled through forest and field, as if testing the hearts and character of all who had been beckoned by the incantation. It whispered *Yes, a thousand times, yes*, and I tried to lift my head, to understand why it would say something like that at such a time as this. Why would it betray me and rejoice in my death?

Then suddenly, miraculously, the tapestry of Darkling flesh parted. Black wings no longer hid the sky from view and the sweet fragrance of life swept over the battlefield. Overhead, the moon broke through and cast beautiful silver beams down, drenching me in nocturnal brilliance. Then I was able to see what had parted the death throng that surrounded me. Two ghost-like figures sailed past the Darklings: two imaginary beings, transparent yet having substance.

They came with a fury, kicking and punching, knocking everyone aside, forcing the barbaric Darklings to move. Cries echoed and wings thundered and enchantments were cast in a flurry.

But none of the Darklings' whispered spells could stop this pair.

I grinned weakly, for I recognized them. Maddie's characters had been following her throughout the evening, her invisible companions, ever faithful to their creator.

Then they pushed and shoved against the wall of Darklings until it opened and she walked in with the ethereal carriage of a queen: Madeline, bathed in moonlight, her face and hands covered in mud, as if she had just been born anew from an earthen womb. Elspeth, Sage and Sienna followed her, while the werebeast clumped in behind them all, carrying the boy in his arms, holding the lad high where none could touch him.

At the sight of them, Thane stopped his feeding, a look of surprise and horror on his face. And in that instant, my heartbeat returned, became a natural rhythm again.

Perhaps my last dream could still come true.

Chapter 94

Crowned with Dreams

Thane:

The wall of Darklings parted as two diaphanous creatures cut through like scythes. These transparent beasts didn't respond to any of my spells or songs. Relentless, they fought against my northern cousins until an opening appeared and the moon shined upon me. I cowered. Silver-white light poured down.

Exposing the sacrilegious ceremony and my hollow heart.

I crumbled to my knees then, at last, when the moon found me, when it scorched me as the traitor I truly was. I had turned against my own clansman. I couldn't bear to look up, to see the brightness blinding me, to feel the wickedness in my own soul, and I held one arm over my head to shield my eyes.

Then Maddie walked in, crowned with dreams like sugar candy. Stained with mud and glowing in moonlight, she didn't look human anymore.

Maybe she never had been.

"Him." She cast a long finger at me and then, like vengeful ghosts, both of the transparent figures circled me. They grabbed me by the arms, their rough fingers digging into my flesh like claws. One of them kicked me in the leg, just for the fun of it, then giggled when I cringed.

These transparent creatures were as solid as any beast or person I'd ever encountered.

Moon magic.

"Take him to the Land of Nightmares and see that he never escapes!" Maddie cried.

"No!" I begged. "Please, not that, don't—"

But pleading only made my captors laugh harder. They jostled, pulled and wrenched my arms, kicked and bit, then laughed in unison. They lifted me high in the air and swung me around and around until I begged them to release me. Then, when everyone had seen my true character and cowardice, they carried me away from the feasting field, away from Ticonderoga Falls, away from everything sweet and good and wholesome.

Into the clouds and the sky, toward the black empty terror that waits just on the other side of every dream gone awry.

Toward the Land of Nightmares.

Never to return.

Chapter 95

Faery Tales

Ash:

Elspeth came forward, tears on her face, her voice so strained she could barely speak. She knelt and wrapped her arms around me and Maddie stood beside both of us. Sage came nearer, tugging a vial that hung around her neck on a cord. She opened the slender flask, then placed it to my lips. The Nectar of the Hunt, the dreams of a hundred Sleepers. My sister fed me until my strength returned.

"Take it," I said, looking up at my daughter when I was finally strong enough to stand again. "Claim the village. It was always your inheritance. Don't let anyone steal it from you."

I watched the wild Darklings who continued to hover and lurk in dangerous, brooding clusters, knowing that their storm of black wings could rain another attack at any moment. I was ready to fight, if need be, to claim what was rightfully ours. Elspeth turned slowly, gazing at the crowd that had surrounded us. I could sense the anger within her, a righteous anger, and I smiled when she brazened a clenched fist over her head.

"You have broken your sacred vows today!" she cried, her

eyes like flames in the darkness. "Life and limb. You dared to attempt the Feast of Forbidden Dreams!"

She took a step forward, one hand pointing in accusation at the horde of Darkings, their voices now a low chattering moan. "I curse you!" she said. "*All* of you—"

The moon seemed to draw nearer as she spoke, until the luminous orb was three times its normal size. It set Elspeth aglow with a silver-blue fire. Strands of thin white lightning danced about her, crackling and sizzling. "—How dare you try to take anything from this village, from this land that is my birthright!"

Then she stared up at the moon, raised both hands above her head, palms open, and she cried out, a primal shout so raw that it cut all who heard it in the belly and few could stay standing on their feet. Like a shock wave, it surged forward, causing the mountain itself to tremble. In the near distance, trees wavered and houses shook, windows near and far rattled and broke.

Both of Elspeth's arms swung down and in that instant an impenetrable darkness fell from the heavens, her enchantment so strong that it wiped out all sound and movement. It forced everyone to stop and listen. The entire crowd of Darklings turned, every one of them facing her now.

"A curse be upon you and your entire clan," she continued. "On those who live here and those back in the homeland. Barrenness shall fall upon your houses and every harvest you gather shall turn bitter in your mouths! A curse be upon each and every one of you, if you do not grant me obeisance on this day."

As one, their heads lowered.

"Kneel!" Elspeth demanded.

And all the Darklings knelt before her. Even her own kinsmen.

I too knelt, until she took me by the hand and nodded for me to rise. From that point on, I stood at her side as each of the wild Darklings came forth, one by one, each pledging that they would never hunt again in Ticonderoga

Falls without her permission. This act of fealty lasted for hours, until the moon hovered on the edge of the horizon, almost ready to slip away and give the world back to her sister, the sun. Then finally, at last, a quiet peace rolled over the field, as if all the venom had been drained from an old wound. Now the humans gathered in small groups, laughing and joking, as if they knew that they were safe from the nightmarish beasts that still roamed the field. Like weary children, the humans began to scatter, free to go home now, their innocence intact.

Just as it should be.

Only a few remained.

Joe Wimbledon ambled forward then, his limp more pronounced than before. His clothes were dusted with snow and dirt, for he had been among those harvested in the field. He knelt before me, although we both knew that I was no longer the ruler and Joe had relinquished his title as Legend Keeper.

"You will always be my friend," I told him as we clasped hands and I lifted him to his feet. "And I promise safety for you and your family for all that you have done for me."

Joe nodded his head quietly, tears in his eyes, perhaps saddened because he could no longer hear the whispering Legend as it cantered among the treetops.

Ross Madera came forward next, concern on his face. Despite all he had been through tonight, my friend approached with only thoughts of my well-being. "Come with me," he said. "Let me bandage your wound. I'll see if I can find something to take away the sting of pain—"

"Not yet," I answered. "I'll stop by later."

Sienna watched the two of us, something in her eyes much deeper than hunger when she looked at Ross.

"Let me see your arm," I said to Ross.

He pulled back his sleeve to reveal the long jagged scar on his forearm. I whispered a singsong poem, words that none but a Darkling could understand, and the mark on Ross's arm vanished.

"I release you," I said with a smile. "Now you're free to choose."

Sienna and Ross strolled away, arm in arm, as if they had known each other all their lives. I could hear her chatting in a low, sultry tone about possibly moving to Ticonderoga Falls and making it her home.

All the while, Sage stood nearby, sacrificing the rest of the Hunt to make sure that both Elspeth and I were truly safe, although we told her she was free to harvest. She merely shook her head and said that the best harvest was right here, right now.

Then a young man came nearer and he lingered at Elspeth's side. He seemed unafraid of the other Darklings, as if his desire to be near her overshadowed any potential danger. I recognized the lad, for I had seen him often at Joe Wimbledon's house. He was Joe's nephew, Jake.

I had been wrong to think that no one would ever love my daughter. There were already strong feelings between the two of them, although they were probably too young to feel this way. Still, I knew better than to argue with her when it came to matters of the heart.

She was the ruler now.

I lifted my head and caught a new fragrance on the wind. A new harvest was growing in the village. Hidden and secret. Somewhere, somehow, on this evening, Darkling seed had been planted in the wombs of twelve human women. This would be an uneasy harvest when revealed, but I knew that those children would be innocent of the crimes of their father—whoever he had been.

Then, when the crowd of Darklings was finally dispersing—as they were all spreading broad wings and sailing through rose-tinted skies, as the humans were wandering off toward home and the promise of soft beds—Maddie came forward and knelt before my daughter. She was the only human who had offered obeisance and the gesture confirmed those deep feelings I already had.

She and Elspeth spoke quietly for a moment, then Maddie rose and came to me.

The field was near empty now. The werebeast meandered back and forth, always within sight, still carrying Tucker in his arms, the lad fast asleep.

Maddie gently placed one hand on my wound and she held it there, ignoring the heat and the sparking light; she pressed it there until the flow of red-black blood finally stopped. Until healing returned to my bones, to my marrow.

And, most important, to my heart.

Meanwhile, the Legend zipped overhead, leaping merrily from one tree branch to the next in the nearby forest. This was the happy ending that I had never anticipated. It was destiny after all. Madeline was meant to be here. Meant to be part of this century-old legend.

"I nearly lost you tonight," she said.

"And I you."

"Promise me," she said then, with a smile that rivaled the brilliance of the setting moon, "if you're ever in trouble again, you will call me."

I smiled.

"I promise," I answered.

Then she cupped my face in her hand, her fingers brushing my cheek and chin, almost exactly like I had held her in the forest. She remembered everything now, even how my Veil had held her still in the forest, she remembered it all and she was unafraid.

She came even nearer, her eyes like starlight, and she kissed me.

And with that, I wrapped my arms about her and pulled her close, held her so tight that no magic could ever separate us.

The dream worth dying for was alive and well.

Epilogue

Eight Months Later

Maddie:

I stood with my hair pulled back, sweat dripping down my neck from an unexpected flurry of Santa Ana winds. Boxes were stacked waist-deep inside the bungalow and a moving van slugged its way out of the driveway, back toward civilization. Meanwhile, the sun was sliding toward the Pacific, the shadows were growing longer and I was wondering where I was going to put everything once I unpacked. This mountain cottage was about a third the size of my Malibu home, the one I finally sold just last week.

Tucker sat on the front porch, an advance reader's copy of *The Dream Eaters* open across his knees. His ten-year-old eyes searched through the pages for the true story written between the lines—the story about him and Samwise and the entire community of Queensbury Falls, a mythical town nestled in the forests of the Adirondack Mountains. Meanwhile, Samwise scampered and rolled in the grass, yipping at the leaves that occasionally sailed to the ground. Thankfully, he'd gotten used to wearing dog skin unless it was absolutely necessary not to—though it had taken him a long time to figure out when that was.

Just then I heard a familiar voice, a lumbering step climbing the stairs.

Sheriff Kyle.

"You need some help unpacking?" he called.

I glanced at him and grinned. He limped now, but fortunately, all the other scars and wounds from his brief battle with Thane had healed.

"Sure," I said.

We worked side by side, ripping boxes open and unwrapping the contents. Every hour or so throughout the evening, a neighbor would drop by to welcome me back to Ticonderoga Falls, giving me cakes, pies and cookies, until the sweets lined my kitchen table and counter. And now, in their midst, two pizza boxes stood open and empty. Tucker fed the last slice to Samwise, despite my protests.

Meanwhile, the moon rose in the heavens and its silver light poured in every uncurtained window.

Until, finally, the last moving box was unpacked.

I stretched and yawned, surprised that somehow everything had been put away. Even my son and the dog had been tucked away for the evening, both of them already asleep. It was hard to concentrate right now. Moonbeams showered the kitchen, brilliant as sunshine, and I kept hearing a familiar song. I glanced at the clock.

Kyle slugged down a last cup of coffee, then got ready to leave. He paused at the front door and glanced awkwardly at his feet. "I don't know if I ever—if I thanked you for what you did," he stammered. "If it hadn't been for you—"

"I think we all played a part in the final resolution," I said, remembering how he had braved the crowd of Darklings, trying to save Hunter.

He nodded, silent, then turned and headed down the stairs, toward his car.

I stretched my sore muscles again, then walked through the house shutting off the lights. The moonsong was so strong now I could hardly think. I entered my bedroom and opened the window, glass shimmering in silver moonlight, while the landscape beyond glistened in a way it never had before. I took a deep breath, let the black midnight flow into my lungs, and I stared into the forest that surrounded the little bungalow. Something sparked in the distance, almost like heat lightning. But it couldn't be. Not down this low.

It was the Legend, looking for me. Circling from one tree to the next, word by word, speaking the next chapter into existence.

It's good to have you back, a voice spoke through the night sky. It was Elspeth. *We've missed our Legend Keeper.*

I smiled. It was good to be back home again, to return from my journey to the real world, the land of deadlines and editors and agents. I much preferred this, the world of never-ending stories, of myth and magic. I thought I heard the distant flap of broad black wings.

Thump.

The noise beat against my chest and clouded my vision.

Thu-thump.

Both hands gripped the windowsill and I leaned forward.

Thump.

"You can come in now," I whispered.

As soon as the words left my lips I saw the view outside change. The midnight horizon of sky, stars and ever-deep forest shimmered and twisted. The landscape began to melt and dark smoke poured over the windowsill into my room, tendrils like liquid swept across the floor, then spiraled into a tall column until it turned into flesh and bone.

Ash.

"Quite an entrance," I said.

"Just a reminder of what you've been missing," he replied.

He took me in his arms and it was like being wrapped in midnight itself, he kissed me and I could taste the forest—the evergreen, the river, the incense of leaves as they whispered in the wind.

"You could have come with me," I murmured. "I was only gone for a few days—"

"You know I hate the city."